MISFITS

GARRETT LEIGH

RIPTIDE
PUBLISHING

Riptide Publishing
PO Box 6652
Hillsborough, NJ 08844
www.riptidepublishing.com

Misfits

Cover art: G.D. Leigh, www.blackjazzpress.com
Editor: Carole-ann Galloway
Layout: L.C. Chase, lcchase.com/design.htm

ISBN: 978-1-62649-247-9

First edition
March, 2015

Also available in ebook:
ISBN: 978-1-62649-246-2

MISFITS

GARRETT LEIGH

RIPTIDE
PUBLISHING

One does not refuse love. It was there,
before we ever knew it . . .

TABLE OF CONTENTS

TOM

CHAPTER ONE

Tom Fearnes shook hands with the estate agent and watched absently as she disappeared into the bustling streets of Camden Town. Around him, busy Londoners jostled each other for space, and none of them took much notice of him blocking the pavement. He tuned them out and scrutinised the vacant building in front of him, frowning. The disused guitar shop wasn't quite what he'd been hoping for, inside or out.

But, but, but . . .

Tom dismissed the boarded-up shop front, and glanced around at Camden's popular markets and music venues. The familiar buzz of a new venture tickled his veins. He was in the right place, he could feel it, but the only vacant premises on the vibrant strip of Camden High Street were *all* wrong. Too small and overpriced, each one was a definitive no-go, which left his plans for a spring restaurant opening a distant dream.

Deep in thought, Tom tore himself away from the unsuitable shop and drifted towards the Tube station. He dodged a few slow-moving people, and swore under his breath like a grumpy native. Camden wasn't his usual stomping ground, but he was an adopted Londoner through and through, and dawdling tourists got on his nerves, especially when—*great*—the sheer number of them closed Camden Town Tube station.

Tom glared at the metal shutters and caught the eye of a nearby Underground worker. "Is Chalk Farm open?"

The woman shook her head. "Closed for congestion. Try Mornington."

Tom sighed. Mornington station was a ten-minute walk in the wrong direction from his Hampstead flat. He'd have to go all the way back to Euston now and get on a different line. Either that or hole up somewhere and wait for the crowds to clear.

He turned south towards Mornington and considered his options. He was bloody knackered and *busy*, and with the guitar shop a nonstarter, he needed to get home and begin the search for a new restaurant site all over again. *Hmm.* Thinking about his company's latest culinary venture reminded him that he hadn't eaten all day. His stomach growled, and he glanced around, looking for a place that wasn't too rammed. A PGB pub caught his eye. It wasn't the kind of place he usually frequented, but he could see a few empty tables through the window.

He braved a zebra crossing and pushed open the restaurant door. The inside of the pub smelled of cheap lager and burned meat fat. A surly hostess showed him to a table by the door, dropped a sticky menu in front of him, and left him to it. Tom watched her stomp away with a wry smile. Checking out the competition was always fun, especially on a Sunday evening. Tired and beat down from a long weekend, it was the sign of a sound kitchen team if a restaurant was still churning out great food.

Tom settled in his seat, shed his coat, and ran his gaze over the menu. To the untrained eye, it appeared impressive—vast and diverse—but Tom knew better. Any restaurant offering steak, pizza, curry, *and* a Moroccan tagine was seriously confused. And lazy. He knew the development manager for this particular brand and had heard most of their food was produced in a factory in Sheffield.

Boil in the bag bollocks . . .

"Can I get you a drink?"

Tom glanced up and blinked, for a moment imagining the words had been spoken in an entirely different context. *Wow.* There was no other word for the streak of masculine beauty waiting by his table with a notepad. Long fingers tapping on the paper, elegant hands and fragile wrists. Slender arms, slim shoulders, and a beautiful, pale neck. And his face, *damn*, his face. High cheekbones and flawless skin were set off by a tiny silver ring curving out of his perfect nose.

"Can . . . I get you a drink?"

"Uh . . ." Tom fumbled with the drinks menu. "Pint of Beck's, thanks."

The waiter disappeared. Given the attitude of the hostess, Tom didn't expect him back anytime soon, so he was surprised when a frothy pint of lager materialised a few minutes later.

"Are you ready to order?"

Not even close. Tom absorbed the young waiter's melodic northern accent and scanned the menu again. "What do you recommend? Anything good?"

"Depends what you like."

"Yeah?" Tom heard the waiter's indifference loud and clear, but the youngster's dark beauty cancelled out any offence he might have felt. "What about the pies?"

"We're out of the beef and ale."

"Is the chicken any good?"

Silence. The waiter wrinkled his nose. Tom glanced at his name tag. *Jake.* Labelling staff like meat was a concept that irritated Tom, but he liked the kid's name; it suited him. "What's the steak burger like?"

Jake shrugged. "It's . . . okay."

The pause said it all. "Just okay, eh? Where's the meat from? Is it British?"

"It's from Uruguay."

"Nice. You've convinced me there's nothing in this place worth eating. How do you know I'm not a mystery guest?"

The kid scowled with barely suppressed derision and shook his head. "We don't have those anymore; they're not cost-effective. We have anonymous online surveys instead. You scan the QR-code on the menu with your smartphone."

Tom swallowed a chuckle. He was familiar with the concept of online guest satisfaction surveys; he owned a stake in a company that hosted them. The QR-code thing was new to the industry, though. Not many businesses had it yet. "I'll have the fish and chips."

Jake made a strange noise and waved his hand. "You don't want to know where the fish is from?"

Is he taking the piss? "No, thanks. I'd rather live in ignorance."

Jake snatched the menu back and disappeared. Tom forced himself to not watch and retrieved his phone from his coat pocket. He was engrossed in a commercial property website when Jake returned with his food a little while later.

"Do—do you want any sauces?"

Tom poked at the anaemic piece of battered fish on his plate, but noticing Jake's mild stutter, he decided to cut him some slack. "I'm good, thanks."

Jake sloped off without further comment. With a healthy amount of trepidation, Tom picked at his supper while he checked his diary and caught up on emails. As the director of his own thriving restaurant business, he had plenty to do.

Jake meandered past a few times. He didn't check on Tom, but the third time, Tom sensed his waif-like presence, he flagged him down, held out the plate of greasy slop, and asked for the bill.

Jake seemed unsurprised by Tom's lack of appetite. He brought the bill with a substantial discount and promptly disappeared again. The restaurant had filled up while Tom had been engrossed in his emails and soggy fish, and Jake seemed to be the only waiter on the floor.

Tom waited awhile for him to come back, but when it became apparent it wasn't going to happen, he gathered his things and made his way to the bar. The unsmiling face of the hostess greeted him. She took the bill folder and put his credit card into the payment machine.

"Was everything all right with your meal today?"

"Nope," Tom said, though he kept his tone light. "It was cold, greasy, and presented on a dirty plate."

The hostess stared, but whatever retort she may have made was cut off by a deafening crash. Tom cringed. He knew the sound of smashing plates all too well. He looked over his shoulder and saw Jake surrounded by a sea of obliterated crockery.

Jake dropped down and punched the floor. He started to gather the shattered plates, but couldn't seem to get a grip on them. A broken bowl slipped out of his hand. "*Bollocks, shit, fuck!*"

Tom took an instinctive step forwards, saw the strain in Jake's shoulders, the angry twitch in his muscles, and felt a sudden, intense urge to help him that seemed beyond humble sympathy. But he stopped himself. There was nothing more humiliating than a stranger acknowledging whatever disaster had befallen you, and Lord knew, the flush creeping over the back of Jake's neck told Tom he was embarrassed enough.

An irate-looking manager—who'd been conspicuously absent until now—appeared from nowhere and shoved Jake aside. "Leave it. Go out the back and pull yourself together."

Jake's arm shot out at an odd angle. "*Wankers.*"

The manager glared. "For God's sake, *go.*"

Jake scrambled to his feet, darted to the kitchen door, and slammed it behind him. Tom relaxed a little. The scene was one he'd witnessed, and performed in, many times over. Who hadn't dropped an armload of plates in the middle of a busy shift? But even as the diners around the mess went back to their food like nothing had happened, Tom got the distinct sensation that he was missing something. And he didn't like the manager's manner. There was nothing more unprofessional than letting a crowded restaurant see your frustration. It could be forgiven in a young waiter, but not a manager.

"Enter your PIN please."

The hostess's bored voice startled Tom. He'd been so engrossed in Jake's calamity he'd forgotten she was there. He followed the prompts on the screen.

"Do you pool your tips here?"

"No. Your server keeps them."

Tom handed her a folded banknote. "Good. Tell Jake I appreciated his candour."

The girl's face remained impassive. Tom sighed and passed the payment machine back. Where did places like this find these people? Even Jake's scornful derision was better than nothing at all.

Tom made his way to the restaurant's exit feeling slightly sick with the weight of the few oil-sodden chips he'd managed to eat. Tired too. A long, lonely weekend of property searching had left him craving a warm bed and missing Cass. Always, always, missing Cass. But his low mood lifted when he stepped outside into the mild September air. He loved London at any time of year, and autumn was his favourite season. Mellow and warm, even when the air turned cooler.

The unmistakable scent of city nightlife got to him too. Camden felt different when the sun went down, heady and exciting. Suddenly, the twenty unanswered emails clogging his inbox felt less important. He checked his watch: 7 p.m. The weekend crowds had eased, and he probably should've gone home, but his abortive dinner—and the pint of beer on an empty stomach—had left him restless. He didn't feel like going home to an empty flat.

He wandered along Camden High Street. A pub caught his eye, one of those oh-so-cool bars with bare brickwork, graffiti, and a bazillion tea lights. The kind of place Tom knew he'd be too old for in a few years' time. He drifted inside. London being London, no one glanced up. He bought a pint of overpriced lager and found a table in a dark corner. The mellow chillstep music was soothing, and for a while, he resisted the call of his laptop and people watched instead . . . analysing the clientele he'd be targeting *if* he ever found the right premises. Camden was an eclectic locale. Hipsters, punks, goths, yuppies, he could see them all in the bar. And he'd seen them out on the street too, dark and edgy . . . too cool for their own good. Camden felt like a place for the young . . . the up-and-coming who wanted to stamp their mark on the world a different way. To make it here, whatever restaurant Tom opened would need to be more than a mainstream brand.

But how? Young people desired luxury, but lacked the money to procure it. And Tom had noticed in recent years that his younger clientele were becoming less adventurous. They wanted safe, uncomplicated food . . . wanted it to look the same wherever they went, and that didn't leave much scope for creativity. Simple, posh, and cheap. There had to be a way to have it all.

Tom tapped his fingers on the table, brainstorming concepts, lost in thought. He nearly didn't notice the appearance of the slender, dark-haired man in the seat beside him sometime later. A twitching bundle of limbs he belatedly recognised as the waiter from the faceless restaurant down the road.

"*Wankers.*"

Tom blinked. "Excuse me?"

Jake winced, and it was a moment before he spoke again. "Hello."

Tom smiled, unsure if he was about to get punched in the face. "Hello again."

"Hi." Jake jerked, like a bolt of electricity had just run through him. "You . . ." he stopped, started again, and slid a leather-covered book across the table. "You left your diary."

Tom reflexively reached for the diary that held his whole life. The diary that rarely left his sight. "How did you know where to find me?"

"I saw you come in here when I was on my break. Figured I'd take a look when I finished work and see if you were still here."

Tom shoved the diary into his laptop bag. Jake muttered something. Tom straightened up. "Sorry, what?"

Jake shook his head. "Nothing. I'm just ticking."

Ticking. Tom had heard the phrase before. A lightbulb clicked on in his brain. "Tourette's?"

"Shit, fuck, bollocks. *Yes.* Shit." Jake winked. "Fly him to the moon."

Tourette's. Bloody hell. That explained a lot—the stuttering, the sudden tremors in Jake's limbs, and the badly timed swearing. "Is that why you called your boss a wanker?"

Jake shrugged. "Sometimes my tics are in context."

Tom grinned, though inside, his mind was reeling. Tourette's wasn't a condition he knew much about, but he'd already seen firsthand how disruptive it could be. Even now, he saw Jake struggling to keep still. "Can I buy you a drink?"

"No, thanks. You left me a fifty-quid tip. I can buy my own."

Jake got up as abruptly as he had sat down, and walked to the bar. Tom watched him go, admiring the liquid way his body moved when he wasn't ticking, and speculating if he'd come back.

It seemed like an age before Jake reappeared with two pints of lager. He set one in front of Tom, then hovered, his left arm rippling. Tom gestured to the chair beside him. "Sit down, please. I could use the company."

Jake sat down. He cradled his drink in one hand and glared at his twitching arm until it stilled. "*Wankers.* Sorry. It's worse when I meet new people."

"Don't apologise," Tom said. "It doesn't bother me." And it didn't. The young man next to him was a far cry from the vibrating ball of frustration he'd been in the restaurant, and his tics seemed natural. As Jake relaxed, Tom could almost see them slowing down and fading in their intensity. "I'm Tom, by the way. In case you were wondering—"

"Why would you think that?" Jake held out his hand. "I'm Jake."

"I know." Tom met his grasp. Felt a spark, like Jake's excess energy had travelled into him. "It said so on your name tag."

Jake twitched and a series of clicking noises escaped him so fast Tom wondered if he'd imagined them. "Yeah, sorry your dinner was pants. The food is always crap in there."

"It's not your fault. You tried to warn me."

"Not on purpose. TS makes me brutally honest."

"TS?" Tom floundered a moment and released Jake's electric hand. The loss of contact defogged his brain. "Oh, you mean your Tourette's."

It wasn't a question, but Jake shot Tom a glance that had "idiot" written all over it. Tom let him have that one. "I don't think it's your Toure . . . sorry, TS, that makes you a terrible waiter."

Jake leaned forwards. "Oh yeah? What did I do that was so bad?"

Up close, he was even more beautiful than Tom had first imagined. Dark, soulful eyes. Wavy hair that hung a little too long. And he smelled good, like cigarettes and youth.

Tom covered his fascination with a pull on his beer. "It's not what you do; it's how you do it. As a guest, I shouldn't know that standing in front of me is the last place on earth you want to be."

"Fly him to the moon."

"Exactly."

Jake rolled his eyes. "Don't indulge me. That's one of my favourite tics. If you play along, I'll forget I'm doing it and they'll all come out."

"Okay . . ." Jake was clearly comfortable talking about his TS. "Is that so bad? The tics, I mean." Tom gestured around. "No one seems to notice them."

"That's because I've found my volume switch. I don't shout anymore, at least not often. A few years ago, I hardly left my bedsit."

"Volume switch?"

"Yep. I didn't want to be a weirdo shouting in the corner all the time, so I learned to mute myself. I had to. It was either that, or walk around with my mouth taped shut, though I *did* do that for a few months."

The image made Tom smile, but the sadness in Jake's dark gaze tempered it. "So what do you hate so much about where you work? What put that frown on your face before you even got to me?"

"What do you care?"

Tom shrugged. It was a fair question. "Call it research. I'm in the industry."

"The . . . *wankers* . . . restaurant industry?" Tom nodded and Jake considered his question. "I hate being told to be the same as everyone else," he said eventually.

"A chain restaurant probably isn't the best place for you, then. They make every high street look the same."

Jake huffed his agreement. "The company I work for has five pubs in the city, and they're all identical. The food, the decor. They even have a script to make us all sound like robots. Winds me up."

This time, Tom didn't bite back his smile. Jake's gripe reinforced the puzzle Tom had been pondering all day. "So if you could redevelop the restaurant you worked in, how would you do it?"

"I wouldn't. I don't care enough. I'm only working there because it was the only job I could get."

"Maybe you would care if it was a concept you liked," Tom countered. "Food you liked, or an ethos you believed in."

Jake snorted, but it was hard to tell if it was a tic or a reaction to Tom's words. He waited a moment, but Jake said no more, so Tom drained his drink and went to the bar for another round.

Jake eyed him when he got back. "You know, you look way too young to care about all this business bollocks."

"I'm thirty." Tom pondered Jake's age. His slender frame and smooth skin made him look eighteen, but his eyes gave him away. He'd seen more of the world than he should've done. "What about you?"

"Twenty-four," Jake said. "Too young for you?"

"Depends what I was going to do with you."

The words slipped out before Tom could stop them, aided by three pints of strong lager. In his head, he heard Cass laugh. *Smooth.*

Tom waited for Jake to rebuke him. Call him a pervy twat. Perhaps even get up and leave.

But Jake just grinned and put his elbows on the table. "I reckon you should start at the top and work your way down."

CHAPTER TWO

Jake was joking, at least Tom thought he was, but the loaded exchange changed the tone of their conversation, and as the beer flowed, the air between them got hotter. It was nearly midnight before Tom realised he'd forgotten to go home.

He leaned away from Jake with a rueful smile. Somehow, they'd ended up almost nose to nose. "I should get going."

Jake stood and passed Tom the jumper he'd taken off during their conversation. "Yeah, me too."

They left the pub and stepped out onto the street. Tom shivered. The temperature had dropped while they'd been holed up inside. Jake put a cigarette in his mouth. Lit it. "Don't mind, do you?"

"Have at it." Tom didn't know what else to say. It was late, but he wasn't ready for the night to end. "Um, Tube station?"

"Sure."

They walked to Camden Town Station. Jake twitched a lot as they ambled along. Tom wondered why. In the pub, Jake's tics had all but disappeared—or maybe Tom had just grown used to them—but outside on the street, it was clear Jake struggled. After a while, Tom took Jake's arm. Whether it helped or not, he couldn't tell.

Jake calmed somewhat when they got underground. He turned to Tom and smiled. "Thanks. It helps when someone touches me. Give me something to focus on."

Tom scanned his Oyster card and slipped through the barriers. He waited for Jake to do the same before he shrugged. "No worries, providing you don't mind a stranger touching you."

"Beggars can't be choosers."

Tom stared at Jake. He didn't believe that for a second. Jake was gorgeous, and even with the TS wreaking havoc through his nervous system, he oozed sex appeal. Who in their right mind wouldn't want to touch him?

"I'm surprised, actually, that you walked this far with me. Most people lose their nerve when we get outside."

Tom frowned, leading the way to the platform. "Is it worse outside?"

"Sometimes. Depends on the situation. My tics are coming out now because I'm tired, but earlier, when I found you in the bar, I was nervous . . ."

"And when you were working, you were pissed off, right?"

"Right." Jake leaned against the grubby platform wall. "That was extreme, though. It's been a while since I've lost my shit that much."

Tom mirrored Jake's position. He closed his eyes briefly, sure he could feel the warmth of Jake's body. "What happened? I mean, I know you hate your job, and I saw the plates on the floor, but what made it worse today than any other day?"

"You ask a lot of questions."

"You make me want to."

Jake smirked. "Fair enough. If you must know, I was pissed off because the barman stole my tip from my biggest table. The bloke's a prick, and when I called him out on it, I ended up ticking like a fucking lunatic instead. I tried to calm down, but then some old bird tripped me up. My boss called me an idiot, and the TS got away from me after that."

"It must be hard to find a happy medium when so much stimulates your tics."

"There are a few things even TS can't spoil." Jake chuckled, deep and low. The gravelly sound reminded Tom of Cass again, but a train pulled in before he could let the thought fully manifest.

They found seats on the train. Jake muttered to himself as he sat down. A woman across the aisle stared, but Jake didn't seem to notice, and Tom was surprised to find that her attention didn't bother him either.

The train rattled through Chalk Farm. They sat in companionable silence for a while, save Jake's sporadic mutterings, until Jake nudged Tom with his elbow.

"Why did you come into the restaurant today? I could tell you were pissed off as soon as you walked in. Thought you were going to be one of those tables that moaned my ear off."

Tom chuckled. "I did moan, at the girl on the bar, but I don't think she noticed."

Jake laughed too. "Yeah, there's not much to Courtney. She knows a lot about hair extensions, though, in case you're ever interested."

"Can't see that happening."

"So . . ." Jake whistled and made a strange popping sound. "Why did you come in if you knew you were going to hate it so much?"

"You're a shrewd one," Tom said. "I always figured I had a pretty good poker face, but if you must know, it was a spur-of-the-moment thing. The Tube station was shut and I couldn't be arsed to walk to the next one."

"Oh." Jake seemed disappointed. "I thought you were spying for head office, or some undercover exposé or something."

"Sorry, mate. I'm not that interesting."

"Yes, you are."

The train stopped in Belsize Park. Jake tore his stare from Tom and frowned. "Shit, I'm going the wrong way. I live in Kentish Town."

He dropped his head and groaned. Alarmed, Tom put his hand on his shoulder. "Are you okay? Do you want to get off?"

A barrage of tics swept through Jake before he straightened up and grinned. "Too late now."

And indeed it was. The train had closed its doors and already left Belsize Park behind. Tom relaxed and took his hand off Jake as his tics faded. He seemed unconcerned with being on the wrong train, like it happened all the time. Perhaps it did. "Where do you live?"

"Hampstead, during the week, at least."

"Where do you live at the weekend?"

"Berkhamsted. I have a house there."

"You sound rich," Jake stretched his legs out in front of him. "I didn't think that was possible from working in restaurants."

Tom shrugged. He wasn't rich, but for his age, he'd done all right. "I don't work in restaurants. Not anymore, at least. I own them. Come on. Let's get off here."

The train rumbled into Hampstead. Tom took Jake's arm as he twitched getting off the train and held on to him until they got to the end of the platform.

"You don't need to babysit me."

"Hmm? Oh, sorry." Tom released the death grip he had on Jake's arm. Jake grabbed his hand and put it back. "You can touch me, Tom, but do it because you want to, not because you feel sorry for me."

Something about the way Jake said his name made Tom's chest feel warm. He stared at Jake, feeling the charge where he held Jake's slender wrist. "I don't feel sorry for you. I just didn't want you to fall."

"Same thing."

"No, it's not."

Tom let go of Jake's wrist again, suddenly aware of how close they were standing. It was late—no early—the early hours of Monday morning, but the Tube station was still busy, like it always was. London wasn't New York, but it was still a city that never slept.

Jake didn't move, not even to tic. The only sign of life in him was his dark addictive gaze and the tiny flicker of his tongue as he licked his lips. His brief stillness was mesmerising. Tom stared at him, lost, until Jake clumsily touched his cheek. "Why *do* you touch me, then?"

Tom didn't answer with words. What could he say? They'd just met, spent only a few hours in each other's company, and yet, Tom couldn't say good-bye. He took Jake's arm for a third time and led him above ground. Outside on the pavement, he pointed to a row of converted Edwardian houses in the distance. "My flat's over there. Fancy another drink?"

The Hampstead flat was old and beautiful—high ceilings, hardwood floors, original fireplaces—but it was also small and expensive; a combination that always wound Tom up.

Not tonight, though. He unlocked the door and waved Jake in, absorbing the forbidden scent of the cigarette Jake had smoked on their short walk home. "Do you want a drink?"

Jake squinted up at the ornate coving in the tiny hallway. "No, thanks. I think I've had enough."

Tom hung his coat on the hook. He didn't want a drink either. He wanted to kiss Jake . . . kiss him hard, but the moment seemed elusive.

"*Wankers.* I like your bum. Shit." Jake slapped his hand over his mouth.

Tom laughed. "Kind of you to say."

Jake stood stock-still for a few seconds, then let his hand drop. "Sorry. You do have a nice arse, though."

"Thanks. Yours is pretty nice too. Can I take your coat?"

Jake shrugged out of his coat, but instead of handing it over, he leaned in front of Tom to hang it behind the door himself. The movement brought his neck within inches of Tom's mouth. For the first time, Tom noticed an intricate tattoo hidden by Jake's shaggy hair. The design was black and moody, with distressed typography. The words gave Tom pause. *Don't ask me why.*

"What does your tattoo mean?"

"Which one?"

Tom touched his finger to Jake's neck. "This one."

"It means I was a pissed-off teenager. I got all my ink when I was angry."

"Are you still angry now?"

Jake shook his head. "No. I found the cure."

Tom traced the script, following it until it disappeared into the complex shading around Jake's spine. Jake shivered, but not like the abrupt shot of a tic that Tom was fast beginning to recognise. "And what was it? The cure, I mean."

"Learn something. Read a book. Explore someone. Anger is just a hole where your life could be."

Something changed. Tom's pulse quickened. He stilled his finger, but left it on Jake's skin, absorbing the rising heat between them. Jake glanced over his shoulder, his gaze a wicked mix of rueful desire, and in that moment, Tom knew Jake wanted him too.

Jake leaned back, and Tom kissed him, but the kiss wasn't as explosive as Tom had played out in his head. He didn't grab Jake's chin or bite his lips. He didn't pull his hair, or press him against the wall. Instead, he fell pliant under the gentle brush of Jake's mouth on his, wound his arms around Jake's waist, and pulled him close. Held him tight like they'd kissed a thousand times over.

Tom felt Jake connect with every part of his body. His scalp tingled, his cheeks, his chest. His dick hardened in his jeans. He cupped Jake's face with his hand and drew a thumb over his cheekbone.

Jake pulled away. "Show me your bedroom?"

Tom didn't need telling twice. He spun Jake in his arms, kissed him again, and backed him through the open bedroom door. They hit the bed. Tom was taller than Jake, wider, stronger, and he steadied their stumbling.

Jake tugged at Tom's clothes. Tom toed off his shoes and unbuttoned his shirt while Jake unbuckled his belt. His jeans fell to his knees. Tom shrugged out of his shirt and considered Jake. He was wearing biker boots, skinny jeans, and a T-shirt as thin as he was. The look was grungy and cool, but Tom had seen enough. He wanted Jake's clothes on the floor, scattered on the polished wood.

He undressed Jake—T-shirt first, *clingy* jeans next—and shed the last of his own clothes. For a moment, they stared, naked and still, and took in each other. Tom was fair haired and solid. Broad shoulders, chest, and thighs. In contrast, Jake was pale, fragile looking, and covered in sinister ink.

Tom closed his hand around Jake's cock, feeling the weight of it. "What do you like to do?"

"I like to suck dick and get fucked."

The bluntness took Tom by surprise, though he couldn't say why. Not that he was disappointed. The girth of Jake's cock was alluring, but Tom didn't bottom. And he *loved* getting head. Who didn't?

Still, he wanted something more first. Wanted to feel Jake everywhere, so if they never touched again, he'd know he'd made the most of this beautiful, enigmatic young man.

He lay back on the bed and pulled Jake over him, kissed him, and ran his hands all over his body.

Jake responded in kind and ghosted his palms over Tom's chest. "You didn't look this muscly with your clothes on."

"That a bad thing?"

Jake hummed around another kiss. "No. It suits your eyes."

Tom shoved his hands into Jake's silky hair and tugged so he could see Jake's face. "What does that mean?"

"What I said."

Fair enough. Tom kept his hands in Jake's hair. It was soft and clean, and Jake seemed to like Tom's nails digging into his scalp.

Tom rolled them over and covered Jake's slim frame with his broader body. He found Jake's cock and captured it in his hand without breaking their kiss. Jake jerked beneath him. *A tic?* To be sure, Tom opened his eyes and squeezed Jake's cock again.

Jake arched his back and groaned. "Fuck yeah."

Encouraged, Tom drove his tongue into Jake's mouth. He'd been intrigued by Jake the moment he'd laid eyes on him, and now he was sure of his path. He was going to fuck Jake, fuck him until he screamed his name.

Jake broke their kiss and tugged on Tom's shoulders. "Bring me your dick."

Tom followed his direction and straddled Jake's chest, which, unlike his back, was untouched by ink. He held his cock a hairsbreadth away from Jake's full lips. "Not going to bite me, are you?"

"No. Touch calms me down. I hardly tic at all if I'm in bed with someone."

That was good enough for Tom. He slid his dick into Jake's mouth and sucked in a breath. The hot, wet heat of Jake's tongue felt amazing, and Jake digging his nails in his thighs made it feel even better. He closed his eyes and let sensation sweep over him. He grabbed a handful of Jake's hair. "Yeah, like that."

Jake teased Tom's balls, then he pulled back with a soft, heated puff of air. "Tell me what you want."

Tom opened his eyes. "You like dirty talk?"

"I'm curious. I told you what *I* like."

Tom grinned and brought his cock back to Jake's mouth. "Maybe I'd like you to figure it out."

Jake took the hint. He drew Tom into his mouth again, lightly at first, with only the gentlest pressure, then he ramped up the volume and grazed Tom's cock with his teeth.

Tom groped around behind him and gripped Jake's cock, wishing he was flexible enough to lean back and return the favour, like Cass had so many times for him. He felt a deep flush heat his skin and knew they couldn't play this game for long.

He pulled out of Jake's mouth and tapped his lips with the head of his dick. "You bottom?"

"Always, at least so far." Jake stuck out his tongue and licked Tom lightly enough to make Tom's eyes roll. "That okay?"

It was more than okay. Tom clambered off Jake, walked on his knees to the bedside table, and fumbled with the drawer. He rolled a condom on, slathered lube onto his dick, and turned to find Jake relaxed and ready for him.

Tom considered his options. True to his word, Jake hadn't ticked at all since they'd taken their clothes off. It was hard to believe he was the same frustrated waiter who'd lost his cool in the restaurant. He offered his hand as he lay back and stretched out. "Come here."

"Want me to ride you?"

Hell yeah. "Yeah."

Tom sat up on his elbows, watching as Jake sank down on him. He took his time easing Tom inside his body. Tom's cock was thick and long, and Jake's brief discomfort was clear, until it faded and he bit down on his lip in a way that made Tom's toes curl.

Jake flexed his muscles, then he lifted himself up so slowly Tom couldn't hold back a low groan.

Jake smirked. "You like that?"

He growled. "Do it again."

Jake obliged, and it was the start of the most languid fuck Tom had ever had. He'd first put his hands on Jake with a clear image in his mind, an image that saw him bending Jake in half and driving into him, perhaps even flipping him over and pushing his face into the pillow. But it didn't happen. Jake worked his magic and with every long, slow roll of his hips, Tom fell deeper and deeper into something he didn't quite understand.

Tom took his weight off his elbows and raised his arms over his head, gripped the edge of the bed, and arched his back.

"You look so hot right now." Jake leaned down and pressed their chests together, trapping his cock between them. "Even more than I thought you would."

Tom thrust his hips up. Made them both gasp. "Yeah? You look pretty fucking beautiful yourself."

Jake's eyes widened, like Tom's words had sent a jolt through him. Or maybe it was something else. With his quivering thighs and sweat-sheened skin, Jake seemed on the edge of release.

Tom gathered himself and drove up into Jake, heeding his spine-tingling pace, but twisting his hips, searching for the angle that would unravel Jake's smirking composure.

He found it on the third go.

Jake fell slack on top of him and moaned, low and plaintive. Tom grinned and pushed Jake's hand towards his cock. "Make yourself come."

Jake resisted. "Don't need to. You're doing it."

Tom thrust harder, and Jake gave in, jacking himself until he seized up and came over Tom's chest. "Oh God . . . *Fuck.*"

"Yeah?" Tom drove his hips up, absorbing every clench and spasm of Jake around him. His world narrowed to the dark, flushed man writhing on top of him, the feel of hot skin on skin, and the heavy scent of sex in the air. Then pleasure twisted his gut, drove the breath from his lungs, and forced a guttural groan from deep in his belly.

He came with a yell that was smothered by Jake's frantic kiss. He met Jake's embrace, and they collapsed together in a tangle of clumsy hands and rough, biting kisses, the kind of kisses he had imagined when he'd first set eyes on Jake.

When it was over, they lay breathless and exhausted. Jake shivered. Tom hooked the rumpled sheets with his foot and drew the duvet over them. Jake hummed his appreciation. "Your bed smells nice."

Tom smiled into the darkness and touched the soft mane of inky hair he felt like he'd known forever. "Stay awhile, if you like."

"Careful. I sleep like a log. You'll need a foghorn to wake me up."

Tom rubbed Jake's shoulder. He didn't sleep much, never had, but he knew someone else who slept like the dead once he finally found rest, and it was a characteristic he found endearing. He tightened his arms around Jake and listened to his unfamiliar breathing even out. Felt the faint tics ripple through him and felt his affection for him grow with each shudder and jolt.

Jake wasn't the man he'd longed for in his bed that night, but though he missed Cass enough for his chest to ache, Jake's slender bones wrapped around him felt pretty bloody perfect.

CHAPTER THREE

It was 9 a.m. when Tom's phone rang the following morning. He fumbled for it among the stacks of paperwork on his desk, prepared to do battle with yet another cowboy supplier, but then he saw the photo ID of the caller and his heart skipped a warm, pleasurable beat. *Cass.*

Tom smiled and pressed the speakerphone button. Cass was the executive chef at their flagship restaurant, his business partner, lover, and soul mate of the last nine years. "Morning, gorgeous."

"Morning."

"You okay?"

Cass hummed in reply, throaty and deep, like he'd just woken up. "You left something pretty in bed."

Tom's grin widened as he checked the time. Cass had spent the night at the flat above Pippa's, their restaurant in Shepherd's Bush, and he wasn't much of a morning person when he didn't have to be. What was he doing in Hampstead so early? "Very funny. How do you know that? I thought you were going straight to the house after the stock take this morning."

"Couldn't sleep. I did the stocks last night instead. More productive than counting sheep, eh?"

"You're preaching to the choir." Tom leaned back in his chair and stretched the kinks out of his spine. His own inability to sleep past dawn was what had driven him to leave Jake alone in bed in the first place.

Tom got up from his desk and walked to the window. He felt lighter, like he always did when he told Cass he'd been with another bloke. Their relationship was a mystery to many, but it worked for them. They shared a life, and from time to time fucked other people. Didn't change the fact that they loved each other to death.

"So, who *is* the pretty thing you left in bed for me?"

Tom let Cass's teasing question hang. Pretty was just the half of it. He'd watched Jake sleep for hours, traced his tattoos, counted his tics, and admired his fragile beauty. Cass was the only man who'd ever captivated him so completely . . . and so fast.

"Earth to Tom?" Cass chuckled, and even through the phone, Tom felt his presence like a second skin. He had the dirtiest laugh on the planet. "Sounds like he's something special. Shame he didn't hang around for me to see it for myself."

"He left?"

"Yep. Think I scared the shit out of him. I offered him a cuppa, but he scarpered like a bat out of hell."

Tom winced. He'd never have left Jake if he'd known Cass was going there. Jake wasn't the first bloke one of them had brought home who'd assumed the other would be out for his blood. "I didn't tell him about you last night. I was going to head back soon, buy him brunch, and do it then."

"Wasn't a one-night thing, then."

It wasn't a question, but Tom considered it anyway. Did he want to see Jake again? Naked or otherwise? Yeah . . . yeah, he did. "Did you get a chance to talk to him?"

"Not really, but I gave him the note you left. He took it with him, if it's any consolation."

It wasn't, and Tom had a feeling Cass knew it. "Anyway, aside from insomnia, what are you doing at base camp? Everything okay?"

Base camp was their nickname for the Hampstead flat, but in reality, Cass rarely made the long Tube ride across the city when he stayed late at Pippa's. He worked hard enough without adding a hellish commute to his day, a reality Tom often found tough to swallow when he was missing Cass as much as he had been recently. Cass sighed, like he'd heard Tom's lonely thoughts. "I thought we could drive home together for Manday Monday. I forgot you had to work today."

"Sorry, babe."

"Any idea what time you'll be back?"

Tom felt a twinge of guilt twist his gut. Monday was the only consistent day of the week Cass didn't work, and Tom did his best to keep the day free so they could spend quality time together at their real home, a ramshackle house away from the city. But life didn't always work out that way, and today he'd be lucky if he made it home in time for supper. "Don't wait up."

Cass sighed again, but it was pissed off rather than rueful this time. "Okay, but don't forget I took tomorrow off as holiday. We should do something."

He hung up before Tom could admit he *had* forgotten Cass had a few outstanding lieu days to use up before Christmas.

Tom wandered back to his desk and tossed his phone on an open folder. He had back-to-back meetings scheduled for most of the following day too, one of the cons of running six businesses that had nothing in common. He rubbed his neck and sighed. Life would be far easier without principles.

Easy. Tom thought of Cass, and, not for the first time that morning, thought of Jake too. Yeah, life could be easy, but who wanted that?

Not Tom. He spent the rest of the morning wrangling with advertising firms and rescheduling his Tuesday meetings. It was nearly lunchtime when his phone rang again. The caller ID for Pink's, the tiny fish café they owned in Covent Garden flashed up. "Morning, Nero."

Nero, the grouchiest chef in the world, grunted a response. "The rep from the recycling company called here for you. Said he was confirming your meeting tomorrow."

"Shit. Is that really tomorrow?" Tom thumbed through his diary and found the appointment—*Barry Herbert, Green Stuff Logistics*—neatly written in for the following Sunday. *Bloody Sunday? What the fuck was I thinking when I wrote that?* "Shit. I had it down for the wrong day. Don't suppose you want to fill in for me, do you?"

"You taking the piss?"

Nero had a point. The bloke was blunt on a good day, and bloody rude the rest of the time. "Did he leave a number?"

Nero reeled it off and hung up. Tom called the rep and tried for a reschedule, but it wasn't good news.

"Could be difficult. I'm heading home tomorrow night. Do you want to liaise with my PA and set something up with head office?"

Not really. In fact, it was the last thing Tom wanted to do. Green Stuff Logistics had their home in bloody Reading, and Tom barely had time for meetings in London.

Still, there wasn't much he could do but agree and make the appointment. He'd built his company from scratch and put everything he had into making it thrive, but nothing was more important to him than Cass.

Even so, it was close to midnight by the time he staggered off the last train into Berkhamsted and caught a cab home. He let himself into the old Victorian house and followed the sound of the TV to the living room, hoping to find Cass awake, but no such luck. He was stretched out in front of the fire, fast asleep. Tom hovered in the doorway a moment, enjoying the view, but Cass's presence reeled him in, like it had the moment they'd met nearly a decade ago. He dumped his bag, kicked off his shoes, and padded across the bare wood floors they hadn't had time to varnish yet. He crouched down and pushed Cass's hood back so he could see his face. Chiselled cheekbones and dark stubble greeted him. He waited a moment to see if Cass would reveal his moody-blue eyes, but the love of his life remained asleep.

With a reluctant sigh, Tom kissed his cheek, dug some breakfast supplies out of the freezer, and went to bed alone.

Tom woke at dawn to find Cass had crawled into bed with him during the night. He held him awhile, breathing him in, but eventually his usual restlessness got the better of him, and he left Cass to sleep.

He trod softly down the stairs, through the unpainted hallway and derelict dining room, and headed for the kitchen, the only finished room in the house. He put the kettle on the range and warmed himself over the hob while the water came to the boil. Then he took his mug of hot tea and stood by the kitchen window, one of his favourite pastimes when he was lucky enough to wake up at home. The garden was wild and beautiful, a tangled mess of gnarled branches and overgrown shrubs, and after a week in the city, watching the birds dance in the trees was a balm to his tired eyes.

There was a scrabbling noise at the back door. Tom wandered over and granted entrance to the lean streak of feline attitude who fought him for Cass's affection.

Souris sashayed into the house, shooting Tom a glare that left him in no doubt of his place in her world. The tiny tabby belonged to Cass, and only deigned to come home when she knew he was there, or at least sensed he was imminent. She spent the rest of her time with the old lady across the road and treated Tom with disdain. This morning, she stalked past the food he put in her bowl and disappeared into the house to find Cass.

Tom returned to his post with a wry smile. Perhaps the cat had the right idea. Was there anything better than a lazy day with Cass? Probably not, but as Tom stood by the unpainted kitchen window, his mind drifted to another dark-haired man who'd recently shared his bed. In the misty light of the early morning, he took a moment to appreciate the similarities between Cass and Jake. Some were obvious—tattoos, dark hair, and slim bones—but others less so. Others were things most people wouldn't notice, especially in Cass, like the vulnerability that drew Tom in until he couldn't let go.

Cass, Jake, Cass, Jake.

Though Cass owned his heart, Tom knew he'd see Jake again. He had to . . . that is, if he could get to Camden anytime soon.

Wiry arms slid around Tom from behind. "What are you thinking so hard about?"

Tom closed his eyes and absorbed the warmth that spread through his chest. "You?"

Cass chuckled and pressed his face between Tom's shoulder blades, biting gently through his T-shirt. "Yeah, and the rest?"

Tom turned away from the window and pulled Cass to him in a long, hard hug. "What are you doing up so early? Thought it would be gone noon before you showed your face."

Cass was silent a moment, his face hidden in Tom's chest, then he shrugged. "The cat punched me. Think she's hungry."

"She's not hungry; she's an arsehole. I already fed her." Tom inclined his head at the full cat bowl. "I'll feed you too, if you like. What do you want for breakfast?"

Cass lifted his head and grinned, his sleep-tousled hair sticking up in every direction. "Make me a cuppa and surprise me."

He sloped off to the shower, leaving Tom to roll his eyes and throw some bangers under the grill for sausage baps. Cass was a typical chef: he worked hard, played hard, and only ate a proper meal when someone else cooked it and put it in front of him. Tom's repertoire was basic, compared to Cass's at least, but when he had time, there was almost nothing he liked more than taking care of his boy.

They spent a lazy morning on the sofa. Cass put his head in Tom's lap and dozed through reruns of *Top Gear* and *Only Fools and Horses*, while Tom balanced his laptop on the arm of the couch and answered the emails he couldn't ignore. True to form, it *was* gone noon before Cass decided he was awake enough to go out.

They wrapped up warm and left the house for their habitual walk through the woodland that surrounded their home. Tom shut the back gate and held out his hand. Cass grasped it, and they set off down the bridle path that took them through the nearby Ashridge country park. The woods were peaceful and almost deserted, populated only by a few dog walkers. A young labradoodle pup ran up to them and pounced on Cass.

Cass laughed and scratched its ears. "I want one."

Tom thought of their contrary cat and snorted. "No chance. You have to come home at night if you have a dog."

"Says you."

Cass kept his gaze on the pup, a longing smile on his face, and Tom had to fight to remain unmoved. His position was fair, in his mind, at least. Cass's insistence on remaining on the front line of their business was a major bone of contention. He was an equal partner in their company. There was no need for him to work seventy-five-hour weeks in the kitchen. He could do anything he wanted—

Tom caught his train of thought and reined himself in. Cass *was* doing what he wanted. Anything else would bore the arse off him, and working seventy-five hours a week was far better than how Cass had spent his time before he'd found his calling selling artisan sausages on London's famous Borough Market. Didn't make being apart any easier, though, and knowing it was unnecessary grated at Tom's nerves, even on a good day. Why was it so hard for Cass to just . . . be?

The dog's owner whistled. The pup woofed and scampered away. Cass reluctantly watched him go. Tom fought again to ignore the yearning in Cass's gaze, and reclaimed his hand. They walked until they returned to the canal and stopped at a pub by the water's edge. Cass went inside and brought back pints of ale and three bags of crisps to the table Tom had claimed.

Tom rolled his eyes. "Quavers? Really?"

"Piss off." Cass ripped the bags open and pushed one bag Tom's way. "I know you're not too posh for Quavers."

Tom gave Cass the finger. His private school education was something Cass liked to poke fun at. Cass'd grown up in the back end of Tower Hamlets, and to him, Tom's childhood seemed like a Disney film.

"So tell me about the lanky hottie in our bed yesterday."

Tom swallowed a mouthful of beer. Though Jake had been on Tom's mind, Cass hadn't mentioned him all morning, which Tom had taken as a sign he wasn't that interested. "What do you want to know?"

"Where did you meet him?"

"In Camden. I grabbed some dinner in one of PBG's places."

Cass wrinkled his nose. "What the fuck for? I'd rather starve."

"I know, I know. The food was rubbish, but the scenery wasn't bad. Jake was my waiter."

Cass smirked. "You picked up your waiter? That's so cheesy."

"Not quite. I went for a drink after. He found me in the bar and brought my diary back to me. I'd left it on my table."

"That's even worse. So, *Jake*, eh? I like that name, and I liked his ink. He has some epic tattoos."

"So do you." Tom took a pull of his pint and considered Cass. He and Jake had different eyes. Jake's were warm and brown, while no one on earth had stormy blues quite like Cass. "Did you notice anything else about him?"

"I didn't get much chance. I told you, he legged it."

"You didn't talk to him?"

"Not really." Cass set down his beer, perhaps sensing Tom was trying to tell him something. "And he didn't say much at all, apart from calling me an arse-bandit wanker, which I thought was pretty rich. Why? What am I missing?"

Tom reached for the crisps between them. "He has Tourette's. You know what that is, right?"

"I think so," Cass said after a moment's thought. "Is that the swearing thing Keith Allen did that documentary on?"

"I don't know, but there seems to be more to it than swearing. Jake called them tics . . . the swearing and stuff, but it was more physical than just shouting, like it went through his whole body."

Tom explained the incident in the restaurant and the behaviour he'd witnessed in the bar and on the train. "It wasn't so bad when we were fucking, though. I forgot about it, to be honest, and it felt like he did too."

"So you fucked him, then?"

Tom chanced a glance around, but there was no one close enough to overhear them. "Yeah, I guess, but to be honest, for most of it, it felt like *he* was fucking *me*."

Cass burst out laughing. "Really? That's bloody brilliant. I wish I'd seen it. You're such a control freak."

"Yeah well, *you* like it."

"True." Cass sobered himself with clear effort. "Is that what's got him under your skin so much? The fucking? Or is it the Tourette's?"

Tom hooked his legs around Cass's under the table, and reminded himself how lucky he was to be with someone who understood him so well. "I don't know," he said eventually. "I had a good time with him, and I liked him, a lot, but it feels unfinished. Like I forgot to do something that really bloody matters."

"Sounds like more than fucking." Cass drained his pint and dropped the glass on the table. "Maybe you should stick around next time."

Next time. They left the pub with the notion swimming in Tom's head, though Cass said no more on the subject. They completed the loop around the town and stopped at the Dragonfly, the bistro they owned on the high street.

Cass wanted to check the kitchen, but Tom stood his ground and parked him in a cosy alcove with a cup of tea while he wandered back of house under the pretence of doing so himself. Gloria, the bistro's head chef, greeted him with open arms. Tom returned her crushing embrace with a wry smile. Gloria didn't need her kitchen checked. Cass aside, she was the best chef they had.

"I saved some cassoulet and dauphinoise. Take it home for you and Cass. You both work too hard."

Tom wasn't about to argue, especially when Gloria was pushing her epic cassoulet on him. He bade her good-bye, retrieved Cass, and together, they made their way home.

They spent the rest of the day painting their bedroom, an activity that ended with Cass bent over the bed and *covered* in sticky white fingermarks. It was late by the time they sat down to the mountain of food Gloria had donated to them.

Cass eyed the overflowing dishes. "We always have too much food. Maybe you should track down your new friend. Feed him up a little."

"You'd be okay with that?"

Cass shrugged. "Why not? You always know when someone needs your help. You've got a sixth sense or something. The fact that he's hot is a bonus. Find him. Fuck him. Fix him. It's what you do."

"That's not what I do."

"Yes, it is." Cass shoved his fork in his mouth like the conversation was done, but then he held out his hand. "You fix me all the time when I listen, and if he . . . Jake wants to see how, bring him home. I'd like to meet him."

The thought of Cass and Jake in the same place together made Tom warm all over. He took Cass's hand. "I'd rather *you* came home more often first." He didn't miss the bleak undertone lacing his words, but he tried to ignore it. "And I don't fix you, babe; you fix yourself."

"Do I? Some days I'm not so sure."

Tom squeezed Cass's hand. "What's on your mind?"

"Hmm? Oh, nothing. Not really. Just hard to believe I'm really here sometimes, you know?"

Tom didn't. He'd tried over and over to get his head around Cass's continual belief that he didn't deserve all that he'd worked so hard for, and still didn't get it. Cass had come from nothing and now he had the world at his feet. Why couldn't he be proud of that? Proud of *them* and all they'd achieved? Lord knew Tom was, but he'd lost this argument with Cass too many times to spoil their precious time together.

Instead, he squeezed Cass's hand again, loved him a little bit more, and tried to find a plausible business reason to pass through Camden the following day.

CHAPTER FOUR

In the end, it was three weeks before Tom returned to Camden, and even then, he had to use the lure of another potential restaurant site and sacrifice a day with Cass to find the time. And it wasn't much of a lure. The newly vacant barbershop was tucked away on Chalk Farm Road; nowhere near the bustling markets that had drawn Tom to Camden in the first place.

He emerged from the Tube station on a dreary Monday morning and looked around. Clear of the weekend crowds he'd battled last time, the air felt different, but still vibrant and full of promise. The barbershop had appeared a dive on the website, but Tom still headed south with a flicker of hope in his belly. The colourful streets of Camden seemed to do that to him.

The estate agent met him at the boarded-up shop. It had been vacant a few weeks, and was already covered in the bright graffiti of London's underground artists; street culture Tom would have to get scrubbed off before Cass persuaded him to leave it right there.

"Have you viewed any other properties since we last met?"

"Hmm?" Tom tore his gaze from the graffiti and caught his runaway thoughts. Christ, the place was a tip, and he was worrying about some poxy vandalism? He focused on the agent. "We've considered a few, but not in this area. There's a site in Putney we might take on if we can't make things work here."

The agent looked offended. Tom wasn't fooled. Estate agents were snakes, every bloody one of them.

"This is a great site," she said. "I know it's a bit off the beaten track, but it won't be for long. We're seeing lots of movement in this area."

Tom let the comment hang and preceded the agent into the dusty premises. She continued to talk at him, but he tuned her out and surveyed the stripped shop front with a practiced eye. First impressions weren't good. Depending on the depth of the structure, the architect he employed would need to do some serious work to maximise the building's potential, work that wouldn't be worth the money unless the site was hiding something spectacular.

The agent cleared her throat. "Come through to the other rooms."

Tom flipped through the printed property details as he followed her to the area that could serve as the kitchen. He'd seen photos online, and knew the back rooms of the building were practically derelict.

"It does need a lot of work," she said.

Tom shot her an irritated glance. "You think?"

The agent met his glare head-on. "Look, I know it's a dump, but it has planning permission to extend another twenty feet, and you could utilise the upper floor too. The building is structurally sound. For the asking price—which I think you can negotiate down—this place is a steal."

A steal. Easy for her to say, because that was the other thing about this building: it was for sale, not for rent and, if they took it, would be their biggest, and riskiest, investment yet. "What was this place originally, before the barbershop, and whatever it was before that?"

The agent checked her notes. "The market tollhouse, and then a fire station, but it closed in the sixties. They built a new one down the road."

Tom walked to the middle of the ground floor and spun in a slow circle. "What happened to all the stuff?"

"Probably in a museum somewhere."

Tom glanced around again and tried to see past the dust and junk. He took in the disused bell clock. Beneath the vulgar modernisation, he was beginning to realise the building was gorgeous. *Are those open arcades original?* He'd heard of a chef up north who had converted an old RAF base into a pizza place, utilising many of its original features. Even the wood-fired oven had been built in the shell of an Apache helicopter.

His gaze fell on the open staircase. "What's up there? Offices?"

"At the moment." The agent consulted her notes again. "You could rent them out, or use them yourself. Are you still working at your place in Greenwich?"

Tom shrugged. He liked his cosy offices above their most recent and daring venture. The stripped-back stew-and-ale bar epitomised the ethos of the whole company, and reminded him every day what the hell it was all for.

An hour later, Tom said good-bye to the agent for what felt like the millionth time. Once she was gone, he lingered, snapping photos of the timbered old building's exterior for Cass to look at when they met up that evening. Tom's head still told him the place was a dump, but his gut said it could be something special, if only they could track down the fire station's original . . .

"*Bastard.*"

The growled, bitten-out curse caught Tom off guard. He jumped a mile and spun around to find Jake behind him, hands clenched, eyes wide, and not looking entirely friendly. "Bloody hell. You scared me. All right, mate?"

Jake said nothing, just tapped his own cheek a few times. Tom couldn't tell if the silence was deliberate. He took a step forwards, his hand reaching of its own volition for Jake's scruffy sleeve. "Was that tic in context, or are you as pleased to see me as I am to see you?"

Jake jerked back and jostled a passing woman. "Piss off."

Tom flinched. This time there was no mistaking the venomous bite in Jake's tone, or the furious flash in his dark gaze. "Something wrong?"

"Where's your boyfriend?"

"At work." Tom kept his tone neutral. "He'll be glad we ran into each other, though. You made quite an impression."

"Are you taking the piss?"

"No."

Jake glowered hard at Tom, his arms trembling. Then he lost the battle he must have been waging against his tics and went off like fireworks.

Tom waited, ignoring the occasional stares of passersby, but Jake's tics didn't fade, and Tom sensed the frustration pouring from him. He'd seen this before, at the PGB restaurant, when he'd dropped the plates.

Tom's phone buzzed in his hand. Cass's devilish scowl flashed onto the screen with an SMS at just the wrong moment. *Any good?*

Tom typed out a quick reply. *Maybe. Need a concept, though. Fast. Bring this bastard to life.*

Cass's response was instant. *Get your arse in gear then, pretty boy. I'll bring the food.*

Despite Cass's very real disinterest in the nuts and bolts of the business, he designed epic menus for every restaurant they'd ever opened. All they needed was a plan . . . a vision. *Tom's* vision; something that felt distinctly lacking right now, barring the sporadic flashes of fire hoses hanging from the ancient exposed beams.

"That's him, isn't it?"

Tom blinked. Somehow, he'd missed Jake calming himself enough to step closer and peer around him at the screen of his phone. "Who? Cass?"

"That's his name?"

"Yeah. Want to see?"

Tom held out the phone. Jake stepped back like it was a poisoned lance. "Fuck off. You could've warned me you were cheating. I wouldn't have stayed over. Fuck, I probably wouldn't have shagged you at all."

"I wasn't cheating—"

"Yeah? Then why did your toy boy walk in on me in your bed? I'm not a bloody idiot, Tom. Is that even your real name?"

Tom laughed; he couldn't help it. "Yeah, my name's Tom. What else would it be? Listen—" He stopped and tried to order his thoughts around the distraction of Jake's misplaced, but pretty damn sexy, temper. "Listen, I wasn't cheating, okay? Cass and I have an open relationship. If you'd stuck around, he probably would've made you breakfast."

"Yeah, right." Jake ticked and slapped his own arm. "It's a good story, but find yourself another mug."

"Looks like you found me." Tom took a risk and closed the distance between them. "Tell you what, how about we get some lunch. I'll tell you all about myself, and if you still think I'm a twat, you never have to see me again."

Jake took some persuading, but eventually Tom managed to coax him into a nearby café.

"You're not buying me lunch, though. I can buy my own." Jake stomped up to the counter and came back with tea and bacon sandwiches. "This posh enough for you?"

You sound like Cass. "Do I look too posh for a bacon sandwich?"

"Not today."

Tom resisted the urge to roll his eyes. He'd woken up in Berkhamsted to find Cass had hidden all his smart-casual business attire in protest at their Monday apart. Tom had retaliated by stealing Cass's only clean jeans and his favourite leather jacket. "Okay, so if you think I'm such a dickhead, why are you buying me lunch?"

"I spat in it."

"No, you didn't."

"I wanted—*wankers*—I wanted to."

Tom chanced a grin. "Well, I'm glad you didn't."

Jake picked up the pot of tea. His hand shook. He put it down again. "What the fuck is an open relationship?"

"You want me to define it?" Tom leaned forwards. "Or tell you what it means to me and Cass?"

"What's the difference?"

"I don't know, because we don't care what anyone else thinks."

Jake finally poured his tea, eyes down, his concentration clear. "Then why tell me? What makes you think I care?"

"I'm not forcing you to stay."

With a low growl, Jake put his elbows on the table and glowered. "Go on, then. Enlighten me."

Tom picked up his sandwich. The bread was plastic, soggy, and soaked in bacon grease. His mouth watered. "Cass is my partner. We live together, own a business together, and we're totally committed to each other." Jake snorted as he picked up his own sandwich, but Tom held up his hand. "Let me finish."

"*Wankers.*"

"If you say so." Tom bit back a grin. "Cass and I have been together a long time. I was twenty-one when I met him; he was nineteen. It was love at first sight, but we were too young to settle down. So we didn't."

"But you live together now?"

"Yes, but we still hook up with other blokes from time to time. Sometimes together, but that's rare."

"Why?"

"We don't often find someone we both like."

Jake's frown deepened. Tom jumped into the awkward silence. "We're very honest with each other. I would've told him everything about you even if he hadn't come home when he did."

"I thought he was going to deck me."

Tom shook his head. Cass had a volatile temper, but it wasn't triggered by jealousy. "Cass is cool. We approach things in different ways, but ultimately, we meet in the middle."

Jake finished his sandwich. "Different? How?"

"Cass would never do this." Tom gestured between them. "He fucks other people, but he likes his own space, mentally, at least."

Jake raised an eyebrow. "He fucks other people . . . because you don't bottom, right?"

"No. We fuck other people because we want to." Tom held Jake's gaze. "But in answer to your question, I *don't* bottom. Cass is versatile. I'm not."

"You shouldn't have to cheat on each other because you don't want to bottom."

Tom suppressed a sigh. *He really doesn't get it.* "It's not cheating, Jake. We choose to live this way. It might not make sense to you, but it works for us."

"Sounds fucked up."

"So?" Tom felt the first flash of defensiveness. He wanted Jake to understand for reasons he wasn't quite sure of yet, but he wasn't prepared to let Jake—anyone—tear his relationship to shreds. "How do you feel when people judge you by how you sound?"

On cue, Jake ticked and growled something Tom didn't catch. "Don't play on my TS. It is what it is. It doesn't define me."

"I know that."

Jake nodded slowly. "Your boyfriend—Cass—he's . . ."

"Bloody gorgeous?" Jake rolled his eyes, and Tom smiled. "He wants to meet you."

The faint trace of humour in Jake's gaze faded like it had never been there at all. "No offence, but I don't want to be part of some weird ménage trip. You're a good shag, but you're not *that* good."

Tom said nothing. He'd enjoyed fucking Jake . . . enjoyed it a lot, and he *knew* Jake had too.

"Bastard, bastard, bastard. I wish you were a prick." Jake groaned and put his head in his hands.

Tom rubbed Jake's shoulder. "I'm not asking you for anything, Jake. You asked me a question. I answered it." Silence. Tom squeezed Jake's shoulder. "All right?"

Jake finally met Tom's gaze. "If you didn't do shit like that, I wouldn't care if I never saw you again."

Tom didn't know what to say. He wanted to see Jake again, but the churning in his gut told him it wasn't that simple. Jake didn't get his relationship with Cass, he didn't *like* it, and Tom couldn't live with that. Cass was everything to him. Always.

"I should go." Jake sat up and rubbed his face. "I need to go home."

"Kentish Town?"

"Yeah."

Tom withdrew his hand. Folded his arms. He knew this should be good-bye, but he couldn't bring himself to say it. Instead he said, "Maybe I'll stop by that cesspit you work sometime."

"Good luck with that. I don't work there anymore."

"No?"

Jake shrugged. "I got sacked this morning. Guess you were right, and I'm not much of a waiter."

"What happened?"

"Same as always." Jake gulped the last of his tea. "They kept me until my probation was nearly up, then found some bullshit reason to get rid of me. It wasn't too hard. My boss kept notes of my fuckups."

"They can't sack you for having Tourette's. That's illegal."

"That's life. I'm used to it."

"Doesn't make it right." Tom absently stirred the dregs of his own tea. He could well imagine Jake's TS made him a challenging team member, but victimising him wasn't the answer. The laws against discrimination were there for a reason. "What are you going to do?"

"Something will come up. It always does. I haven't worked on a building site for a while. Maybe I'll try labouring."

The thought of Jake shivering on one of the city's many construction sites, ticking halfway up some perilous scaffolding, churned Tom's stomach. "You don't have to do that. I'm sure I can find you work."

Jake kicked back his chair with an abrupt screech of wood on tile. He dumped a tenner on the table and stormed out of the café.

Tom wasn't altogether surprised. He toyed with the idea of letting Jake choose his own good-bye. Then he shoved his own chair away and followed Jake out. He found him by the zebra crossing and caught his arm. "I didn't mean to offend you."

Jake squirmed and pushed Tom away. "I don't need a fucking sugar daddy."

The frustration in Tom's veins boiled over. He grabbed Jake's flailing arm and held it tight. "I'm thirty years old, dickhead, I'm no one's bloody dad, got it?"

Jake said nothing. Tom took his chance and pressed his business card into his hand. "I don't feel sorry for you, but I can help you. I *want* to help you. Call me. I'll be there."

CHAPTER FIVE

oft bites woke Tom; gentle bites, like little bugs blowing warm air over his back. He smiled into his pillow and felt the first vibrations of a delicious morning stretch creep over him.

Cass ramped up his ministrations and dug his teeth into Tom's shoulder, slid his hand down his spine, under his waistband, and squeezed his arse. "I know you're awake."

Tom's smile widened, but he played possum a moment longer, enjoying Cass's attention. The morning didn't often find them cuddled together like this. Tom liked his space when he slept, and most days he was up and at 'em long before dawn.

Cass ripped the duvet from Tom, shocking him with the frigid, early morning air. "Don't ignore me, Tommy-boy."

"Bastard." Tom rolled over, surprised to find Cass wide-awake and grinning at him. "What are you so chirpy for?"

"I'm not chirpy; I'm horny. You fell asleep on me last night."

It was true. They'd met up at the flat only for Tom to inhale the plate of risotto Cass had brought him from Pippa's and pass out in front of *Breaking Bad*. Another switch in their usual roles, but a long week of wrangling with estate agents and accountants would exhaust any man.

Not that there was anything bad about falling asleep in Cass's arms, or waking up under the spell of his lips and tongue.

Despite Cass's devilish ministrations, though, Tom reached for his phone. It was a big day. As of eleven o'clock that morning, they would be the proud owners of a derelict old fire station in downtown Camden. A decision Tom had made just moments after leaving Jake. A call he'd made with little conscious thought. Camden, Jake. Camden, Jake. Somehow it all felt right.

"Put that fucking phone down." There was mirth in Cass's tone before he closed his lips around Tom's dick.

"Fuck!" Tom's eyes rolled, and he arched his back from the bed. Cass knew his body well, his pleasure spots and weaknesses, and it wasn't long before Tom was desperate for more. "That all you got?"

Cass pulled his mouth from Tom's cock with a wet pop. "You can't handle all of me." Cass squeezed Tom's balls and trailed his fingers lower. Tapping. Stroking. *Pressing.*

Tom squirmed. He could take a finger or two, but he had to be in the mood or drunk . . . very drunk. "Don't push your luck."

Cass chuckled, and Tom took his moment to turn the tables. He tugged Cass up and flipped him onto his back. They wrestled a moment, neither man prepared to yield dominance. Then, as so often happened when Tom was naked with Cass, the world seemed to stop. He stared at Cass, his heart hammering in his chest.

I want you.

Cass stared right back.

I know.

They did this from time to time: tried to deny the enduring desire they had for each other, all the while screaming for more.

Cass blinked first. He rolled over and raised himself up on his hands and knees. "What are you waiting for?"

Nothing on this earth would keep me from you.

Tom retrieved condoms and lube and got them both ready. Cass needed little preparation, but Tom took his time anyway. Playing Cass was the best kind of fun, hearing him gasp, feeling him jerk and shudder.

He sat back on his heels, easing Cass down on his cock. They'd danced this dance more times than he could remember, but though Cass liked—craved—it rough, Tom would never truly *hurt* Cass, to take their game beyond a little dirty pain.

Cass shivered. Tom wrapped his arms around him and pressed his chest against his back. "Okay?"

"Yeah." Cass lolled his head on Tom's shoulder, and Tom felt him relax from the inside out. "I wanted you to fuck me until the damn bed collapsed. Now, I want to stay right here."

Tom smiled into the arch of Cass's exposed neck. He felt the same.

He kissed Cass's sweat-sheened skin and stroked his cock, slow and languid. He had a full day ahead of him, but he was in no hurry. Cass hummed around some deep breaths, and then rose up on his knees. Tom followed and thrust slowly in and out of him, watching his cock breach Cass over and over.

Cass fell forwards, raising himself up to meet Tom's thrusts. "Fuck yeah."

"Yeah?" Tom moulded himself to the curve of Cass's body, took Cass's hands and placed them on the bed frame. "What about this?"

He rolled his hips and drove into Cass with a biting, twisting thrust. Cass groaned and dropped his head, and Tom knew he had him. Cass wielded a power over him like no other, but this was a game Tom knew well—he knew Cass well. In the end, no matter who won the struggle for dominance, Tom would never feel like he'd lost. Cass was any man's ultimate fantasy.

Tom picked up the pace and pounded Cass the way they'd both been craving for weeks. He steadied himself with one hand on Cass's tattooed hip, and kept the other busy, roaming his glorious, sinuous back. Stroking. Scratching. The heat between them rose. Sweat trickled down Tom's chest. He shoved his hand into Cass's hair. Tugged. "Touch yourself."

"No." Cass ground the word out through clenched teeth, still resisting the inevitable.

Tom smirked, released Cass's hair, and reached around him. "Do it myself, then."

He gripped Cass's cock and slid his slick hand up and down, working him in time with the push and pull of his own hips.

Cass growled, low and desperate. A violent shudder jolted him. "What are you trying to do to me?"

"I'm not trying, Cass. I *will* make you come."

"Ugh, God, you're such a smart-arse."

Cass panted through some harsh, sharp breaths. Tom rubbed his back until, finally, Cass cried out and wet warmth coated Tom's hand. Watching Cass come was his own undoing. He slammed forwards once more and came hard, leaving bruising fingermarks on Cass's hips.

Tom slumped on top of Cass's trembling form. They stayed still a moment, gasping for breath, then Tom pried Cass's hands from the bed frame and toppled them both to their sides. He wrapped his arms around Cass from behind and held him tight until his shaking calmed.

He stroked Cass's sweaty hair back from his face with his clean hand. "Love you."

Cass blew out a breath. "Love you too."

They washed up and lay quietly for a while, exchanging lazy kisses. Tom felt wide-awake and ready to start the day, but Cass dozed until the alarm on his phone startled them both.

"Bloody hell." Cass fumbled on the bedside table and turned it off. "It can't be time to get up."

Tom laughed. "Some might say you'd been up already."

"Piss off. I've got a big order to do today for the weekend. I need to get in the fridges before everyone else is there to get in my way."

Cass started to get out of bed, but Tom caught his arm. "Oh no, you don't. I need you today. We've got to sign for the keys to the Camden place, and we've got a meeting at Bites straight after, remember? You need to be there."

Bites was their organic snack company: a crazy, harebrained scheme, cooked up over one too many bottles of wine. It was two years old, a lot of work, and expanding so fast Tom could barely keep up.

Cass scowled. "I'll come to the estate agent's, but you don't need me in some stuffy, bigwig meeting. I've got shit needs doing."

"I do need you," Tom protested. "They're your products. You need to have a say in how they're packaged. You'll only get the arse if we do it wrong."

"They're flapjacks, Tom. Just put them in a bloody box."

"Don't be a dick." Cass, with the help of the trusty team of cooks that staffed their production kitchen, had developed every one of the Bites products, which were now being delivered to offices around the capital. Organic, nutritious, and cheap, every single line had been a winner. They may have started with flapjacks, but things had moved faster than anyone had expected and Tom couldn't handle it all on his own.

Cass sighed. Tom didn't often drag him into the corporate world, but he still fought every time. "How long will it take? I don't want to be stuck in Shoreditch all morning."

"Takes as long as it takes. Be quicker if you contribute."

A few hours later, Tom kicked Cass under the table that separated them from the designers the packaging company had sent. Glared at him to still his drumming fingers. Cass was bored, he could tell, but he didn't much care right now. Didn't Cass realise Tom was bored to tears too? "Do you like those boxes? Or do you prefer the plastic?"

Cass shot him a withering glare. "No plastic. There's no point producing organic food, and then coating it in slimy cellophane crap."

"It's recyclable," one of the designers put in. "Your clients can dispose of it in their green bins."

"If they have them," Cass said. "Most of our stuff goes to office blocks. I don't think they dispose of their own rubbish. Use cardboard. If it ends up in landfill, it'll biodegrade."

The designer made a note, and Tom smiled to himself. Cass thought he was no good at this, but in reality, he was far better than Tom. He didn't waste his time negotiating, or trying to keep everyone happy. He said what he wanted and expected it done.

The meeting drew to a close. Tom glanced at the time. Despite Cass's dire prediction, they'd wrapped it up in ninety minutes.

After the designers left, Tom slugged Cass's shoulder. "Wasn't so bad, eh?"

Cass rolled his eyes. "It was bollocks. Couldn't they have emailed you all that?"

"Maybe, but we've not used this firm before, and it's better they get to know us a little. Makes the process easier, especially if there're any problems down the line. Besides, email or no, I wouldn't have known the answers. It had to be you."

Cass defied the lecture with an insolent smirk that drove Tom up the wall, and shoved his hands in his pockets. "Can we have brunch now?"

"Thought you had an order to do?"

"Adam can put it on the system. I'll check it later."

Tom leaned over and kissed Cass on the cheek. The scratch of Cass's stubble and the smell of his skin brought their morning fuck rushing back. "Let's check in with the girls downstairs, then we can go to Kat's."

Cass led the way down to the production floor. Their ten-strong team of cooks met them with warm hugs and smiles, especially Cass. Women of a certain age always loved Cass. He donned the appropriate garb and disappeared into the kitchen to check what was cooking.

Tom lingered in the break room by the admin area. Ethel, the oldest staff member they employed across the whole company, made him a cup of tea, and they settled down on the communal sofa for a catch-up. Ethel was a true cockney and had known Cass for most of his life. Bites had started with a batch of the old family recipes she'd taught him when he was a boy.

"So what's been going on around here? Have we missed anything good?"

"Go on with you." Ethel pinched his arm. "You know nothing ever happens around here. Work and sleep, that's all we've got in this life."

"You should retire." Tom added more milk to the builder's brew Ethel favoured. "Let Donny look after you."

Ethel snorted. "That daft apeth can't look after his silly self. Have you seen your old nan recently?"

Tom craned his neck and glanced through the window that separated the office from the production floor. Beyond the preparation area, he could see Cass peering at something one of the girls had pulled out of the ovens. From a distance, it appeared to be the new aged-cheddar oatcakes he'd devised to come packaged with chutney dip—cheese and crackers without the worry of perishable cheese. "I went last week."

"Cass go with you?"

"What do you think?" Tom blew out a frustrated breath. Dolly was Cass's grandmother, not his, and she'd taken Cass in when he was just a baby and raised him like a son. But things had changed in recent years. Dementia had taken hold, and the lady who'd once been the brightest light in Cass's life had faded to a frail bag of bones in a

Clapham nursing home. "He won't even talk about her. It's like she doesn't exist."

"Cass is just like her, you know," Ethel said. "Silent and stubborn. It's in his genes."

Tom felt the familiar low burn of grief in his heart. "Dolly didn't look good when I visited her last. She doesn't know who I am anymore."

Ethel clicked her tongue in a way that reminded Tom of Jake. "The old bird's not long for the world now, I can feel it in me water. I just hope there's some closure before she passes. No mother should go to the grave not knowing the fate of their—"

Tom's phone cut her off, and he was grateful for the distraction. Cass had carried the shadow of his mother's disappearance since he was fifteen years old, and the weight of his grief had been a heavy load for him and Tom both. Sometimes Tom thought it would be easier if she'd just bloody died.

He pulled the phone from his coat pocket. He didn't recognise the number lighting up the screen, but that wasn't unusual for his business phone. He touched the screen and waved Ethel an absent good-bye as she cleared her mug away and drifted back to work.

"Tom Fearnes." Silence, then a similar tongue click to the one Tom had heard just moments before. "Jake? That you?"

"*Wankers*. How did you know?"

"A hunch. I was hoping you'd call."

"Yeah?"

"Yeah. How are things?"

More silence. Tom sat up straighter on the couch. He and Cass had talked about Jake a lot since Tom had last seen him a fortnight ago.

"*He's on your mind, I can tell.*"

"*Does that bother you?*"

"*Only because it bothers you, because you're worried about him. You wouldn't be you if you weren't.*"

"*Wouldn't be me?*"

"*Yeah.*" Cass shrugged like it was obvious. "*I know you. This isn't just a hookup for you. You won't rest now until he's sorted, and I'm good with that. I told you . . . you need to fix him.*"

Fix him. That conversation had been the second time Cass had uttered those words in the last couple of weeks, and Tom remained unconvinced. And he wasn't sure how he felt about Cass being so magnanimous either. Though they'd always been open with their sexual relationships, something... everything felt different about Jake.

Who cleared his throat at last. "You said you could help me find a job."

"Okay." Tom could fix that at least. "Doing what?"

"Anything... *shit, fuck, KAPPOW!*"

Jake's sudden exclamation made Tom smile, and he was glad Jake couldn't see him. "I can meet you this afternoon?"

"I don't need to see you. I just need a job."

The rejection should've stung, but Tom had expected it. Between them, he and Cass had figured Jake wasn't the type to ask for help unless he had no other choice. In that, Cass and Jake were *very* similar. "Fair enough. How about you meet me anyway, and I'll show you a few options."

The most sensible thing would be to send him to Rascal's, their street food canteen at South Bank. The place was casual, teeming with students, and Jake's best chance of blending in unnoticed, but would he want that? And did Tom want to be complicit in hiding Jake away from the world?

It didn't feel right.

"I have an office in Greenwich. Can you get there?"

Jake made a strange noise, then he sighed, though Tom couldn't be sure if he was as frustrated as he sounded, or ticking. "Got nothing else to do. Where is it?"

Tom gave Jake directions to the Stew Shack and hung up after agreeing to meet him at noon. He checked the time. If he was going to make it, he needed to leave now.

"Sacking me off?"

Tom whirled around to find Cass right behind him. "How much did you hear?"

"Enough. Is Jake okay?"

"Hard to tell. He's looking for work."

Cass found Tom's hands. He seemed thoughtful, which was always dangerous. "What are you going to do with him?"

Tom shrugged. "I don't know."

"I could find him something at Pippa's?"

The fact that Cass even thought to offer made Tom's chest warm. Cass was his fallen angel come good, and Tom was so proud of him it hurt. "He's not much of a waiter, and I don't think his TS could stand the heat of your kitchen."

Cass narrowed his eyes, but took Tom's point with good grace. He ran Pippa's back of house team with a volatile iron fist. Probably not the best place for a vulnerable young man. "Maybe something in admin then. You need a new PA."

"I don't need a PA. Besides, with the new site I won't have time to supervise him."

"Then get him to help you with it. Jesus, Tom. You can't do everything yourself, especially now you've bought the Camden place."

"*We've* bought the Camden place. You signed your name this morning too, remember?" Tom reluctantly pulled away. The Tube ride into central London wasn't particularly long, but he'd need to change lines. "I better go. I'm meeting Jake at the office."

"I know. I heard."

Tom saw a flash of something in Cass. "Come with me?"

Cass hesitated. "No, not yet. I show up now, he might end up agreeing to something he's not cool with because he's down on his luck. Help him get straightened out first, if he'll let you, then let him decide what he wants."

"I'll miss you."

"Yeah?" Cass grinned, and whatever Tom thought he'd seen faded. "I'll be missing you too when I can't sit down all day."

CHAPTER SIX

"*How* many restaurants?"

Tom grinned and clicked through the company website. He turned the screen around so Jake could see it. "Five. Not so many when you consider the company who just fired you has more than a hundred."

Jake peered at the screen. "Yeah, but you're way too young to own so much shit."

"I don't own anything." Tom pointed to a logo in the top left corner of the screen. "The company owns them."

"The parent company is Urban Soul?"

"That's right."

Jake whistled. "And you own Urban Soul?"

"Not on my own."

Jake shot Tom an inscrutable glance. "With your boyfriend?"

"Cass, yes. He's my partner."

It was the first time either of them had mentioned Cass. Tom let the silence hang a moment, then he clicked on the Bites logo. "We own this business too. Have you seen the posters on the underground?"

Jake peered at the screen. "Maybe. Is it the snacks you can get by post?"

Maybe it's time to increase the ad budget for the Tube stations. Jake was far from their target audience. It was good news if he'd absorbed enough of their campaign to tell Tom how they worked. "Yeah. Organic snacks. Healthy and cheap. I just came from our production kitchen, actually. It's in Shoreditch, not too far from you."

Jake scowled, like he'd forgotten the purpose of their meeting was to find him a job. "What would I do there?"

Tom shrugged. He hadn't thought the idea through, and now that he had Jake in front of him, he found himself struggling to picture him in any role he had to offer, though a vision of the maternal gang at Bites taking Jake under their wing made him smile.

"What's this?"

"Hmm?" Tom focused on the enigmatic question mark posted at the bottom of the company home page. "Oh, that's our new venture. We just bought a place in Camden. Not sure what we're going to do with it yet, though."

"Another restaurant?"

"That's the idea."

Jake straightened up, ticked a few times, and walked to the small office window. He stared out over the heated decking where the Stew Shack's patrons sat, enjoying their lunch. "You said this one was your favourite. Why not open another one in Camden?"

"We never open the same restaurant twice. It's not what we do."

Jake looked over his shoulder, perhaps remembering the long night they'd spent huddled in the corner of that Camden bar, talking Tom's company ethos to death. Did Jake feel betrayed now he knew it was something Tom shared with Cass? Tom couldn't tell. Behind the vulnerable belligerence, Jake had put up a wall that hadn't been there the first time they'd met.

"Um, besides," Tom went on when Jake didn't speak, "the location wouldn't suit an alehouse. The venue is pretty vintage, but . . ."

"But what?" Jake finally turned and gave Tom his full attention.

Tom sighed. "That's the problem. We haven't got that far. We probably should've had a plan before we bought the place, but we didn't."

"You don't seem the type to make mistakes like that."

Don't I? "Yeah well. I don't know what came over me. I think I figured it would work itself out, but Cass has been busy at Pippa's, and we haven't had much time to brainstorm."

Jake took the second mention of Cass in stride. He took another look at the Stew Shack's outdoor seating area. "What do you like best about this place?"

"The simplicity, I guess." Tom resisted the urge to join Jake at the window, but the simmering current between them was as strong as ever. "We serve just three daily stews and casseroles here, a few simple sides, and four guest ales that change every week. No fuss, no gimmicks. Just a bowl of hot food and some beer."

"So what's stopping you from taking that theory and applying it elsewhere? A bowl of stew could be anything, right?"

"Right." Tom let the idea seep into him and take hold. "We developed the stew and ale concept because it suited Greenwich. We launched it during British food week last year. Camden's different."

Jake frowned. Tom could almost see the cogs spinning in what he was fast learning was a sharp, intelligent mind. "There's nowhere like Camden."

Tom remembered the words that had come to mind when he'd wandered down Camden High Street the day he'd met Jake. Colourful. Vibrant. On impulse, he shut down his computer and felt in his pocket for the keys he and Cass had picked up on their way to Shoreditch. "Want to go see?"

It felt good to be back in Camden with Jake. Tom had visited the new site several times since he and Cass had put their offer in, but passing under the iconic bridge with Jake by his side seemed to make it better.

He unlocked the arcade doors and waved Jake in. "This place used to be a fire station. We're trying to track down some of the old equipment, but we're not having much luck."

Jake drifted to the centre of the main ground floor space much like Tom had when he'd first entered the old building. He gazed around, ticking a few times for good measure, glanced up at the high ceilings, and then at the ornate windows. "There's a vintage fire engine in the library, one of those motor car ones from the twenties. Maybe it came from here."

Camden Town Library was just down the road. Tom made a mental note to check it out. "So what do you think? If we put your theory to the test, how would we do it?"

"My theory? You mean copying the Stew Shack? 'S'not my idea, mate. You came up with it in the first place."

"Semantics." Tom beckoned Jake to the staircase. "You've planted a seed."

He showed Jake upstairs. Jake wrinkled his nose at the office space. "They've fucked this right up, haven't they?"

Tom grinned. Cass had said the very same thing. "We're going to clear it out. Put a massive long table in for big parties. Maybe a private bar."

"You need lights." Jake stared up at the ceiling. "Hanging lights."

"Modern or vintage?"

"Modern."

Tom thought of his aversion to fusion food. "Modern lights in a vintage building. Would that work?"

"How would I know?" Jake treated Tom to one of his trademark scowls. "I'm a working-class northerner. You're a pair of posh boys."

"Not Cass," Tom corrected. "He's an East End boy. Grew up on pie and mash."

Jake seemed surprised. Perhaps he hadn't heard Cass speak when they'd encountered each other at the flat. "You could do that? Pie and mash is simple enough."

Tom wandered to one of the beautiful old windows and drummed his fingers on the sill. It was a good idea, but it wasn't quite right. Tom studied Jake's back. He felt like his grip on a brilliant concept was just out of reach, and Jake had all the answers. "What do *you* eat in restaurants?"

"I'm unemployed, remember? I don't go out."

"Humour me?"

"You're not funny."

"*Jake.*"

Jake turned around. "Don't say my name like that."

"Why not?"

"Just don't."

A heavy silence coated the air. Tom felt it touch every part of him. He swallowed hard. Words failed him, but Jake broke the pregnant pause with a sigh.

"Burgers," he said. "Real ones, not that McDonald's crap."

"Burgers?"

"Yep. Told you I wasn't posh."

Tom grinned. "Trust me, burgers can be poncey."

"Not the good ones."

Jake had a point. Tom mulled it over. He liked the idea of a hipster burger bar, but there had to be more to the concept than that. A hook.

Jake appeared like a clicking ghost at his side. "You look pissed off."

"Hmm? Oh, I'm not pissed off. I'm frustrated. This place has many faces, and I can't quite envisage them all." Tom spoke mostly to himself, so he was surprised when Jake touched his arm.

"Okay, so you're posh and I'm not. So, if I eat burgers, what do you drink?"

"Beer? No, that's not it. "

Jake nodded. "Exactly. What do you drink when you're being a toff?"

"I'm not a toff."

"Whatever. Even if you're not a toff, you must know some."

Tom thought of the corporate functions he sometimes cajoled and blackmailed Cass into attending. Tom despised them as much as Cass, but they were a necessary evil from time to time. The last one had been a dinner put on for the city's youngest entrepreneurs. They'd both hated every minute. They'd stuck around for the canapés, then swiped a bottle of high-priced fizz and snuck off home to fuck all night.

Burgers and . . . "Champagne—fuck, that's *it*. Burgers and champagne. Nothing else. Fuck, fuck, fuck."

Jake raised a dark eyebrow, clearly bemused. "You think that would work?"

Tom didn't answer, his mind whirring too fast to articulate what he was thinking. He opened a drawer of an abandoned desk, found a pen and paper, and sketched out a convoluted mind map. Branding, construction, logistics—

Jake cleared his throat. "You look like someone else."

"Yeah?" He made a note to contact local organic meat suppliers, then Jake touched Tom's face and the gesture hit him like a sledgehammer. He stilled his manic scribbling and covered Jake's hand with his own. "Who do I look like?"

Jake opened his mouth, but a tic got there first. His free arm lashed out and smacked a nearby filing cabinet. "Bollocks!"

Tom winced. The few times they'd met, he'd noticed Jake's arms and hands were often littered with bruises. Now he knew why. "You okay?"

"I'm fine."

The heavy air between them faded. Tom went back to his planning, and Jake wandered across the room. Tom let him be. He had plenty to do, and Jake seemed like he needed some time to calm down.

A little while later, his phone rang. Cass. That was unusual. Cass rarely called when he was at work.

"What's up?"

"Nothing. Just wondered how your, uh, meeting went."

Ah. Tom glanced at Jake. He was out of earshot and appeared to be cleaning something off the wall with his sleeve. "Still going on. I couldn't find anything that felt right for him, so I brought him to Camden to see the new site."

"And? Does he like it?"

"Hard to tell. He did devise a concept for me, though, and I bloody love it."

"Let's hear it, then."

Tom took Cass through the fledgling model for their new venture. Cass listened, then he fell quiet while Tom waited with baited breath. If Cass didn't like the idea, the whole thing was toast. Despite his disinterest in corporate duties, he was always right when it came to their business.

"I like it."

Tom leaned back on a dusty filing cabinet. "You do? Thank God for that, because I bloody love it."

"Yeah, you said." Cass chuckled. "So what are we going to do? A streamlined core menu with some trendy specials?"

"Probably, but that's up to you, isn't it? I've done my bit."

Cass snorted. "Hardly. I'm not getting involved with poncey champagne. You're on your own there, and you've got to turn that bomb site into a restaurant."

"You're all heart."

"I know—shit—hang on a sec." Cass muffled the phone and snapped at someone. Tom wondered where he was. He didn't allow mobile phones in Pippa's kitchen, so he must've been in the bin yard or the office. He sounded rattled when he came back on the line. "Bell end. How hard is it to put rubbish in the right bin?"

"You've got bins on the brain today."

Cass growled and there was the distinctive clang of him kicking something—always quick to break something, anything, even himself, to vent his frustrations. "Don't be fucking cute. If we can't get it right in the businesses we have, what's the point in opening more?"

"Why are you having a pop at me?"

"I'm not. You know stupid shit like that winds me up."

Tom did know it. Of course he knew it, but he wasn't in the mood to be on the receiving end of Cass's temper today. "Okay, I need to get going."

Silence, then Cass sighed. "Don't go. I'm just pissed off because of the mess I came into here. It's no wonder I'm always bloody working." Cass sounded like the spirited grin he'd had when he left Tom had never been there at all. How quickly things could change in a few hours. "Okay, back to the Camden thing . . . What are you going to do with the place? We might be selling burgers, but I don't want any cheesy diner crap."

Tom absorbed the abrupt shift in Cass's mood. He loved Cass to death, but his temper gave him whiplash. When would Cass learn that anger broke the stuff he wanted to fix? *Anger is just a hole where your life could be . . .*

"Tom?"

"Hmm? Oh, the Camden thing? I'm still working on that. Jake thinks some of the stuff from the old fire station might be at the library. I'm hoping they might let us take it back if we can convince them it belongs here."

"If anyone can do it, it's you. What about the layout issues downstairs?"

"I haven't got that far yet. Bloody hell. What's with you today? Did you eat a bag of Skittles before you woke me up?"

Cass chuckled. "All right, all right. I'll leave you to it. Just keep me posted. Oh and I'm going to come home tonight. Meet me at base camp."

He hung up, leaving Tom to ponder the sudden rush of communication. It felt a little odd. Good, but odd.

Tom glanced around. He'd lost track of Jake while he'd been on the phone, and now he was nowhere to be seen. He gathered his stuff and made his way downstairs. He found Jake by the defunct back area, staring at the mess of dust and poky rooms.

"Is this the kitchen?"

"That's the plan."

"And the restaurant's over there?" Jake jerked his head to the main space in the building.

"Yep."

"Then you need to take this wall down. The building is listed, but this isn't original. It's plasterboard. Listen."

Jake knocked on the wall, and sure enough, it produced the telltale hollow tap that came from cheap, bodged construction.

Tom looked out over the ground floor space and pictured what Jake had in mind. It made sense. "What if we took all the walls down and had an open kitchen?"

"Like the chicken shop down the road?"

"Cleaner, I hope."

"That could work." Jake walked a few paces and pointed to the floor. "It would have to be somewhere around here, though. This is where the water pipes are, and you're not allowed to dig around too much."

Suddenly, Tom could see it: an open kitchen, alive with flame grills, lively chefs, and eclectic waiting staff . . . young waiting staff, with punky hair and tattoos. "How do you know so much about building regulations?"

"My dad's a builder."

Tom raised an eyebrow. It was the first time Jake had ever mentioned his family. "Did you grow up watching him work?"

"Watching?" Jake buzzed out a tic. "No, I was free labour until my TS made me too embarrassing."

Tom had clearly touched a nerve. "Still, seems like you know more about this than I do. Want to sit down and sketch out some ideas?"

The speculative look on Jake's face faded. "I can't do that."

"Why not?"

"*Rat-faced wankers.* Sorry."

That appeared to be Jake's only answer. Tom took advantage of his silence. "I could use the help."

"I'm supposed to be looking for a job."

"This could be your job." Tom trod carefully. Jake had let slip on the Tube ride over here that he'd blown a few interviews because of his TS. His explosions of tics had taken prospective employers by surprise when he'd failed to disclose his condition. "Work for me. Help me develop this place. I'll pay you what I'd be paying the PA I'd have to hire."

"PA? As in, like your fucking secretary? Following you round like a dog, photocopying and making your tea? No thanks."

"There's more to it than that. And I've got all the other sites to manage. You'd be on your own most of the time. You'll probably hardly see me."

Jake thought on it a moment, like Tom's presence, or lack of it, was the deal-breaker, then he narrowed his eyes. "I don't need your charity."

"No, but I need yours."

"Liar."

Tom said no more. He leaned against the offending plasterboard wall and waited for Jake to think it over. Part of him knew he *was* offering Jake the job because he felt sorry for him, and because he still felt insanely attracted to him, but beneath all that, common sense won out. Tom needed help, and Jake had already proved his knowledge and vision.

"You can't pay me. I'll work for you, but you can't pay me."

Tom raised an eyebrow, sensing victory. "I have to pay you. It wouldn't be right if I didn't."

"I don't want your money."

"How will you live? You've got bills and rent. No one can afford to work for free in this city."

"I have some savings. They'll tide me over for a while."

"Then why did you call me?"

Silence. Tom didn't dare let himself speculate if Jake had called him with a motive besides the need for a job, that perhaps he *wanted* to see Tom again. Something told him if he pushed Jake too hard, he'd simply walk away. "How about I pay you after the event? We'll develop and open the restaurant, and you'll get paid when the job is complete."

"How long will that take?"

Tom considered the question. It was October now, and they'd launched the Stew Shack from concept to opening night in a little over two months, but that wasn't going to happen here. The rebuild would take weeks, maybe months, on top of everything else that needed to be done. "Six months," he said. "Maybe more."

"Fine."

Jake seemed annoyed for reasons he kept to himself. Frustrated, Tom made yet another mental note to negotiate a living wage for Jake, and pulled out his phone to type a message to Cass. *I just employed Jake as my project manager, kind of. That cool?*

Tom didn't expect a response till much later. Wherever Cass had been when he'd called, he was bound to be back in the kitchen now, but Tom's phone buzzed within moments of him hitting Send.

It's cool. Always. But I want to meet him.

CHAPTER SEVEN

om stood on the train with his shoulder wedged between a statuesque woman's breasts and his face downwind of a ripe-scented vagrant. Peak time on the Tube was always hellish. He usually did his best to avoid it, choosing to start his day at dawn and finish well after the evening rush, but tonight he had somewhere to be.

The train rumbled into Belsize Park. Tom jostled his way onto the platform and let the crowd carry him through the station and above ground. From there, it was a five-minute walk to one of the oldest gay bars in London.

Tom pushed open the door. The King William was cosy and traditional, and smelled of proper brewed ale. It reminded Tom of the Stew Shack. Jake had chosen this pub to meet Cass in, and it was perfect. Cass was never happier than when he was snuggled up somewhere warm with a pint of real beer in his hand. With any luck, Jake was the same.

After scanning the bar, Tom spotted Jake sitting alone in a quiet corner, head down, shoulders hunched, and he found himself glad Cass was running a little late. Jake had surprised Tom when he'd finally agreed to meet Cass; Tom had figured it would be a lot longer than a month before Jake wanted that, *if*, indeed, he ever wanted it at all. He'd made his thoughts on Tom and Cass's unconventional relationship perfectly clear.

Tom grabbed a couple of pints from the bar and made his way to Jake's table. "All right, mate?"

"Hey . . . *wankers*." Jake stopped and shook himself. "It always sounds weird when you say that."

Tom slid onto an antique leather-cushioned bench. It felt good to sit—it had been a long day—and it felt even better to see Jake. It had been nearly a week since they'd last met up. "Say what? 'All right, mate?' What's weird about that?"

"You sound like someone else."

"Probably Cass. I told you he's a proper cockney ruffian; I pick up all his bad habits."

"Better his habits than mine." On cue, Jake muttered something under his breath. "Where is he, anyway? I thought he'd be with you."

"He got held up at Pippa's. He'll be here soon. Why? Are you nervous?"

Jake scowled. "No."

But his restless gaze gave him away. Tom studied him over the rim of his glass. Aside from the week just gone, they'd seen a lot of each other over the past month. Jake had proven himself a gold mine of undeveloped skills and had drawn up construction plans for the Camden site worthy of any architect. Tom was thrilled. Shame Jake didn't seem to know he was the bloody dog's bollocks.

"Cass was up early this morning," Tom said. "He's *never* up early. I think he's worried you won't like him."

That got Jake's attention. "He's worried *I* won't like *him*? That doesn't make any sense."

"Doesn't it?" If Tom was honest with himself, he was probably more nervous than Cass and Jake combined. He'd spent the three days since Jake had finally agreed to Cass's request for a meeting feeling like his whole world was tilting on a precipice. "Why do you think that?"

Jake shrugged. "Because he's got nothing to lose. Even if he hates me, he still gets to keep you. What's going to happen to us? He'll tell you to ditch me, and I'll never see you again."

Us.

Tom knew in his heart Cass would never *tell* him to ditch anyone, but before he could reassure Jake of Cass's good intentions, the man himself took a seat at the table.

"Evening." Cass reached for Tom's pint and downed half of it in one. "Anyone want another drink?"

"I'll get them." Jake jerkily rose. His chair hit the wall. "Bitter, yeah?"

He brushed past Tom and was gone before anyone could answer. Cass raised an eyebrow. "That went well."

"He's nervous." Tom kissed Cass's stubbled cheek. "Be nice."

"I'm always nice." For a moment, Cass appeared offended, then his face softened. "Honest. Best behaviour, okay?"

"You'd better." Tom treated Cass to the rueful frown he often sent his way during the corporate meetings Cass hated so much, the frown that had precious little effect on Cass's propensity to misbehave.

Jake returned to the table. He set two pints of ale down, then dropped back into his seat.

It didn't escape Tom's notice that he sat on his hands. Perhaps Cass noticed too, because his greeting was a simple nod.

"All right, mate? I'm Cass."

"I'm . . . *Jake*."

Jake looked like he was fighting something, like he couldn't breathe. Cass touched his arm. "Don't be shy about your TS. You can't be more antisocial than me."

"It's true," Tom said when Jake didn't respond. "If Cass didn't spend so much time shut up in the kitchen, he'd have an ASBO for sure."

Cass chuckled, though it seemed a little forced. He let his hand fall away from Jake's arm. "That's why you bullied me into selling my market stall, isn't it? So you could hide me away?"

"Keep you out of trouble, more like." Tom grinned. "You're a lairy bastard."

Jake glanced between Tom and Cass, absorbing their exchange. He seemed to steel himself. "What did you sell on your stall?"

"Sausages," Cass said. "Among other things. British street food. Tom fell in love with me over my toad-in-the-hole sandwich."

Tom wasn't about to argue with that. As a skint, hungry student, there'd been nothing better than the cheap comfort food a feisty young Cass had sold from his stall at Borough Market. "It was a bloody good sandwich."

"How old are you?"

Jake's question was abrupt, and followed by a muted run of clicking, but Cass remained unfazed.

"Twenty-eight." Cass punched Tom's arm. "So way younger than this middle-aged, middle-class git."

Tom caught Cass's hand in his own, and again, Jake seemed transfixed by their easy display of affection. They were pretty safe in a gay bar, but Tom and Cass had never hidden themselves from the world. Out and proud. Family, friends, and work. Tom wondered what Jake's reality was. Wondered what he was thinking behind that shrewd brown gaze. Wondered about all sorts of things until Cass decided to make an awkward situation ten times worse.

"When did you develop TS?"

Tom kicked him under the table. They'd agreed beforehand to leave Jake's condition well alone. What the hell was Cass playing at?

Though the sharp kick to his shin had to hurt, Cass ignored Tom and focused on Jake. "Did you have it when you were a kid, or did it come later?"

If Jake was offended by the question, he hid it well. "I was diagnosed when I was thirteen. I don't know how long I'd had it before then. I've always been weird."

"Weird is good," Cass said.

"Yeah? I shouted 'crunchy tits' at my brother's girlfriend in church."

Tom felt his eyes widen. He managed to control his reaction, but Cass had no such restraint, and his laughter burst out of him in much the same way as Jake's tics.

"Shit, sorry. It's not funny, really." Cass tried to calm himself with a mouthful of beer. Failed.

Tom kicked him again, hard, but Jake cut him off with a deep chuckle of his own.

"It's okay. It *is* funny. My brother laughed at the time, but his girlfriend's parents, not so much. I didn't get invited to their wedding."

Tom couldn't find any humour in that, but Jake's smile seemed genuine, so he let it go.

Cass gathered himself at last. "Do you mind talking about it?"

Jake shook his head. "No, I'd rather talk about it than have people stare at me. It's never going to go away, you know?"

"I know." Cass smiled, and for a moment, Tom sensed something flare between him and Jake, a camaraderie, perhaps the first blooms of friendship. Then Cass took Tom's hand, and Jake's tentative grin faded.

Tom breathed a silent sigh. Watching Cass and Jake interact felt good, despite the tension, but at the same time, guilt gnawed in the pit of his stomach. He'd always measured his words when it came to Jake's TS. But had he made things worse? Made it harder for Jake to be himself? Did he feel invisible when Tom pretended not to notice his twitching and muttering?

Jake groaned and dropped his head. Cass jumped, startled. He reached for Jake, but Tom stopped him. He was familiar with this tic, and true to form, it was over before Cass had retracted his arm. Tom could tell Cass wanted to ask more questions, but something stopped him, and Jake broke the silence first.

"How long have you two been together?"

"Nine years," Cass said. "That's right, isn't it?"

Tom nodded. "Something like that."

"That's a long time." Jake took a pull on his beer. "When did you start fucking other people?"

And boom, there it was, the subject that made Jake squirm in his seat. Tom eyed Cass warily, but Cass surprised him with an easy shrug. "We've always done that. It's not a big deal for us. Having sex with other people doesn't negate a committed relationship."

Jake clicked his tongue. "It *is* just fucking then."

"Is it?" Cass retorted mildly. "Then why are you here?"

It was the million-pound question, and one Jake apparently didn't have an answer for. Tom intervened before Cass could dig them a deeper hole. "You've never told me where you're from. You sound Mancunian."

The distraction worked. Jake broke his stare off with Cass and scowled at Tom instead. "Leeds, you idiot. I'm not a fucking Manc."

"Sorry." Tom couldn't help his grin. "North of Hemel Hempstead feels like the other side of the world to us."

"Bloody southern fairies." Jake let his accent lapse into a broad Yorkshire drawl, deep and melodic.

Tom glanced at Cass. He was a sucker for accents. Cass caught his gaze, but turned away before Tom could gauge him.

"How long have you been down here?" Cass asked.

"A few years." Jake finally brought his left hand—the one that seemed to twitch the most—up to the table. "I thought I'd blend in better. It's the cockney way to repeat yourself, isn't it?"

"We don't do that," Cass protested. "I don't do that, do I?"

He looked to Tom for help. Tom smirked. "You just did, you numpty."

"Twat." Cass gave Tom the finger, but switched his attention back to Jake. "I haven't noticed you repeating yourself. Do you do that a lot?"

"Not at the moment."

Cass raised a curious eyebrow. Jake thought on it a moment before he elaborated. "My tics run in cycles; they come and go. I've only got a few that live with me all the time."

Cass smiled. "Keeps life interesting, eh?"

"Like the wankers thing?" Tom said.

"Yeah, it's my only swearing tic at the moment."

"So you mean it every time you call me a bastard?"

"Probably." Jake grinned at Tom for the first time that evening, and warmth bloomed in Tom's belly.

"So . . ." Cass let the word hang long enough for Tom to get uncomfortable. "This Camden project. Have you two thought of a name yet?"

Jake raised an eyebrow. "Why are you asking me?"

"Tom said you're doing most of the work. I figured you might have some ideas by now. Tom and I are both shite at names."

"I'm only answering the phone."

"You're doing a lot more than that," Tom protested, and it was true. Jake wasn't great on the phone, but his sharp, articulate emails got things done, and he knew his way around a building site. "Besides, Cass wanted to call our last place 'Chernobyl,' so the less input he has, the better."

They talked shop a little while longer. Cass managed to feign interest in the colour schemes the designers had sent through, and Jake showed genuine curiosity in the menu Cass was devising.

"So, you've got five types of beefburger already?"

"Yep, and I've got a venison one we serve at Pippa's that I can adapt. I'm working on a pork patty at the moment. It's kind of Thai, but it's not quite right yet."

"What about sides?" Tom put in. "Did you go with the shoestring chips?"

"Yeah, but I've got some gourmet wedges you can charge an extra couple of quid for. I know you like all that up-selling buggery." Cass shot a glance at Jake. "Tom likes to get the most out of every mouth we feed."

Jake seemed sceptical, but Tom wasn't about to bore him with statistics, or maybe he was, until Cass programming Jake's number into his phone stopped him.

It made sense, they were all working on the same project, but Tom couldn't help but wonder what it all meant. Cass and Jake were very different men, but seeing them together, leaning over the same table, with their matching dark hair and contrasting eyes . . . it stirred something in Tom, something he'd been trying to ignore.

Eventually the discussion wound down.

"I need a piss," Jake said at last. He threw an unreadable glance at Tom, pushed back his chair, and left the table.

Tom watched him go and noticed Cass doing the same. "What do you think?"

"Of Jake?"

"Yeah."

Cass nodded slowly. "I think I should go home."

"What?"

"I'm going to go back to the house tonight."

Of all the things Tom had expected Cass to do, bailing on him wasn't one of them. "Why?"

"He's trying to hide his tics. He's exhausted."

Tom darted a glance between Cass and the gents' toilet door. "How can you tell?"

"I Googled Tourette's. He can suppress his tics for a while, but it only makes them worse in the end. He's had enough for one night."

Tom didn't know what to make of Cass researching Jake's TS. It was something he'd considered himself, but he'd never got round to it. "What else did you find out?"

"Nothing that you need to know today." Cass shrugged into his coat and kissed Tom's cheek. "I'm going to take the car and check on Souris. She was giving me evils on Sunday. Think she misses me."

Bloody cat. "*I* miss you."

Cass rolled his eyes. "Yeah, yeah. Stay here, okay? Spend some time with Jake."

"I thought we were going to do that together." It wasn't a plea. Tom knew Cass and knew there was nothing he could do to make him stay, but Jake's words came back to haunt him all the same. *If he tells you to ditch me...* Tom caught Cass's chin in a gentle grip and held his gaze. "Something you're not telling me?"

"No."

"Sure about that? Because there's nothing more important to me than—"

Cass sighed. "Fuck's sake, Tom. I don't want to be the most important thing in your life; I just want you to love me, and I know you do."

Tom let his hand drop. Cass *was* the most important thing in his life, but it wasn't a sentiment Cass often thought himself worthy of. "Jake seems to like you."

Cass snorted. "Does he bollocks."

A ripple of frustration ran through Tom. "It takes him a while to get going. Stay a bit longer, please?"

"Tom, it's not going to happen. He doesn't want me here."

"Then we should probably both go." Tom didn't know why the thought of leaving Jake hurt so much. "I don't want to do this without you."

Cass shook his head. "No, that doesn't feel right either. I watched you together before I came in. He's different with you, comfortable; he trusts you. I think he needs that."

"What are you saying?"

"I'm saying, stay here and be what he needs. You've got a big heart, babe. There's plenty of you to go around."

Tom grabbed Cass as he started to turn away. "I love you."

Cass smiled. "I know. That's why I'm totally cool with this. I can see it, Tom . . . I can see what draws you to him, and it's fucking beautiful."

There wasn't anything left to say, not tonight, at least. Cass left to catch the Tube to Hampstead, pick up their car and drive back to Berkhamsted, and Tom stayed where he was and waited for Jake to come back from the longest piss in the world.

And when he finally did, Tom realised Cass had been right: he was exhausted. They sat and talked for a little while longer, but when Jake started to look like he might fall asleep where he sat, Tom escorted him home to Kentish Town.

"You don't have to walk me all the way to my door, you know," Jake said as they stepped off the underground train. "I'm a big boy."

"Maybe I want to." Tom took Jake's arm. "Do you live far from here?"

"Five minutes."

And indeed it was. Jake led Tom to a low-key block of flats a few streets away from the Tube. "I'd invite you in, but the place is a tip."

Tom smiled. "That's okay. I just wanted to see you home all right."

Jake leaned back on his front door. Tom felt a pull in his chest and somehow found himself caging Jake with his arms. They stared at each other for a long moment. He took in Jake's bottomless brown eyes and the silver ring in his nose. Fuck, he was gorgeous.

Jake cleared his throat. "I know what you want."

"Yeah?"

"Yeah. You want to kiss me."

Tom watched Jake unconsciously bite his lip. "Would that be bad?"

"Doubt it."

Tom leaned down and brushed his lips over Jake's, a barely there kiss that felt more like a whisper.

Jake let out a soft, needy sound, then pushed Tom away with a groan. "I can't get you out of my head, but then I think of Cass, and I don't understand how I feel. I know what you want, but I can't, Tom. I bloody can't."

CHAPTER EIGHT

Cass: *You don't have to be scared of me*
Jake: *I'm not*
Cass: *So why are you giving Tom a hard time?*
Jake: *I'm not*

Cass: *Do you need anything?*
Jake: *Why?*
Cass: *Why what?*
Jake: *Why are you asking?*
Cass: *Why shouldn't I?*

Jake: *Me and Tom aren't fucking*
Cass: *Doesn't mean you can't be friends with him*
Jake: *I don't understand you*
Cass: *You haven't tried*

Cass: *What are you doing today?*
Jake: *Tom's taking me to your production kitchen*
Cass: *Be nice to Ethel. She makes the best tea*
Jake: *Ethel said hello*

Cass: Did you like the kitchen?
Jake: Big ovens
Cass: Size isn't everything

Cass: Feed Tom today
Jake: Why are you telling me that?
Cass: He's stressed
Jake: Why?
Cass: He's about to hit his project wall
Jake: What's that?
Cass: You'll see

Jake: Do you work every day?
Cass: Not Mondays. Mondays are Sundays

Jake: Does Tom take sugar?
Cass: No. Weak and white

Cass: Tom wants a name for the Camden project. Any ideas?
Jake: No
Cass: Think of some. Anything cat related. He loves cats
Jake: Are you taking the piss?
Cass: Maybe
Jake: I don't understand you
Cass: YOU HAVEN'T TRIED

CHAPTER NINE

"**F**at Cat."

Tom glanced up at Jake, irritated. "Excuse me?"

"For the restaurant." Jake jumped down from the counter he'd been perched on. "But with a 'ph,' so it's like 'Phat Cat.'"

Tom shook his head. "I like that even less than Top Cat, Smack Cat, and every other feline connotation you've cooked up. No bloody cats."

Jake shrugged and turned his attention to the branding designs Tom was leafing through. Jake had devised some himself, and was instantly immersed in them, but Tom couldn't focus. It had been nearly a month since the tense meeting in Belsize Park, and for a while afterwards, Jake had been aloof, cold, even. Tom had resigned himself to Jake becoming nothing more than a regular employee, only for him to perk up in the last week or so. That morning, he'd arrived for work with a big grin on his face, and his bouncy good mood was giving Tom a headache.

"I like this one." Tom tapped his finger on an edgy black-and-white design. "I like the fonts. Is this one of yours?"

Jake peered over Tom's shoulder, apparently oblivious to the effect his close proximity was having on Tom. "Yeah, it's not finished, though. I wanted to add some purple, but my laptop crashed. It can't handle the design software Sofia sent me."

Sofia was the interior design consultant Tom had drafted in from the company he'd used for the Stew Shack. She'd taken a shine to Jake, much to Jake's amusement and Tom's surprised chagrin.

"You're just jealous because he won't let *you* flirt with him," Cass had said.

Tom didn't want to admit how right he was. He sighed and scrubbed his hand over his face. Even with Jake's help, the Camden project was starting to get on top of him. Christmas was fast approaching, and Cass's free time was in short supply. He'd developed most of the menu for the new project, but he was still working on the dessert concept.

Jake put a hand on Tom's arm. "What's the matter?"

Tom jumped. He hadn't shared much physical contact with Jake since their near kiss on his doorstep a few weeks ago. "Hmm?"

"You seem weird." Jake let his hand drop. "Are you okay?"

It was an endearing switch in their usual roles, but Tom wasn't in the mood to talk anything other than business. "You either need a crappier design program, or a better computer." Jake stared at him, and Tom belatedly realised it had been longer than he thought since Jake had mentioned his crashing laptop. "You can borrow mine, if you want."

"Don't you need it?"

Jake had a point. Tom's whole life was on his laptop, and recently he'd felt surgically attached to it. "Cass never uses his, maybe . . ."

Tom caught his mistake too late, but rather than the blank look Jake usually plastered on his face when Cass was mentioned, he shrugged. "Sounds like a plan."

It does? Tom hadn't seen Cass for a couple of days, both of them too swamped with work to make it back to the same bed, and it had been a while since they'd talked about Jake. With the barrier Jake had put up so impenetrable, there hadn't seemed much point.

Frustrated, Tom shoved the brand designs into a folder, Jake's chunky fonts at the top of the stack. "Ask him yourself, then maybe the two of you can come up with a name for this place that isn't fucking ridiculous."

A week later, Tom found himself in a strange state of flux. He was spending almost every day with Jake, but though Jake's abrupt change in attitude meant Tom was growing more and more attached to his enigmatic assistant, something felt off. He didn't want to lead two separate lives, damn it. He wanted . . . Fuck, he didn't know what he wanted.

Tom sat across from Jake on the Tube train heading east to Shoreditch, watching a slow grin spread across his face as he typed furiously into his phone. In fact, he'd been glued to his phone for most of the day, texting with someone who made him smile like he had the world's best secret.

I wonder what they're talking about. Whatever it was, the distraction seemed to have eased the tics that often plagued Jake on the cramped underground trains, and Tom couldn't help the burn of jealousy in his gut. Seeing Jake grin made his day, but fuck if he didn't want to be the one making his eyes shine like that.

The train pulled into Shoreditch. Tom stood and, as had become his habit even when Jake had been blanking him, took Jake's arm as they stepped off the train.

"You're quiet again today."

Tom glanced at Jake. "Am I?"

"Yeah. Are you worried about Camden?"

Tom waited until they'd passed through the ticket barriers to get out of the station. "What makes you say that?"

"You seem moody."

"Moody?"

"*Fly him to the moon.*"

Tom couldn't help but grin. He liked that tic. It always seemed to come out when Jake seemed happy. "I'm fine. Come on, let's go find Ethel."

They made their way to the industrial unit that housed Bites. Ethel came out to meet them and whisked Jake away to ply him with tea and biscuits. Tom let him go and set to work on what proved to be a long afternoon of number crunching and product design.

It was 6 p.m. when Jake came to find him. "Are you done yet? I want to show you something."

Tom glanced up. Jake stood in the entrance of Bites open-plan office, holding the laptop he'd borrowed from Cass. "What is it?"

"I've finished the branding layout. I put it through the architect software so you can see it on the finished restaurant, if you want?"

Tom nodded. Now that, he did want to see. The builders had fallen behind on the Camden site, and it was hard to envision how the project would ever be finished at all, much less what it would look like.

Jake shuffled over with Cass's laptop. Tom opened it up, and blinked a couple of times as an image of his own face, smiling and drunk on holiday in Ibiza, filled the screen. He shot a wary glance at Jake, who shrugged.

"What? It's not like I don't know he's your boyfriend."

Fair enough. Tom clicked on the open design files and studied the mock-ups Jake had created. They were perfect. Startling, urban, and cool, all the things Tom had first imagined when he'd drifted down Camden High Street. He clicked through the pages, from the incomplete menu designs to the full layout of the unfinished restaurant. If they pulled it off, it was going to be bloody brilliant.

Beside him, Jake fidgeted, and Tom realised he'd left him hanging. "These are awesome. You're really good at this."

"*Wankers*. I did web design at college for a while."

"What happened?"

Jake slapped his neck. "What do you think?"

Tom gazed at him, for a moment transfixed by all that was Jake. He was wearing his trademark skinny jeans, a softly worn jumper that smelled like magic, and a dark woollen hat over his shaggy hair. As ever, he took Tom's breath away.

Tom shut the laptop with a snap that made Jake jump. "It's late, and I'm starving. Want to get some dinner?"

Jake chewed on his lip. His usual retort was a 'thanks, but no thanks.' "I'm pretty wired from staring at a computer all day. I'm not sure you want to sit in a restaurant with me right now."

He buzzed out a few tics as if to emphasise his point.

"You know that doesn't bother—" Tom stopped. Sitting in a restaurant with Jake's muttering *didn't* bother him, but perhaps it bothered Jake. "Actually, I'd rather grab a bag of chips and head home. You're welcome to join me."

Tom unlocked the flat. Beside him, Jake leaned against the wall, languid, nonchalant, a crumpled chip paper in one hand, his ever-present phone in the other.

"How long have you lived here?"

Tom held open the door and waved Jake inside. "A couple of years, but we don't really live here—"

"Yeah, yeah, I know. You've got your mansion outside of the city."

Tom snorted and dropped his keys on the little table in the entrance hall. "Trust me, it's not a mansion. The place was a wreck when we bought it, and most of it still is."

"Thought you didn't like mess?" Jake followed Tom into the living room and poured himself onto the sofa.

Tom forced himself to look away. "Yeah, well. Sometimes there aren't enough hours in the day. You want a beer?"

"Maybe. Who's that?"

"Hmm?" Tom followed Jake's gaze to one of the only photographs that had made it into the Hampstead flat, a photograph Tom had forgotten was there. "That's Cass's Nana Dolly."

"I feel like I've seen her before."

Tom shrugged. "Not unless you were down the East End markets ten years ago. She was an institution there for decades. Didn't retire until she hit eighty."

Jake got up and peered closer at the photograph. "Is she still alive?"

"Yeah, but she's in a home now." Tom yawned and felt his jaw pop. He'd forgotten how exhausting building a restaurant from scratch was, or maybe it was Jake. The past week or so, Tom had struggled to match his energy "Do you want a beer, or not?"

"Sure. Want me to get it? You look dead on your feet."

"I'm fine."

Tom moved through the small flat to the tiny kitchen, pondering Jake's sudden concern for his well-being. He retrieved two beers from the fridge—the only constant in the hardly used kitchen—and returned to the living room to find Jake cross-legged on the floor, scanning through the sparse DVD collection in the TV cabinet. "See anything you like?"

"You're joking, right?" Jake buzzed through a few tics and held up a DVD. "*The Last Samurai*? Really? Tom Cruise is a dick."

Tom sank onto the couch. "Don't look at me. Cass likes the other bloke, the head Samurai guy. Says he has a fuck-me voice."

Jake grunted in answer, though in agreement or not, Tom couldn't tell. He tipped his head back and closed his eyes. Jake moved around, fiddling with this and that, and somehow it didn't feel strange. Tom wondered if Jake was remembering the last time he'd been here, when they hadn't made it past the bedroom door. When they'd ended up kissing and fucking, until they'd both fallen asleep.

Then Jake had woken up alone with Cass in his face.

"Are you awake?"

Tom opened his eyes. Jake was still on the floor, but he'd crawled across the rug on his knees and positioned himself between Tom's legs. "Huh? What?"

Jake laughed, and Tom felt the vibration rumble up through his body. "You're so out of it today, you're making me feel sharp."

"You are sharp." Tom sat up and scrubbed his face, aware of how close Jake was. "You've just got used to people treating you like you're thick."

Jake tensed, and Tom realised he'd spoken his mind without measuring his words.

"Sorry—"

"Don't be. I know you're right."

Jake sat back on his heels. For some reason, the new distance between them felt like a punch to his gut. He leaned forwards, chasing it down. "How are you getting on with the work you're doing? Enjoying it?"

Jake shrugged. "Some of it, but I don't know how you handle your inbox."

"I don't," Tom said dryly. "It's still there when I get up the next day. You can only do what you can do."

"Yeah, but you do loads." Jake drank some of his beer. "I never know what to write back."

"Bollocks. You're better at it than I am." Tom mirrored Jake's action and took a long pull on his beer. "But I think answering emails is a waste of your skills."

"Yeah?"

"Yeah." Tom put his beer bottle down and put his hands on his knees to stop himself reaching for Jake. He'd spent weeks resisting the desire to touch him, he wasn't going to falter now. "I have a bunch of websites that need updating and rebuilding. Fancy it?"

Jake stared at him. "I haven't built a website in years."

"So? You're working for free at the moment, remember? If you balls it up, I'll be no worse off than before."

"What if I don't?"

Tom grinned. "Then you'll get paid what I would've paid the designer on my books."

"What about the Camden project? Don't you need me there?"

"I do, but we're waiting for the builders at the moment. Unless you want to plumb in the bogs, there's not much you can do for the next week or so."

Jake still seemed unsure. Tom gave in to temptation and took his hand. "You could start with Pink's website. It's pretty small and basic."

"Like the restaurant, eh?"

Tom smiled. Pink's was a tiny fish café, ten tables, no set menu. They cooked and sold whatever fish Nero bought from the market every morning. "You're learning. I've got a spec folder, and I know you understand all this coding crap better than I do. I'm sure you could make it more functional."

"Like, so they could upload their menu every morning? Do they have a Twitter? Or a Facebook page? They could put it on there too."

"Exactly. Think you can make that happen for me?"

A tic rippled through Jake. "*Wankers*. I could try."

Tom sat back and closed his eyes, satisfied. Regardless of his attraction to Jake, the website at Pink's really *did* need a total overhaul, and he didn't have time to sort it out. If Jake was hiding the skills Tom suspected he was, this was the perfect solution.

"Why do you care?"

"What's that?" Tom opened a lazy eye.

Jake took his hand again. "Why do you care what I do? Look at all this." He gestured around the tiny flat. "You have your business, your property . . . Cass. You have everything. What am I to you?"

Tom considered Jake through heavy, half-lidded eyes. He'd expected Cass to ask what Jake was to him before Jake ever did, but though he'd thought about it, he still didn't have an answer he could verbalise. He sat up again and cupped Jake's chin with his hand. In the dimly lit room, Jake's eyes gleamed like a wolf's. Tom let himself be drawn in so they were inches apart, then he kissed Jake, once, twice, until Jake whimpered and pulled away. "This," Tom said. "*This* is what we are."

The first time they'd fucked had been measured and sweet, and a far cry from the scene Tom had pictured when he'd first realised his attraction to Jake. His imagination had proved nothing on reality, but even as Tom pushed Jake down on the rug, uncertainty crept over him. The sensation was unfamiliar, and Tom wasn't sure he liked it. He and Cass knew each other well. Their sex life was passionate, charged, and the one thing Tom had never, ever doubted.

Jake tapped Tom's temple. "You think too hard."

Tom hummed and kissed the tips of Jake's fingers, sucking one into his mouth. He waited for Jake's eyes to roll before he pulled off and searched out Jake's lips.

Jake's gasp of surprise was light, and laced with an innocence that made Tom want to hold him close and never let go, but there was nothing sweet about the way Tom kissed him. Tom held Jake's face tight in his hand, rough and needy. It had been three months since they'd last truly touched, and the long weeks of pent-up discord were about to explode.

He pulled Jake's grungy T-shirt over his head, leaving his arms raised. "Don't move."

The command was whispered, and Tom only half expected Jake to obey—Cass never did, at least not on the first try—but Jake didn't stir as Tom roamed down his body, exploring the lean curves of sinuous muscle.

Tom traced every inch of Jake's torso with his tongue and lips. Grazed his smooth inked skin with his teeth. Tom had spent too long resisting the call of his slender bones, and now he couldn't touch him enough.

Jake finally quivered beneath him, his soft moan barely audible. Tom smiled into Jake's flat abdomen, blowing warm air over his protruding hip, then he unbuttoned his own shirt, stripped Jake of his jeans, and dug around for supplies under the sofa. It wasn't the first time he'd fucked on the living room floor, and Cass had a thing for being bent over the arm of the couch.

He found what he was looking for and threw it down beside Jake.

Jake met his gaze and licked his lips. "Take your jeans off."

Tom shed his remaining clothes. For a moment, he felt cold. He didn't spend enough time in the flat to bother with the central heating timer, and the slow, ancient pipes combined with the late November air was enough to make him shiver.

Or perhaps it was something else.

Jake opened his legs, inviting Tom closer. Tom crawled over him and kissed him again, losing himself in Jake's gentle, demanding touch. He put his hand on Jake's chest and gauged his heartbeat, feeling it quicken with every stroke of his tongue. In that moment, Tom was certain there was room in his life with Cass for this precious man. There had to be.

He poured some lube onto his hand and warmed it between his palms before he took hold of Jake's cock. He pumped him slow and sure, like the beat of a drum, watching the sensation travel through Jake until he was pushing up into Tom's hand, widening his legs. Tom squeezed Jake's balls and moved lower, using more lube to work Jake open.

Jake let out a frustrated groan. "Just fuck me, will you? I can take it. I need it."

Tom curled his fingers in Jake one more time before he withdrew and reached for a condom. He rolled one on with shaking hands. He'd been careful with Jake up until now, but he knew all bets were off the moment he slid inside him. He remembered his smooth, tight heat too well, remembered the rush, and he *ached* for it.

Jake raised his legs and brought his knees to his chest. He trembled.

Tom leaned over him, their cocks sliding together. "I'm not going to hurt you."

Jake smiled. "I know."

Trust. It bloomed between them for the first time. The sensation shocked him. Jake had been in his life for months, fucking the first night they'd met, and working side by side ever since. Had it really taken Jake this long to realise Tom wasn't going to fuck him over?

Jake rocked his hips up to Tom's cock. "Stop bloody thinking."

Tom absorbed the command, though it didn't escape his notice that he'd once again lost control of an encounter with Jake. He lined his dick up with Jake's body and pushed inside, inch by inch, watching Jake swallow him up.

Jake threw his head back and clutched Tom's shoulders. "I forgot how big you are."

"Oh, I'm going to make you remember." Tom rolled his hips a fraction. "You ready?"

Jake dug his nails into Tom's skin and met his gaze. "Hell yeah."

The eye contact changed everything. In a split second, Tom became a man possessed by the feel of Jake wrapped around him.

He thrust hard into Jake, savouring every breath and sound, until Tom was scrambling for purchase on the rug. The rough surface dug into his knees, but the pain was pleasurable and added to the fast-growing heat coiling deep in his belly.

Jake grasped his cock, his hand sliding easily with the lube Tom had left there.

The sight of him jacking off, neck arched, head thrown back, made Tom groan and pound him harder. "You look so hot like that."

"You've said that before. Get some new lines, old man." Jake's eyes were wide, but the dark glint in them told Tom he knew exactly what effect he was having.

Like that, is it? Tom canted his hips, changing the angle.

Jake faltered and grabbed Tom's wrist. "Oh God."

Tom smirked, but his smugness was brief. His muscles were locking up, and he knew he was going to come soon. He gritted his teeth and gripped Jake's leg. His balls tightened, Jake clenched around him, and Tom let go with a gravelly groan.

Heat pulsed between them as Tom came. Jake let out a strangled cry and shot over his stomach. He thrashed his head from side to side as his body jerked. Awe warred with alarm in Tom. He'd noticed that the first time, the way Jake's release hit him like a train. Without the blissed-out stare, he'd have looked in agony.

Tom waited for Jake to calm, then reached for an errant piece of clothing to wipe him down. Jake watched him through heavy-lidded eyes, silent and spent, chest heaving with harsh breaths. Tom kissed his chest, withdrew carefully, and padded to the kitchen to chuck the condom. Jake was still sprawled on the floor when he came back. Tom considered him. He was long limbed, but made up of sinew and bone. *I want to carry him to my bed.*

As though he'd heard the thought, Jake held out his hand and let Tom haul him to his feet. They shuffled into the bedroom and crawled into bed. Tom lay on his back with Jake draped over him. The darkness enveloped them, and Tom let it take him until Jake moved. Tom felt him rise up on his elbows and opened his eyes to a soft kiss.

"Do you feel better now?" Jake asked.

"Better?"

"Yeah. You didn't seem yourself earlier."

Tom pushed Jake's hair behind his ears. "I'm fine. Just tired. It's been a busy few weeks."

Jake seemed satisfied with Tom's answer. He curled himself around Tom and put his cheek on his chest. "Cass says you get like that when you work too hard."

Tom blinked, unsure if he'd heard right. "Cass?"

"Yeah. He's been texting me. We've talked every day for a while now. I want to meet him again."

CHAPTER TEN

Tom pushed his way through the early morning bustle of yet another London station. Sometimes it felt like his life was ruled by the bright lines of the Tube map and the packed trains, but today he paid his usual frustration no heed. Today, he was a man on a mission, and it would take more than a crowd of sour-faced commuters to slow him down.

He made it above ground and braved a zebra crossing. He dodged a slow-moving bus and headed west. In the distance, he saw the signage for Pippa's. It was early, barely 8 a.m., but Thursday was a busy day in the restaurant trade—the day the weekend started early—and Cass would already be in the kitchen.

It began to rain, one of those intense showers that soaked through even the thickest pair of jeans. Tom felt it seep into his bones as his phone buzzed in his pocket. He pulled it out and read the message from Jake.

I'm gonna be offended if you keep leaving me in bed. Stay next time. Sleep with me.

Next time. Fuck. Tom shook himself. Despite Jake's best efforts, he was still bone-tired, agitated too, and unable to think beyond the next ten minutes. Last night, he'd watched Jake sleep for a while before he'd caught a few hours himself, but he'd crept away from the bed when dawn came, scribbled a note, and caught the underground across the city to Shepherd's Bush. Cass had been on his mind from the moment Jake had uttered his name in that lazy, postcoital moment, and there was only one way to get to the bottom of that.

Tom let himself in the front door of the restaurant. A few staff members smiled and waved. Some said hello. Tom nodded at them and continued on his way. He strode through the dining area and pushed open the kitchen door, gaze roving until he found Cass behind the main pass, knife in hand, prepping meat.

Cass looked up at just the right moment and saw Tom in the doorway. His expression remained unchanged, but he set his knife down, like he knew what was coming next.

Tom pointed at the ceiling. "I need a minute."

On any other day, he'd expect Cass not to follow him, but something in Tom's tone obviously compelled him to do as he was told for once. Tom led the way to the accommodation above the restaurant and kicked open the door. Cass followed him into the flat and locked it behind him.

"Something wrong?"

Tom turned to face him and folded his arms to stop himself reaching out. "I fucked Jake last night."

Cass raised an eyebrow. "So?"

"Why didn't you tell me you were talking to him?"

"Oh." Comprehension flickered over Cass's features. "I wondered if he'd mention it."

"Why didn't *you*?"

"I was going to."

"Uh-huh." Tom glared at Cass and took in his troubled gaze. "I don't understand." He gestured between them. "This works because we're honest. We don't hide things from each other. Why did you keep this from me?"

"I didn't keep it from you, I just . . . Fuck." Cass took his bandana off and ran his fingers through his hair. "I didn't think he'd respond to me, and when he did, I was here and you were somewhere else. I didn't want to talk about it over the phone."

"Why not? Don't you think a phone call is better than nothing?"

"Nothing is all I fucking know. I've hardly seen you for weeks."

"And whose fault is that? No one forces you to chain yourself to the bloody kitchen."

Cass's gaze darkened as his temper began to burn, but when he spoke, there was no fire in his tone, only a tired bewilderment Tom had never heard in him before. "It's not a crime to do an honest day's work. You taught me that. What exactly are you angry about?"

Tom remained silent, not all together sure of his answer. *Was* he angry? Or just bloody confused? Shutting people—shutting *Tom* out—was Cass all over, but clandestine messages to Jake didn't fit his MO. Tom sighed and scrubbed a frustrated hand down his face. Why couldn't Cass just fucking *talk* to him?

"Look." Cass stepped closer, but kept his hands to himself. "I wanted to get to know him better. You can't give him up, so I figured we should at least be friends."

Tom's stomach clenched. "I *would* give him up, if you asked me to. I'd do it in a heartbeat."

"I'd never ask you to do that." Cass raised his voice as his temper boiled over. "I like him. Why is that so hard for you to understand?"

"You like him? How?"

"What do you mean, how? How do you think?"

Cass balled his hands into fists and set his jaw. Tom took a deep breath. This was the Cass he saw in his dreams, lost and wild, searching for something he'd never find. "Just tell me, Cass. Please?"

The quiet plea reached Cass like nothing else could, and the fire in his gaze faded. "I talk to him every day. We have a lot in common, mainly you, but other things as well. It's a shame you met him first."

Cass grinned, dark and wry, but Tom couldn't find his sense of humour. "Why?"

"Why what?"

Tom backed Cass slowly into the door and pressed their foreheads together, craving the comfort of a physical connection. His frustration had eased, and now he just felt tired again, too tired, even, to care much that Cass had deflected his question. "Why is this so complicated?"

"Because you bagged a blinder. You shouldn't seduce blokes you actually like."

"Don't take the piss out of me." Tom pushed himself into Cass and felt every curve and angle of his body in just the right places. "I've missed you this week, but I'll still make you regret it."

"Yeah?" Cass licked his lips, a challenge if there ever was one. "Then stop yelling at me and kiss me like you fucking miss me."

Tom kissed him once, hard, then spun him around and wrestled him against the door face-first. Cass fought him briefly, jostling the bookcase by the door. Tom caught the bowl Cass kept his keys in with his elbow. It fell to the floor and shattered, but Tom barely noticed. Right now, he only had room for Cass.

Tom won the struggle. He shoved Cass into position and tugged his chef trousers down. Cass was heavier than Jake, with more meat on his bones, but in moments like these, Tom dwarfed him. "Is this what you want? Like this? Against the door?"

Cass pushed back, grinding himself on Tom's cock. "You wouldn't dare."

Tom chuckled. They both knew how wrong that statement was. "Stay here."

Tom stepped away and opened the bathroom door, found what he needed, and returned to Cass, who hadn't moved a muscle.

"You'll have to be quiet." Tom lubed his fingers and slid them easily into Cass, stretching him out as he unbuckled his jeans. He rolled a condom on and replaced his fingers with his cock, slow but steady, and all the way, stopping only when he could go no further. "Think you can manage that?"

Cass squirmed, his body clenching and flexing around Tom. He lolled his head back. "Shit, yeah—"

Tom swallowed Cass's groan with a kiss. They'd never fucked up here. Cass was apt to get loud, and with a restaurant full of staff and guests below them, it had never felt right. But for once Tom didn't care about right. Despite a scalding hot shower, he felt sure he could still smell Jake on his skin, but he wanted Cass like he'd never wanted him before. Cass, Cass, Cass; his best friend, lover . . . soul mate.

He drove into Cass, waiting a brief, heart-stopping moment before he did it again, and again, setting a furious rhythm that made his toes curl. Cass braced himself on the door and took it all, arching his back and grinding against Tom, like he wanted, *needed*, more.

Neither of them lasted long. Cass came with a strangled grunt, and Tom followed seconds later, muffling his groan with a bruising bite to Cass's neck.

"Arsehole." Cass hung his head, panting. "That better be under my collar."

"It is." Tom withdrew. Cass swayed. Tom held him tight and kissed his neck, soothing the mark left by his teeth. "You make me crazy, you know that?"

"Mmm." Cass sounded spacey. "I need to sit down."

Tom double-checked the door was locked, then peeled Cass's hands from the wood, pulled his trousers up, and turned him towards the living room. "Sofa. I'll be there in a sec."

Tom ditched the condom in the bathroom bin and washed his hands. There was broken crockery all over the place and jizz splattered on the door, but it could wait. It could all wait. He half lifted Cass from the couch and slipped in beneath him. Cass lay boneless on top of him. Tom slid his hands under his chef jacket and T-shirt and rubbed his back. "Better?"

Cass hummed. "Yeah. That was awesome."

Awesome. Yeah, fucking Cass was always awesome, but as Tom stared up at the ceiling of the flat he rarely visited, the reality of why he was there came rushing back. "We still need to sort out this craziness with Jake. It's driving me nuts."

Cass sighed and kept his face hidden in the crook of Tom's neck. He seemed relaxed, but the tension in his shoulders gave him away. "What have you got to moan about? You're the one getting the best of both worlds."

"That's how you see it?" Tom nudged Cass until he met his gaze. "I don't want both worlds, Cass. I want one, one where everyone's happy."

Cass shook his head. "That's your problem. You want to keep everyone happy, and you freak out when you can't." Cass shifted so he was wedged between Tom and the back of the sofa. "But you don't need to worry about me. I *am* happy."

I wish. Tom wasn't fooled. The mood swings, the sleepless nights, the endless fucking silence saw to that. Cass seemed content enough most of the time, but happy? Those moments were all too rare. "Don't bullshit me. This thing with Jake is different, and it's going to affect— it *is* affecting—*everything*. Neither of us has ever had a . . . bond with someone else before."

"I had Dean for a while. I was fucking him for months before he moved back down south."

"Dean was your fuck buddy. There was nothing else there, and you didn't miss him when he was gone."

"Do you miss Jake now?"

Yes. "That's not what I meant." Cass's expression was unreadable. Tom nudged him. "Jake's special, I know that, but I don't get why *you* want this to work out so much. Makes me think you might be using him to distract me."

"Distract you?"

"Yeah, to stop me bugging you to come home, when it's clearly the last place you want to be."

"What the fuck?" Cass sat up, and Tom's postcoital haze evaporated. "Why would you think that?"

"Why wouldn't I?" Tom fought to keep his tone even. "You'd rather be here alone than come home to me. What am I supposed to think?"

"You're the one who told me not to bother schlepping to Hampstead."

"That's because I don't want to be in bloody Hampstead either!"

Cass jerked away and scrambled off the sofa. "Don't give me that shit. The flat was your idea."

"So? What did you expect me to do? Kick around the house by myself while you roamed the streets, fighting the world and God knows what? Wait for the next call from the police station?"

It was a low blow. Cass had been out of trouble for years, but the damage was done, the words out before he could stop them.

Hurt coloured Cass's gaze before anger took its place. "How long are you going to punish me for that?"

Tom closed his eyes and counted to ten, then he opened them and tried to find something, anything, in Cass's baleful gaze to hold on to. "I'm not punishing you, Cass. I just don't want to be alone, and neither do you, so why are we both so lonely?"

Cass had no answer. Tom held out his hand. Cass drifted back to the sofa and took it. He lay back down and wrapped himself around Tom, but the mutinous silence remained. For a while, Tom imagined a gaping rift, a hole he couldn't fill, then Cass stretched up and kissed him, lightly at first, but then deeper, bruising himself on Tom's lips.

"I don't know why I do what I do, sometimes."

Tom found a smile in the pit of his stomach. "I know. I just miss you, all the bloody time, and I feel like you don't give a shit."

"Oh God, Tom. It's not that. I feel like I've lost a bloody limb when we're not together."

"Then why are we apart so much?"

"I . . . I don't know. I just . . ."

Tom touched Cass's cheek. "Just what?"

"I feel like I've got to earn it, you know? I'm so happy when I'm with you, it scares me."

Some days, most days in fact, Tom felt like he'd never come close to understanding the dark, broken boy who owned his soul. Why was it so hard for him to feel loved? To feel worthy of love?

Cass shifted in his arms and knocked his head on Tom's shoulder, as if clearing the fog from his brain. Then he met Tom's gaze with a grin that warmed and broke Tom's heart in one swoop. "Stop fretting. It'll be fine. Don't you think these last few months have been easier with Jake around?"

"Sometimes," Tom admitted. "He's a quick learner, and he's really good at the stuff he already knows."

"It's more than that," Cass said. "What usually happens when we open a new place, eh? You work like a dog, and we fight like a pair of bitches. It's been different this time. You've enjoyed it, and I know it's not me putting that smile on your face."

"I'm sorry I've been busy."

Cass let out a growl of frustration. "You're not listening to me. We've *both* been busy, and I'm not jealous. I don't want to piss around building sites all day, not even with you. And I like Jake. I can picture you fucking him, and it feels right."

"But—"

"But *what*?" Cass put his chin on Tom's chest. "Why are you so scared of how you feel about him? It's not wrong."

"Isn't it?" *I love him.*

"No, it's not, and I don't want you to feel bad about it, because I don't."

"I don't want two relationships. I don't want a separate life from you."

"Then let me and Jake be friends. He doesn't want me any other way, and I'm okay with that. These past few weeks . . ." Cass stopped and gathered his words. "I feel better knowing you're together, that he's helping you, distracting you from working yourself into the ground."

"What about you? Who's looking after you?"

"You." Cass traced a spiky pattern on Tom's chest, jagged and sharp. "I know you're with me whether we're together or not. That's enough."

Tom turned his gaze on the ceiling and played with Cass's hair. It was shorter than Jake's, but just as soft. Smelled just as good. Did Tom deserve so much? Probably not. And the by-now-familiar sensation of Cass shutting him out stung as much as it ever had. "I don't know if we can make this work."

"We won't know unless we try, and I want to try. Jake taps into a part of you I've never seen, and I don't want you to give that up."

Tom watched Cass carefully. His affection for Jake ran deep, but Cass was the love of his life. If it came down to a choice, there was none. "It could get messy."

"Only if we let it. We love each other, and Jake's amazing. All this feels right, just . . . don't leave me behind."

Tom took in the apocalyptic—if deserted—scene of a restaurant in the making: a dusty mess of exposed pipes, dangling wires, and haphazard piles of bricks, a far cry from the clean white walls and shiny wooden floors of the imagined finished project. Tom walked through the main seating area and opened the newly installed double doors that led to the food prep and storage area. More chaos greeted him.

Great. Tom shut the door and returned to the dining area. It felt strange to be alone in the eerily quiet shell of the old fire station. It was Friday afternoon, and the builders had taken advantage of POETS day and knocked off at lunchtime. Without their noise and disorder, the abandoned construction site felt like a ghost town.

But it wouldn't be that way for long. Tom was due to meet with the interior designers in a few minutes, and Jake *and* Cass would be joining them.

A tremor of nerves ran through Tom. It had been a week or so since he'd slept with Jake again, and though things were good between them, he still couldn't get his head around the prospect of loving a man that wasn't Cass. Not knowing how Jake felt didn't help, and he wasn't convinced by Cass's easy acceptance either. They'd lived with other men in their relationship from the very beginning, but not like this, and however much Cass told him it was all right, Tom didn't believe it. He knew Cass, and beneath it all, Cass needed the security of Tom's love for him. Deserved it.

And what about Jake? Didn't he deserve better than being the third wheel of an unconventional relationship? Didn't he deserve someone who loved him, and only him? Didn't they all deserve that? Before Jake, Tom would've been sure of his answer, but now, with Jake kissing him good-bye every night and sending him home to Cass, he wasn't sure of anything. All he knew was his heart ached for both of them.

A knock at the shuttered arcade doors brought Tom out of his musings. He went to answer it, glad of the distraction.

Tom let the designers in and glanced at his watch. Cass would be as late to the meeting as he was to everything else, but Tom had expected Jake before now. His timekeeping was usually pretty good, and he had the main plans for the dining area on Cass's laptop, so the meeting was pointless without him.

The designers took a walk around the restaurant while Tom called Jake. His call went straight to voice mail. Tom left a message, sent a text, then sought out the trio of women milling around the dining area.

"Sorry, folks," he apologised. "Jake's running late. Did he send you any of the blueprints for the interior?"

Karen, a designer Tom had worked with before, retrieved a tablet computer from her briefcase. "He sent me a few files. They weren't complete, but I think the dining area was set to go. Why don't we start there, and pick up the rest when he gets here?"

They pulled up the plans and got down to business. Even incomplete, Jake's designs were a dream to work with. It didn't take long for the team to size up the task at hand.

"Who does your guy work for?" Karen asked. "We're headhunting this month. Think he'd be interested?"

"You can ask him when he gets here. He's self-taught, and freelance at the moment."

"He's good." Karen put her tape measure down and swiped through a few screens on her tablet. "We're crying out for talent like this."

Tom smiled. Jake often seemed like the world's best-kept secret. "You're not poaching him just yet, and I think he's more into web design, though I'm sure he'll take your number."

Karen rolled her eyes, but said no more. Tom heard the door open. He turned around expecting Jake, but it was Cass, late as ever, but for once not the last to arrive.

Tom frowned. Cass raised an eyebrow. "Pleased to see me?"

Tom absently squeezed Cass's arm as soon as he was close enough. "'Course I am."

"What's wrong?"

"Jake's not here."

Cass pulled out his phone. "Have you rung him?"

"Yeah—" Tom cut off as the second designer shot him a pointed glance. "Shit. We need to get this done. They don't have any more slots before Christmas."

Cass pushed him forwards. "Go and do it, then. I'll find Jake."

"Really?" Despite a healthy texting relationship, Cass and Jake hadn't set eyes on each other since that awkward first meeting all those weeks ago. "Where will you look?"

Cass stretched up and kissed Tom's cheek. "I know where he lives. If he wants to be found, I'll find him."

There wasn't anything else to say. Cass left, and Tom spent the next few hours wrapping up a meeting he no longer gave a damn about. It was 6 p.m. when Cass finally called, and the designers had only just left.

"Did you find him? Where are you?"

"I've got him. We're in the car."

"In the car? Where are you going?"

"Home," Cass snapped. He muttered something, to Jake, presumably. "Just meet me back at the house, okay? I've got to go; I'm driving."

Cass hung up, leaving Tom more confused than when he'd answered the phone, but there was nothing he could do but lock up and make a dash through the evening drizzle to the Tube station.

It took Tom an hour and a half to get to Berkhamsted. At the station, he caught a cab back to the house. Cass met him at the front door and tapped his finger on his lips. "Shh. Jake's asleep on the sofa."

"Asleep?" Tom dropped his bag. "Is something wrong?"

"You could say that." Cass tugged Tom into the kitchen and shut the door. "He got evicted from his flat. The landlord chucked him out on the street and changed the locks with all his stuff inside. I found him shivering on the pavement."

"Evicted? Why?"

Tom started for the door. Cass stopped him, his gaze hard. "Why do you think? He missed a rent payment because some douche bag has been letting him work for free. What the fuck, Tom? You weren't paying him? How did you think he was living?"

"That was his decision, not mine. I have a salary plan set up for him in payroll, but he won't take it. He said he had enough to get by until the project was finished."

Cass hissed through his teeth. "Of course he said that. Do you think he could ever ask you for a handout? He bloody idolises you."

"You think this is my fault?" Tom turned his back on the kitchen door and gave Cass his full attention. "Do you honestly think I just let it happen? Bloody hell, Cass. Jake and I bicker about this crap every day. He won't take our money."

"Then make him."

"How?"

"I don't give a fuck how, just bloody do it."

Tom wanted to scream. "It's not that easy, and you know it. I've tried to force things on you before, and what happens? You run from me and start fucking up everything you care about."

"Jake isn't me."

"Isn't he?"

Cass made a noise low in his throat. In better circumstances it might've got Tom excited, but now, coupled with fatigue and frustration, it made him feel like weeping.

"I'm doing my best, okay? You must know I didn't want this for him. I want him safe and happy, more than I bloody know what to do with."

In answer, Cass glowered, his hackles still up, furious, like he could make Tom feel any worse than he already did. Tom resisted the urge to step closer, knowing Cass couldn't be placated until he'd run out of steam.

"I need you to promise me something."

"What?"

Tom measured his words. "I need you to promise me you won't run off if this, whatever it is, gets heavy. It was different before, but if Jake's here with us, there's nowhere to hide."

"There's always somewhere to hide, Tom." Cass punctuated his words with a humourless grin, a grin that made Tom's skin tingle.

"I mean it," Tom said. "I have to know you're in this with me. I can't go through—"

"I made you that promise years ago," Cass snapped. "That bullshit has nothing to do with Jake. I wouldn't have brought him home if I didn't want him with us."

"Fair enough." Tom suppressed a sigh. Cass had missed the point, or done his best to ignore it. "What happened tonight? How did you end up back here?"

Cass's expression softened a little. "I didn't know what else to do. He was shaking, banging his arm on the wall, and he could hardly talk. You said his TS is worse when he's upset, right?" Tom nodded. "Yeah, well, I think the landlord saw he was vulnerable and took advantage."

"Damn." Tom scrubbed a hand over his face. "Don't tell Jake you think that. He's a pugnacious git when he thinks I feel sorry for him."

"I don't feel sorry for him, at least, not like that. I'm just pissed off this shit is allowed to happen. Do you know how much he was short by? Fifty fucking quid. Fifty quid and that bastard would've taken everything he owned and left him on the street."

Tom took a moment to tame the anger surging through him. Cass had enough temper for both of them. "What did you say to the landlord?"

"Not much. I paid him what he wanted to give Jake's stuff back, then I punched him in the face. The guy was a prick."

"Did you call the police?"

Cass scowled. "What do you think?"

Of course he hadn't. Cass was a true East End boy. He didn't do police. "What about the landlord? Are you going to get arrested again?"

"I doubt it. I don't think the guy was legit. The place was crawling with damp, and I swear I could smell gas."

Tom closed his eyes briefly. Though Cass had a criminal record as long as Tom's arm, it had been years since his last misdemeanour. An assault charge now was the last thing either of them needed, but the urge to lecture Cass was drowned out by the horrible image of Jake shivering in a dank, filthy flat. "So, now what?"

"I don't know." Cass glanced at the door. "I told him he can stay with you, if he wants to. That's okay, isn't it?"

"Fuck no. If he stays here, it's with *us*, not me. This is your home. For this to happen, we both need to be here."

Cass nodded slowly. "I told him he could have the spare room and we'd figure the rest out later, but he was so tired, I think he'd have agreed to anything."

Tom reached out and tugged Cass into a tight embrace. "I'm glad you brought him here, okay? You did the right thing. I'm just fretting about the bigger picture, you know me."

Cass stood silent and still in Tom's arms for a long moment, then he pulled away and offered Tom a soft smile that belied the anger Tom had seen in him minutes before.

"I promised Jake I'd come home every night while he was living here. He asked me why I've never promised you the same thing."

"You did promise me once; it just never happened."

Cass's smile faded. "We need to work on that, but we can talk about it later. Go look in on Jake, will you? I think he needs to see your face."

He turned away to mess about with the stove. Tom left him to it and moved to the living room. He pushed open the door and was greeted by the haunting lyrics of Cass's favourite Smiths album, and the heartbreaking sight of Jake curled up at the end of the sofa, half-hidden by the hood of his sweatshirt.

He was a few feet away when Jake jumped awake, his eyes wide. Tom took the last few steps and caught him before he could fall off the couch. "Easy. It's okay. I didn't mean to wake you."

Jake clapped a hand over his mouth, like he could stop the string of tics that escaped anyway, like he could shove them all back in. "*Wankers*. Shit. I didn't mean to fall asleep."

Tom held Jake a moment, then eased him back on the couch. "Don't blame you. It's been a long day."

"I'm sorry I missed the meeting. I tried to get there, but I didn't have my, shit, I didn't have anything."

Jake met Tom's gaze with red-rimmed eyes. Jake didn't seem the type to cry, but there was no hiding his distress. Tom saw the fresh bruises on his renegade left arm and his heart ached for him.

"It's okay. Cass told me everything." Tom gave in to Jake's squirming and let him sit up. "Forget about the meeting. There'll be plenty of others. Everything Cass said to you counts for both of us. You can stay here as long as you like, and we don't expect anything from you in return, okay?"

Jake ticked, but even his trademark buzzing whistle sounded tired. "I like Cass. You won't let him stay away, will you? I don't want to be the reason he doesn't come home."

"That's not going to happen." Tom kissed Jake's hand. "He wants you here, and we'll be here for you as much you want us."

"Both of you?"

"If that's what you want."

Jake nodded, the gesture so slight Tom thought he'd imagined it.

Cass ghosted into the room and put a plate of homemade pizza on the coffee table, then he dropped onto the other end of the couch and put his arm around Jake. Jake met his gaze and smiled. Cass smiled right back and suddenly, Tom felt like a door had opened; a big wide door with the whole world on the other side.

Jake put his head on Cass's shoulder and closed his eyes. Tom stood, his mind spinning, and drifted to the hall to ditch his coat and shoes. Then it felt like a magnet drew him back to the living room doorway. He leaned on the peeling frame and watched them together, Cass and Jake, his two dark mysterious boys. Huddled up on the couch, they almost looked like brothers.

Almost.

JAKE

CHAPTER ELEVEN

Jake Thompson rolled over in an unfamiliar bed. His hand bumped something furry and warm. *What the fuck?* He jumped, startled, until his vision cleared enough to make out the tiny tabby cat curled up beside him.

He extended his hand on instinct. He'd grown up with cats, though he'd never seen one quite so small. The cat stared at him, sphinxlike, then flicked its tail and went back to sleep.

A warm chuckle from the doorway startled Jake for a second time. "That means she likes you. She usually slaps Tom in the face."

Cass. An emotion he couldn't name crept over him. After an afternoon spent beating himself up against the wall the drive out of London in Cass's souped-up Toyota felt like a dream.

Jake stroked the cat again and traced the dark lines that striped her ribcage. "What's her name?"

"Souris." Cass ventured further into the room and set a steaming mug on the bedside table. Jake started to sit up, but Cass stopped him. "Shh, it's early. I just wanted to say good-bye before I left for work."

Jake glanced at the window. It was dark. "What time is it?"

"Half five. Even Tom's still asleep, but I've got to hit the motorway if I want to get into the city by eight."

Jake wriggled his way upright despite Cass's protests. "Are you coming back tonight?"

"Do you want me to?"

Jake nodded. Yesterday afternoon was the third time they'd ever laid eyes on each other, but the thought of Cass leaving made Jake nervous. He felt safe with Tom, but Cass... Cass was fierce and strong, and in the cold light of the early morning, his hand on Jake's arm felt like it had always been there.

Cass smiled a strange half smile. "I'll see you both later then. Now relax, it's the weekend."

He left, but Jake didn't go back to sleep. Instead, he absently stroked the sleeping cat and ticked away until he heard Tom get up and turn the shower on. Then he closed his eyes. From what little he'd seen so far, Tom and Cass's house was old and half-derelict, but Jake had always liked the sound of creaking pipes and ancient groaning boilers. It soothed him, and it wasn't long before he slipped back into a deep and dreamless sleep.

It was midmorning by the time he woke himself with a bruising punch to his chest. He shuffled downstairs and found Tom at the kitchen table, laptop open. By the empty mug and tired lines around his eyes, he'd clearly been there awhile.

Jake thought about creeping away and leaving him undisturbed, but a tic gave him up. "I like your bum. Shit."

"Good morning to you too." Tom looked up from his work. "Sleep well?"

No. "Yeah." Jake shifted his weight from one foot to the other. Dressed in pyjama bottoms and a sweatshirt, blond hair ruffled, Tom looked more at ease than Jake had ever seen him, but despite his TS-induced daze, he hadn't missed the tension between him and Cass the night before. "*Wankers.* Are you okay with me staying here?"

"Of course." Tom leaned back from the table. He considered Jake a moment, then held out his hand, beckoning him closer. "Trust me, if either Cass or I wasn't happy about it, it wouldn't be happening. We both want you here."

He let Tom pull him into an off-balance, one-armed embrace. "I thought you and Cass hardly ever come home?"

"Yeah, well, maybe it's time that changed. Cass and I had a bit of a barney after you'd gone to bed last night, and we both know we need to put more time into things at home."

"Cass said that too, yesterday, in the car, I think. Why's it so hard for you? Can't you just sleep at Pippa's with him?"

Tom shrugged. "Because that's all I'd be doing. Cass works till midnight most nights, and Shepherd's Bush is miles away from where I need to be."

It sounded to Jake like Tom and Cass needed some alone time to reconnect without a twitching idiot interfering, but with Tom's arm warm and solid around his waist, he couldn't find the will to pull away. "Can I have a shower?"

Tom sighed. "This is your home for as long as you want it to be. You don't have to ask to do anything."

Jake said nothing. Tom released him from his grip and picked up an envelope. "I have something for you."

"What is it?"

"Wages, and don't even think about tearing it up or giving it back. Cass just about ripped me a new one last night for letting you work for free. I'm not doing it anymore, got it?"

Jake bristled, but the edge in Tom's tone stopped him from protesting. "What about rent? I don't want to skank off you."

"Figure it out with Cass. Whatever I say is bound to be wrong."

A tic bubbled in Jake's arm. He thought about fighting it, but he didn't have the energy. His arm shot out and sent Tom's empty mug flying. "Shit, fuck. Sorry. *There's rats in here*. Fuck!"

Jake clamped his hand over his mouth, mortified. *Rats, really?* That was a new one. He bent to retrieve the shattered cup. Tom dropped down beside him.

"Sorry," Jake said. "I break stuff. That's why I haven't got any."

Tom picked up a few fragments of porcelain. His face was a study in diplomacy. "Jake, I see your TS every day, and I've seen you break stuff before, okay? Don't worry about it. Besides, have you seen Cass cook in a domestic kitchen? There's a dent in every pan in the cupboard."

Jake whistled and smacked his aching arm. "It hasn't been this bad for a while." *Since I met you.* "I feel like I've lost control of it."

"Maybe you have." Tom piled up the shattered cup and pried the final piece from Jake's fingers. "But that doesn't mean you can't get it back. Is there anything we can do to help you?"

Jake shook his head bleakly and sat back on his heels. Cass had witnessed the worst of his TS the day before, but Tom had only ever seen a fragment of how bad it could get. "The doctor gave me some drugs a while ago, but I don't like taking them. They make me feel dead inside."

Tom rose and fetched a dustpan and brush. He swept up the broken cup, helped Jake to his feet, and put his hands on his shoulders. "Listen, you're an adult, and you know what's best for you. Just promise me you'll tell us, either of us, both of us, whatever, if you need help. You might be used to coping on your own, but that doesn't make it right."

Cass: FYI: You can still text me
Jake: Thought you'd be busy
Cass: I am
Jake: Tom is too
Cass: Cook some sausages. That always distracts him
Jake: He said you had a row
Cass: Did he?
Jake: Yeah
Cass: We're okay, mate. I promise
Jake: I believe you

Cass's texts petered out in the afternoon, but Jake had grown as used to that as he had to the daily contact with Tom's lover. He questioned his deepening feelings for Tom every day, but Cass? Somehow, their virtual relationship had begun to feel normal.

As normal as anything ever felt, at least. Jake spent his first day at Tom and Cass's house in his room, working on the new layout for the Pink's website. He'd taught himself coding years ago, but his skills were rusty. Combined with a relentless stream of tics he couldn't control, he'd about driven himself crazy by the time Tom came to find him.

"You done for the day?"

Jake turned away from Cass's computer screen. He'd been staring at the same set of code for the past two hours, and he'd given himself a headache. "Sure. This is doing my nut in, anyway."

Tom smiled. "Hungry? I owe you dinner after you made me lunch."

"I didn't make anything. I put some sausages in a pan and opened a tin of beans."

"Still counts. Come on. I'll buy you dinner at the Dragonfly."

"The Dragonfly?" It took Jake a moment to remember it was the name of Tom and Cass's bistro here in Berkhamsted. "Um . . ."

He rolled over and sat up, stretching the kinks out of his spine. He'd been flat on his stomach most of the day, trying to control his wayward arm by lying on it until it was completely numb. Even alone in his room, his tics were still off the scale.

Perhaps sensing the war going on between Jake and his nervous system, Tom stepped further into the room and sat on the edge of the bed. "What are you worried about?"

Jake snapped Cass's laptop shut. He didn't want Tom to see the Pink's website until it was finished. "What do you think?"

"I think that I understand, as much as I'll ever be able to, but there's way around it, at the Dragonfly, at least."

"You want me to sit in the car park?"

Tom chuckled. "Not quite, but owning the place has its advantages. I have the best table in the house. No one will even notice us."

A ripple of excess energy buzzed up Jake's arm and across his face. The jolt shook the bed and knocked him off-balance.

Tom frowned. "Did that hurt?"

"No."

Tom opened his mouth. Shut it again. "All right. Let's start this conversation over. Do you want to come out and get some dinner?"

No. "Um . . ."

Tom sighed. "Do you trust me?"

Yes. "No."

"Humour me, then." Tom stood and pulled Jake to his feet before he could protest. "Let me show you, and if you don't like it, we'll get a pizza and come home, deal?"

There wasn't much Jake could say when Tom looked at him like that. They left the house and walked along the canal that ran parallel to the high street. On the way, Jake distracted himself by taking his first look around the distinctly middle-class town Tom and Cass called home. With its Tudor buildings and vintage streetlamps, it was nothing like the places Jake had ever lived before. Nothing like the bleak northern cities he'd grown up in.

"This way." Tom guided him around the lock. "I'll show you the front, then we can go in the side door."

Jake wondered if the side door was part of Tom's way of sneaking inside unnoticed, but found himself distracted again once Tom had steered them to the front of the restaurant. He stared at the simple white branding, and then at the subtly intricate dragonfly signage and frowned. "Where have I seen that before?"

Tom raised an eyebrow. "That fact that you think you have confuses the hell out of me, but I like it."

"Eh?"

"Never mind." Tom took his arm. "Let me know when you see something that jogs your memory."

Jake let Tom lead him back down the alley they'd come from and to a door he hadn't noticed first time around. Tom retrieved a set of keys from his pocket, let them in, and beckoned Jake into what appeared to be a corridor.

Tom pointed left. "Kitchen's down there, dry store behind it. Dining room is this way."

He took Jake's arm again. Another door, another corridor, and then they were in a warm, secluded alcove. Tom pulled out a chair at the solitary table and guided Jake into it, hands on his shoulders. "Look around," he said. "You can see it all, but no one can see you."

Jake gazed at the crowded restaurant, at the packed seating area and buzzing bar. A nervous tic ran through him, but no one glanced his way. Tom was right: hidden in the alcove, no one knew he was there.

Tom massaged his shoulders. "This okay?"

"Yeah." Jake nodded, letting out the breath he'd unconsciously been holding since they'd slipped in the side door. He whistled and tapped his chest. "I like it."

"Good, 'cause I'm bloody starving. Get settled, I'll get some drinks."

Tom left Jake in the alcove and went to the bar. Jake watched him weave through the tables, nodding and smiling to people he knew, oozing the confidence and composure that had attracted Jake to him in the first place. Tom was a cool dude with a massive heart, a heart that seemed hell-bent on tying Jake up in knots. Why did being with Tom feel right and yet so wrong at the same time? Jake felt safe, comfortable, and like he belonged, but then he thought of Cass, pictured him and Tom together and knew he was intruding on something beautiful. Jake had only seen them together twice, but he knew they loved each other in a way he could only dream of ever understanding.

Tom dropped into the seat beside him and set two glasses down. "It's nice here, isn't it? Best of both worlds."

"*Wankers*. Sorry. Yeah."

Tom squeezed Jake's shoulder. "You like chicken, don't you? Gloria has loads of coq au vin going spare."

"Gloria?"

"The chef here. She'll be out in a minute."

Jake took a nervous gulp of the beer Tom had brought him.

Tom squeezed his shoulder again and left his hand there. "Relax."

The sensation of Tom's big, warm hand on his skin was hypnotic. Jake settled back in his seat and took another, more sedate, sip of his beer. "What *is* coq au vin?"

"French chicken stew, but Gloria style. She's Jamaican, so expect some heat."

"And the rest, my darlin'. Here you go, boys." A statuesque woman with red braids appeared from nowhere and set two steaming plates on the table. She kissed Tom's cheek and sat down. "Let me hide here a moment. It's been a long shift."

Tom offered Gloria his beer, grinning when she waved it away. "Many more booked in?"

"Too many." Gloria scowled, but Jake could tell she was pleased. She pulled a zipped plastic bag from her apron pocket. "Can you take these home for Cass? He said he needed them for tomorrow."

Tom took the bag and stuffed it into his coat pocket. "Bloody typical. He's coming home tonight. I'll put them in his car so he doesn't forget them."

Jake watched the exchange with wide eyes. The contents of the bag had looked like shrooms, but that couldn't be right.

Gloria noticed him staring and pushed his plate towards him. "Eat up. You need some meat on your bones, you all do."

Tom laughed as she got up and kissed him again. "Jake and Cass, maybe. If I ate any more than I do already, I'd be in trouble."

Gloria chuckled, ruffled his hair, and left them to go back to her kitchen. Tom picked up his fork, relaxed and easy. "You look like you've just seen a naked woman. What's up?"

"What's in the bag?"

"Mushrooms."

"Mushrooms?"

"Yeah, dried porcini. We source them from a place down in Kent, but Cass always uses his stocks up before the next order is ready. Lucky for him, Gloria looks after him."

"Oh." Jake shoved a bite of chicken and mashed potato in his mouth to hide his embarrassment. "I thought they were a different kind of mushroom."

Tom rolled his eyes. "You sound like Cass."

"Really?" Tom had said that before. "I don't do drugs. I tried them when I was at school, though. Weed was good for my tics, until the TS found a way around it."

Tom said nothing for a moment, absorbed in his dinner, then he smiled a sad little smile Jake had never seen before. "Cass doesn't do drugs either, but he was a wild child when I met him. Took me a while to tame him. Some days, I'm not sure I have."

"He loves you." Jake spoke the words without thinking, and the light in Tom's face faded.

"Oh, I know he does, but life gets in the way sometimes. Cass isn't like me. He grew up fighting for everything he ever had. I think he forgets sometimes that it doesn't have to be that way anymore."

The sadness in Tom's gaze made Jake want to cry. He didn't understand the convoluted mess between the three of them, but he knew Tom was a good man, and that he loved Cass to death.

Jake nudged Tom. "Gloria's nice. Did you mean to put a strong woman behind every business you own?"

Tom chuckled, though the shadow in his eyes remained. "It wasn't intentional. I do think every business needs a mother figure, though. It helps with staff morale."

It seemed to Jake that Tom spent too much of his time making sure his staff were happy. "So who mothers you?"

"My own mum, when I let her. My parents live in Bedford, but I don't get home as much as I'd like."

"Work gets in the way?"

"Always." Tom sighed. "You know me too well. I talk to them every few days, though. My mum called this morning, actually. She invited you to lunch on Boxing Day."

Jake choked on his food. "Me? How does she know about me?"

"Because I told her." Tom rubbed Jake's back. "All right?"

Jake gulped some beer. "What did you tell her?"

"The truth, the clean version, at least. I told her we had a friend staying with us for a while. She asked if you were going home for Christmas, I said I didn't know, so she told me to bring you home with us."

"Did you . . ." Jake stopped. Was he really going to ask Tom if he'd told his mum they'd had sex? "*Wankers.*"

"So . . ."

Jake shovelled the last of Gloria's coq au vin in his mouth. "So what?"

"Christmas." Tom stopped, like he was measuring his words. "Oh and Cass would love it if you came to Pippa's with me on Christmas Day. He only works till five, then we usually go out and get pissed."

Jake drained his beer. Getting wasted sounded appealing, but there were some major flaws in Tom's plan. "You want me to get drunk with you, then visit your family when I'm tired and hungover? Yeah, that's a great idea."

Tom rolled his eyes. "Don't get shitty. This is how it is: Cass and I are going to my mum's on Boxing Day. I have two sisters and a brother, so with all their spouses and kids there's loads of us. Plenty of room for you if you've got no other plans."

Jake scowled in answer and pushed his plate away.

"So have you?"

"Have I what?"

"Got other plans. God, you don't make this easy, do you?"

Jake had no other plans, but the thought of taking his TS to a family gathering horrified him. He'd ruined too many to feel anything else.

Tom rubbed his back again, reminding Jake his hand had been there all along. "It's not really Cass's scene either, but once you've drunk enough, it's not so bad. He'll look after you."

More silence. Jake felt his unnatural energy crackle in his nerves and bubble out of him in a series of popping tics. "My mum hasn't asked me to come home. I didn't go last year, or for Easter."

Tom finished his supper in one big bite. "When did you last see her?"

"Eighteen months ago."

"Are you close?"

Jake shrugged. "Not really. My dad left her when I was thirteen. She remarried and had more kids, and my stepdad couldn't deal with me. I think they were all relieved when I ran away to the big city."

"Families are strange things," Tom mused. "No two are ever the same. Where's your dad?"

"Don't know. Haven't seen him in years." Jake took Tom's plate, stacked it on top of his, and brushed some stray crumbs from the tablecloth.

Tom smiled. "I do that. Drives Cass mad, but once a waiter, always a waiter."

"Thought you said I was a crap waiter?"

"You are, because you hate it." Tom pushed a small laminated menu into Jake's hands. "Have some pudding and stop your moaning."

Jake gave Tom the finger, but was grateful for the change of subject. He'd grown used to his self-imposed solitude, but his time with Tom had made him soft, and being alone was harder now, the nights longer, and the silence louder, punctuated only by the tics that had isolated him in the first place.

"Anything you fancy?"

"Hmm?" Jake leaned back in his chair. Tom's arm was around him, and combined with the alcohol and his full stomach, he felt a little sleepy. "What's your favourite?"

"The plum clafoutis. It sounds posh, but it's just a fruity cross between a pancake and Yorkshire pudding. Cass makes it for breakfast when he's being nice to me."

"I thought you were always nice to each other."

"I never said that." Tom grinned, but his expression had turned blank by the time he got up to order Jake's pudding. Jake had noticed that a lot tonight, and it felt like he was unwittingly touching Tom's rawest nerves. After months of Tom being the coolest bloke Jake had ever known, the change was unnerving. Or, at least, it would've been if Tom's rare moments of vulnerability lasted long enough to convince Jake he hadn't imagined them.

Tom returned with pudding, two spoons, and two glasses of something strong and sweet. He settled in his seat and pulled Jake close again. Jake let him, and forbade himself from glancing around to see if anyone noticed. Did it matter if they did?

Tom didn't seem to think so. He drew Jake back into the present with a light touch to his cheek, the kind of touch that often set Jake on fire. "Did you look into those online courses we talked about yet?"

Jake shivered, glad for once he could blame his overreaction on his tics. "I found a few, but the good ones cost loads. I'll have to save up for them."

"Not necessarily," Tom said. "We usually fund further education for our employees, if the courses they want to take relate to the job they do for us."

"Really?" Jake was sceptical. "I want to learn about typography. You don't need me to do that for you."

"Maybe not, but bear it in mind when you make your plans. Nothing is ever impossible."

Jake picked at his half of the sweet, fruity bowl of loveliness, and downed his sticky wine. The nectar-like booze warmed him. "You know that's not true."

"Do I?" Tom said. "I don't think we ever know anything for certain."

Again with the cryptic melancholy. Jake watched Tom drink his wine, and suddenly wanted nothing more than to wind his arms around Tom's strong body and hold him until the sadness went away. "Can we go home now?"

"Sure." Tom stood and retrieved his wallet from his pocket. "Let me just pay and leave a tip behind the bar."

"Pay? I thought you owned the place?"

"Doesn't mean we get a free ride. That's where most restaurants go wrong. Greedy managers eating the profits. It's not fair on the staff either. They don't get free two course dinners, why should I?"

Jake refrained from pointing out that Ethel had told him all Tom's full-time staff did in fact get a meal with each shift. Tom disappeared briefly, but he was back before Jake had put his coat on . . . back in time to wrap Jake's scarf around his neck and drag the pad of his thumb over his bottom lip. "All right? Sorry things got a bit heavy. I really only meant to feed you, honest."

Jake fought against the thraldom of Tom's touch. "I know."

"Come on." Tom took his hand and led him to the side door of the restaurant. They slipped outside, and Jake waited while Tom locked it behind them.

"When will Cass be home?"

Tom checked his watch. "Not for a while yet."

"Oh." Jake frowned and fell into step beside Tom as they circled the lock and joined the canal path. "It's pretty late."

"I know, but that's how it goes. He won't be out of the kitchen until at least eleven, then he has to do all the due diligence and drive home."

"That's why he stays at Pippa's."

Tom shrugged, though Jake hadn't meant it as a question. "Pippa's kitchen is intense, and working keeps Cass busy. Keeps his mind occupied and his bad habits in check. Trouble is, he doesn't give himself enough credit. He's changed so much, he just hasn't bloody noticed."

"Bad habits?"

Tom shook his head. "Not my story to tell."

Curiosity burned Jake's soul. "Do you think he'd tell me?"

"Perhaps, if you told him why you wanted to know."

And there was a question. Could Jake admit that he was fast becoming obsessed with all things Tom and Cass? Nope. Not tonight. "What about you? Why do you work so much?"

"What else is there? Maybe I need occupying too."

"You shouldn't be fucking about with me if you need to spend more time with Cass."

Tom didn't answer, and they walked the rest of the way to the house in silence. He let them in. Jake shed his coat and shoes and took them to the cupboard under the stairs. He found Tom in the kitchen when he came back, wrestling with a tin of cat food and fending off a fractious cat.

Jake clicked his fingers. Souris cast Tom a baleful glare and sauntered over to him. He tickled her chin. "Hi, sweetie. Is that nasty man taking too long?"

Tom rolled his eyes and scraped the food into a dish. "Don't encourage her. Bloody cat's an arsehole. She's lucky I feed her at all. And see? She doesn't even want it now."

Jake scratched the cat's head as she rubbed herself against his arm. He felt Tom's gaze all over him, and almost didn't dare look up.

But he did look up, and in the softly lit kitchen, Tom's eyes drew him in. He left Souris to her dinner and drifted to Tom's side. Despite the half-arsed conversations and unfinished sentences, he sensed a change, like an invisible tie between them was strengthening, solidifying, and becoming impossible to walk away from.

Tom wrapped his arms around Jake and put his chin on his head. "Everything you say is right, and I've said it all to myself and Cass a thousand times. I wish I knew the answer, but I don't."

"Maybe there isn't one." Jake made the most of the embrace, knowing it wouldn't be long before he went to bed alone.

"Hmm, maybe you're right."

Tom sounded defeated. Jake traced his strong jaw with the tip of his finger. He wanted to say something profound and reassuring, but the words weren't there.

So he kissed Tom and felt a spark meld with all the excess energy in his body and become something warm and wonderful. It flowed through him like liquid gold until Tom pulled away with a soft sigh.

"Good night, Jake."

CHAPTER TWELVE

The bare floorboard on the landing creaked. Jake froze, one foot in the air. It was Thursday morning, and not that early, but Cass was still in bed and Jake had heard him come home only a few hours before Tom had left for the city at dawn.

Jake didn't want to disturb him. If he was being honest, he was nervous of what would happen when Cass did wake up. Despite their near-constant texting, they'd hardly seen each other since Cass had punched Jake's landlord and bundled Jake into his car. Cass had worked the last six days straight, and it was always well past midnight by the time he came home.

Jake knew this, because he'd found he couldn't sleep until he heard Cass tread softly up the stairs and open Jake's door. What he was looking for, Jake didn't know, because he'd yet to find the nerve to do anything but pretend to be asleep.

Perhaps he was checking that Jake was in his own bed.

Shit. Jake had promised himself he wouldn't think about that, not today. Today was the first day Tom had left him alone with Cass, and he didn't need another reason to freak out.

God no.

He tiptoed his way to the bathroom. He took a quick shower, but got out before the hot water pipes could make too much noise. When he was done and dressed, he crept back, but this time, the half-open door to Cass and Tom's room proved oddly tempting. He let a run of silent tics ripple through him, then snuck across the landing and took a peek around the door. Cass lay sprawled on his stomach, dark hair in his face, the cat draped over his neck, and his arm flung out over what Jake assumed was Tom's side of the bed.

I wonder if he's lonely. Probably not with Souris keeping him warm.

Jake felt a warning buzz in his arm. He quit while he was ahead and retreated downstairs to work on his coding.

It was nearly noon when Cass sloped into the kitchen and chucked the kettle on the stove. "Morning."

Jake stared at him and apprehension warred with a strange sense of relief. It had taken him a while to figure out he felt a little lost without his morning text from Cass today, but did Cass feel the same? Jake had no idea. He pushed his work aside. "Do you want me to make you some tea?"

"Nah. You're not a houseboy, mate." Cass grabbed a couple of mugs from a cupboard and turned to the stove. Jake took in the curve of his spine and hunched shoulders. Even from behind, Cass looked tired.

"Houseboy?"

Cass faced him, and Jake realised with a start it was the first time he'd seen him in daylight. Fuck. Why did that seem so important?

"Tom said you were worrying about rent," Cass said. "Do you take sugar?"

"No. And I'm not worried about it. I just want to pay it."

Cass finished his tea making and came to the kitchen table. "There's no rush."

Easy for him to say. Jake didn't want a free ride. Fuck that.

Cass moved around the table and peered over Jake's shoulder. Oddly, though Jake had gone out of his way to conceal the Pink's work in progress from Tom, he didn't mind Cass seeing.

"I like that it's not pink," Cass said. "The first designer couldn't handle the idea of not creating the fucking obvious."

"Tom told me you named the restaurant after your teacher at school, so I figured the colour was irrelevant."

"Mr. Pink was my woodwork teacher. I bloody hated that bloke."

"Why?"

"Because he wouldn't let me bunk off and smoke weed." Cass gestured around the warm, stylish kitchen. "Thanks to him, I built most of these units myself."

Jake didn't know what to say to that. The kitchen was the only finished room in the house, and it was gorgeous. "How much is the rent?"

Cass took a step back. Jake thought he heard him sigh. "The mortgage is nine hundred a month, so if you really want to be equal, you can pay three hundred."

"What about bills?"

Cass rolled his eyes. "Fine. Four hundred, but that's it. No more."

Jake clicked through to his online banking, and waited while Cass fetched the account details for the direct debit. While he was alone, he let a few tics escape, though he didn't know why he was hiding them from Cass. It had only been a few days since Cass had seen him head-butting a wall.

"You don't have to wait until I'm out of the room. I know that makes it worse."

Jake took the cheque book Cass held out and tapped the account details into the computer. "How do you know that?"

"Does it matter?"

"*Wankers. Tosser.* Probably not." It did, though. Tom did everything he could to ignore Jake's TS, but Cass was the opposite, and it had been a long time since Jake had talked about his condition so frankly. It felt refreshing, and he liked it, but the sensation of Cass hovering unnerved him.

Wind your neck in. It's his bloody house.

"What are you doing today?"

Jake jumped, lifting himself briefly right out of his seat. Cass looked like he wanted to ease him back down, but he didn't.

"Um, working," Jake said. "You?"

"DIY, probably, when I've got my arse in gear. That's how I usually spend my days off when Tom's not home."

Cass's grin dimmed, reminding Jake that neither Tom or Cass had managed to take Monday off that week, and despite Tom's best efforts, he was absent now for Cass's only free day before Christmas. "Tom told me Mondays are your Sundays."

"Manday Mondays," Cass said. "We go for a walk, drink some beer, eat, and fuck. Best day ever."

Jake choked on his tea. Cass seemed to realise what he'd said and shifted, his easy candour fading to the awkwardness Jake had always feared.

"Um, anyway." Cass backed away from the table. "I'll leave you to it. Come find me if you need anything."

And then he was gone.

Jake stared after him in consternation. He knew Tom and Cass had sex, of course he did, but hearing Cass talk about it so bluntly had caught him off guard. Being fucked by Tom was the best sex Jake had ever had, the kind of sex he'd dreamed about when he was alone in his crappy flat in Kentish Town.

But he wasn't in Kentish Town anymore. He was in Berkhamsted, with Cass, the man Tom had been in love with for nearly a decade. Thinking about having sex with Tom felt . . . wrong? Maybe? Who knew?

Jake didn't know how he felt. The paranoid part of his brain told him to pack his bag and run for the hills. With Tom gone for the day, he wouldn't have to see his face as he walked away from him. Instead he could remember the kind smile Tom had given him that morning when he'd crept into Jake's room to touch his cheek and whisper good-bye.

But Jake didn't move. Instead, he stared at the HD screen of Cass's laptop, and spent the afternoon listening to him crash around. It would never take him long to find Cass in the big old house. Tom was a quiet man, often found in the corner of a room, silent and working. Cass was different. A trail of chaos, mess, and music followed him wherever he went.

He checked on Jake a lot too. Sometimes overtly, and sometimes not so much. Sometimes he padded quietly to the kitchen doorway and stared at Jake's back until Jake thought he would explode.

The fourth time it happened, Jake lost his cool. "Stop bloody staring at me."

Cass chuckled, low and easy. "Can't. Tom told me to keep an eye on you."

Jake glanced over his shoulder. "Why? I've been here by myself every day this week and I haven't pinched your family silver."

Cass blinked, clearly taken aback. "Easy, mate. I think he meant in case you needed anything. You are in a strange town, after all, miles from the last place you called home."

Jake felt like a tosser; he knew why Cass was keeping an eye on him . . . had known all along. "Sorry. I slept like shit last night, and I'm a twat when I'm tired."

Cass ventured into the kitchen as Jake cracked his jaw on a massive yawn. "Something bothering you?"

"No." But it was a lie, and one punctuated by a bruising punch to his chest, his third that day. "*Fuck.*"

Cass winced. "Do you do that a lot?"

"Only when I'm sleeping most of the time, but it's coming out in daylight today. Must be something in the air."

"Anything make it better?"

Jake looked away. He wasn't about to explain to Cass what eased his nighttime tics, and it seemed he didn't have to. Cass put yet another mug of tea on the table and squeezed Jake's arm. "You can sleep with Tom if you want, Jake. I'm not going to get back every night, and I know you don't like sleeping alone."

"How do you know that?"

"Because I don't like it either, and Tom would love it if you slept in our bed."

A strange disappointment crept over Jake. Hadn't Cass promised he'd come home to Tom every night? To both of them? "What about you?"

Cass thought on it a moment. "Tom likes his space when he sleeps. I like a proper snake pit, and you've got epic legs."

"You've got epic legs."

What the fuck did that even mean? Jake had no idea, and he understood the way Cass's throwaway comment made him feel even less. Cass had meandered, unconcerned, out of the kitchen after turning Jake's head upside down, but Jake had found himself unable to sit still, and with his tics having a party, he'd retreated to his room.

He thought he heard Cass start up the stairs a few times, but it was 5 p.m. before Cass knocked on Jake's bedroom door. "You don't have to hide up here, you know. And how the hell are you comfortable, lying like that?"

Jake glanced up from his screen. He was on his stomach, his chin on a pillow he'd wedged under his arms while he typed away. "I always lie like this, and I'm not hiding. I'm working."

"Yeah, well, you look like a drunk cat, and it's late. Even Tom's calling it a day. The butcher's is open till eight o'clock tonight. I'm going to run out and get something for dinner. Coming?"

After their awkward afternoon together, Jake wanted to say no, but something in Cass's expression told him he was probably fighting a losing battle. Besides, he was using Cass's laptop. What was to stop Cass from taking it back? "What are you going to get?"

Cass waited for Jake to shut the laptop and pull a sweatshirt from the open bag he had under the bed. "Something nice for Tom. He's been stuck in meetings all day. You know, there's some drawers in the garage we could bring up here for your stuff. You don't have to live out of your bag."

"It's fine." Jake buzzed and popped a few times, before he pushed past Cass and jogged downstairs.

Cass followed him, unfazed. "It's bloody ridiculous," he said. "We have drawers. You might as well use them."

"*Wankers*. It's fine."

"Suit yourself." Cass went to the cupboard under the stairs and retrieved Jake's coat along with his own, but avoided looking at Jake.

Jake chewed on his lip. Cass had been nothing but nice to him. Did he really deserve to have it thrown back in his face? Besides, they had much in common, and one thing most of all.

"Cass?"

"Hmm?"

"What's Tom's favourite meal?"

Cass tossed a smile over his shoulder.

Jake frowned. "What?"

Cass shook his head. "I know it's mad, but I love that you want to know that, that you give a shit. That whatever this is means so much to you."

Jake felt heat flush his cheeks, unnerved that Cass had seen through him. He tried not to let Tom see how he felt. How had Cass read him so easily? How did Cass know that Tom's gentle kisses—their only physical interaction since Jake had come to his home—meant the world to him? "He's been good to me."

"He's good to everyone. That's why we have to look after him." Cass opened the front door. "And he's a traditional boy. His favourite meal is steak and chips."

They walked into town in silence. Jake found himself scrutinising the sign outside the Dragonfly before he thought of anything to say. "*Wankers*. Sorry. I heard you cook the best steak in London."

Cass rolled his eyes. "Tom tell you that?"

"No, I read it on Twitter."

"Twitter?"

Jake followed Cass across the street. "I set up an account for Pink's last week and searched the hashtags for all your businesses. Pippa's is huge."

"Really?" Cass grinned. "I think we had a Facebook page once, but the bloke who set it up moved on, and we never got round to getting the password off him. What else did you find?"

"Quite a bit. Your snack boxes are really popular in Canary Wharf."

"Ah, see, I knew that," Cass said. "Tom was wittering on about it a few weeks ago. I think he wants to expand the Bites delivery zone outside of the city."

"What do you want?"

Cass shrugged. "Whatever he wants. He's normally right. Here's the butcher's. You coming in?"

Jake trailed to a stop. He wasn't in the mood to face a crowded shop in the poshest place he'd ever been. "Not today."

Cass didn't look surprised. "All right. Wait here. I know the bird behind the till, so I'll only be a minute."

Jake leaned against the wall a little way from the door and lit a cigarette. He hadn't smoked much since coming to live with Tom and Cass, but he had a few left in the last pack he'd bought in London. He blew smoke into the sky and watched the middle-class Christmas shoppers go about their business. Snippets of their conversations reached his ears. They spoke like Tom, smooth and posh, but they sounded nothing like him.

Cass plucked the cigarette from Jake's fingers. "If you're going to smoke, you have to share."

Jake blinked. "Wow. That was quick."

"Told you." Cass puffed on Jake's cigarette and closed his eyes. "I know people in high places. Don't tell Tom I smoked. I'm only allowed to smoke at Pippa's."

"Allowed?" Jake had seen Tom be stern with staff and builders, but he couldn't imagine him forbidding Cass to do anything. Or Cass obeying.

"It's a compromise. I couldn't get through a weekend at work without killing anyone if I didn't sneak a couple of fags. That's hassle Tom doesn't need."

"*Wankers.*"

"Exactly. Let's swing by Waitrose and head home."

Jake watched Cass unpack the remaining shopping. He'd already tackled the mammoth bag of potatoes and the green beans with the biggest knife Jake had ever seen. "What did you get in the butcher's?"

"There wasn't much left, but I scrounged up a few rib eyes. Want to see?"

Jake shrugged. His coding project was calling him, but he was hungry too, and watching Cass make his own brand of oven-baked chips had turned out to be a fascinating distraction. There was a poetry to Cass in the kitchen.

Cass laid three steaks out on the red board he'd placed over the wooden block he'd cut the vegetables on. "See this eye of fat in the middle?"

Jake wrinkled his nose. He liked eating meat well enough, but the raw product had always freaked him out. "Is that where the name comes from?"

"Yep." Cass checked the time and took a pan down from the hooks above the stove. "Tom won't be long. If we cook these now, they can rest while we do the beans and find some booze."

"We?"

Cass smirked. "Sure. Why not? Come here."

Jake hesitated a moment, then slid off the kitchen stool he'd made himself at home on and rounded the island.

Cass passed him the pan and pointed at the gas burners. "How do you like to eat your steak?"

Jake whistled and slapped his arm a few times before he answered. He couldn't remember the last time he'd eaten any red meat that wasn't a burger. "Dunno."

"Good answer." Cass lit the front burner. "Means I get to boss you around. Contrary to popular belief, the fat in a rib eye means it's better cooked medium, rather than rare-as-you-dare. All right with that?"

Jake nodded. "What do you want me to do?"

"Now there's a question. Um, grab that oil and the salt and rub some on the steaks."

Okay. Jake followed Cass's direction and rubbed olive oil and salt into the slimy surface of the meat. Then he brought the red board to the stove. "Do you want oil in the pan?"

"Nah. It'll smoke like hell." Cass narrowed his eyes and gauged the thickness of the steaks with his finger and thumb. "Cook them four minutes a side, then we'll wrap them in foil and leave them a bit."

Jake took the tongs Cass held out. "You want me to put them in?"

Cass held his hand over the pan. "Yeah, I'd say so."

Under Cass's guidance, Jake placed the steaks in the pan and seasoned them with pepper while they cooked. Then he wrapped them in a foil parcel and set them aside. "Is that how you cook them at Pippa's?"

"Not quite." Cass lit the burner beneath the green beans. "The pans don't get as hot at home. The meat will cook a bit more in the foil."

Jake took it all in. Despite his aversion to the raw meat, dinner was starting to look like the best meal he'd had in years. Cass threw some spices over the chips in the oven, then showed Jake how to make boring green beans taste amazing with olive oil and lemon.

When they were done, they sat at the counter with some strange Japanese beer—samples from a supplier—Cass brought up from the cellar. They made small talk for a while, but it turned out that Cass was even worse at it than Jake. Cass, it seemed, liked to speak his mind.

"Do you ever forget about your TS?"

Jake swallowed some of the pale, super-fizzy lager. "Sometimes. If I'm distracted or absorbed in something, I don't notice the tics."

"Ah." Cass nodded slowly, as though he was having a silent conversation with himself. "Maybe I'm picking up on that. You were ticking loads this morning. I haven't noticed it at all since we started cooking."

"Fly him to the moon. Fuck. It's all over."

Cass stared at Jake a moment, then he burst out laughing. Jake laughed too, and let his favourite tics get the better of him until both he and Cass were crying and gasping for breath.

Cass grabbed Jake's arm. "Sorry, mate. I'm not laughing at you, I swear."

Jake shook his head and attempted to calm the fuck down. "It's okay. I like laughing at it. Makes me feel normal. Shh."

Cass fought with himself, but his laughter seemed as irrepressible as Jake's tics. Only the sound of a key in the front door sobered them both. Jake turned his head, his gaze fixed on the kitchen doorway. Tom's footsteps echoed on the bare wood of the hallway until he appeared, smiling, and took in the scene of Jake and Cass hunched over the kitchen counter, their faces bright with laughter.

Tom's smile was a mile wide. "Something smells good."

"Jake made us dinner," Cass said.

"Did I bollocks," Jake protested. "Cass taught me to cook steak."

"Bossed you around, more like." Tom's smile deepened and a flash of something suspiciously like relief coloured his features. He ventured further into the room and embraced Cass, kissing him soundly.

Jake averted his eyes, wondering if he should leave them to it. He'd never seen them kiss before, and the reaction deep in his gut was a little disturbing. He'd expected to hate it, to be jealous, but those emotions were strangely absent. He liked it. He wanted to look back, stare at them, and absorb it all. He wanted to wind his arms around Tom from behind and press his face between his shoulder blades. Feel the effect Cass's kiss had on the steady beat of his heart, and pretend Cass's love was for both of them.

"*Wankers*. Shit. Sorry." Jake slapped his hand over his mouth, and the feeling was gone as abruptly as it had arrived.

Tom pulled away from Cass with a rueful grin. "Don't ever be sorry. Come here."

He drew Jake into a warm, tight hug, before he rested their foreheads together. "It's good to be home. Let's eat."

CHAPTER THIRTEEN

few weeks later, Jake battled through the Christmas Eve crowds at Covent Garden Tube station. It was the first time he'd been back to London since Cass had rescued him from his landlord, and though he'd missed the vibrant city, he hadn't missed the sensation of a stranger's elbow in his ribs, or the smell of a packed underground train.

He fought his way out of the station as he let the tics he'd suppressed on the train escape. It felt strange to be in London without Tom. Daft, really, considering he'd spent the past four years on his own.

Jake followed the flow of tourists and Christmas shoppers to East Colonnade Market. His favourite magician's stall caught his attention, but he ignored his natural instinct to stand and stare and pressed on to a secluded corner of the market he'd never noticed before.

He smelled Pink's long before he saw it, and even when he spotted the small cluster of tables, it took him a moment to find the teeny tiny open kitchen, doling out paella to the bustling crowds. Tom had described it as "a real hole in the wall," and he wasn't wrong. There was no branding, no logo, nothing to link the chef and single waitress to Pink's or Urban Soul. Only a small wooden sign, lost in the chaos of the market, identified the restaurant at all.

Hmm. Jake leaned on a railing. He'd been over Pink's accounts and knew it was profitable, but the way Tom told it, there was an air of unfulfilled potential, a missed opportunity that made Tom twitchy. Jake took out his phone and pulled up the Twitter account he'd set up for Pink's. He'd spent his time on the train following the surrounding businesses, food blogs, and London media outlets. Most of them had followed him back. Some had tweeted, recognising the name, and querying the bespoke hashtag Jake had devised a few nights ago, over some beers with Cass.

Cass. Yeah, he was more food for thought. Things had mellowed since steak night, and they'd resumed their habit of daily texts. But each night now, after a lingering kiss from Tom before bed, Jake found himself waiting downstairs for Cass. They'd meet in the living room, have a drink, and talk long into the night about music and movies until Cass fell asleep on the couch. Then Jake would creep away to the big bed he had all to himself, and hope that Cass eventually found his way upstairs to spend some time with Tom.

Time that was precious to them.

Time they seemed all too willing to share with Jake.

It felt like a weird limbo, and Jake wondered if this was really how Tom and Cass had lived before he'd come along.

He checked himself for unresolved tics, and then descended the stairs to the dark corner where Nero, the chef, was working. The Spaniard glanced up as Jake approached, alerted to his presence by Jake's buzzing whistle, but to his credit, his expression didn't change at all. When Jake held out his hand, he even smiled.

Huh. Cass said he was grumpy. "Hey, I'm Jake. I've come to take some pictures of you for the new website."

Nero snorted. "Not me, mate, the food. My ugly mug won't do you any favours."

Jake grinned. With his copper skin and soulful eyes, Nero was far from ugly. Jake peered into the *huge* pan he was working with. "This is paella, right? Are you doing anything else today?"

"Hake and chorizo. Here, stir this. I'll go and get some for you to try."

Nero thrust what looked like a canoe paddle at Jake and disappeared into the back area of the tiny kitchen. Nonplussed, Jake stirred the plump saffron-scented rice until Nero returned with a plate of food—which smelled amazing—and a bucket of shellfish.

"Keep stirring, mate. I need to chuck these in."

The shellfish clattered into the pan. Jake recognised prawns and mussels, but a strange elongated shell caught his eye. "What are those?"

"Razor clams. Shame we've only got the ten tables, because they were cheap as chips. I bought loads. Couldn't help myself." Nero dolloped some paella from a second pan into a bowl and held it out with the plate of hake.

Jake smiled his thanks. "You don't have to feed me."

Nero shrugged. "How can you sell something you haven't tried?"

Nero had him there, and both dishes were *amazing*, like all the food he'd tried at Urban Soul's various outlets. Tom and Cass were definitely fulfilling their vision of a unique experience for every guest they served.

Jake snapped a few pictures with his smartphone, honouring Nero's wishes and sticking to the food. He did get a few inadvertent close-ups of Nero's hands, though, and it took him a few glances to realise that Nero only had three fingers on his left hand.

That gave Jake pause. He knew from the state of Cass's hands and forearms that chefs were, by nature, covered with scars and burns, but to lose a whole finger? Jake shuddered. Though, with his missing finger, Nero looked like a rogue, the best kind of rogue. Like a gangster, or . . .

Like a pirate.

Jake sniggered, and it bubbled into a tic he could tell took all Nero's discretion to ignore. With that in mind, he quit while he was ahead and bade Nero good-bye.

He jostled his way through the market crowds again and back out into the open air. The street performers tempted him, but it was getting late, and he had a few things left to do before he caught the train back to Berkhamsted.

It had been a few years since he'd last celebrated Christmas, but though Tom and Cass only took a few days off and it was a holiday steeped in their own brand of tradition, they'd made it clear it was tradition they wanted to share with him. Jake had the impression their routine hadn't changed much over the past few years: Work for Cass, then a late meal and a boozy night out. Neither of them had mentioned presents, but Jake had already bought Cass a remastered Morrissey album. He'd seen it in Camden and hadn't been able to resist. Cass loved the Smiths, and Jake enjoyed watching him drift around the big house in Berkhamsted, singing to himself with a faraway look in his eyes.

Yeah, in that respect, Cass was easy. Getting a gift for Tom was proving more difficult. Jake spent more time with him, worked with him, kissed him—they'd fucked, for God's sake—but Tom's interests outside work and Cass remained something of a mystery.

Jake meandered through the festive lights of Covent Garden. He bypassed the designer shops and stuck to the boho independent stores. He'd just about given up when his gaze fell on a simple glass photo frame in the window of an artisan home wear shop. It called to him, though he couldn't say why.

Perhaps it was the price. At twenty-five quid, it was the cheapest thing he'd considered so far.

Cheap, *but* . . .

Jake slipped into the shop and picked up the frame. Tom worked all over London, but when he wasn't traipsing around the city, he spent most of his time in his office above the Stew Shack, a tiny space that held nothing but computers, phones, and filing cabinets. Jake figured a photo of Cass would brighten the place up, and anyway, he was bang out of time and ideas.

He bought the frame and headed for home, stopping at a post office on the way to buy sweets and send a belated card to Leeds. Jake felt pretty ambiguous as he let the festive red envelope drop into the postbox, but both Tom and Cass seemed to think the small contact with his family was important.

"Don't burn bridges that don't need to be burned," Cass had said. "You can't fix what ain't there anymore."

Whatever the hell that meant.

Jake braved Euston and caught the fast train home. He settled in his seat and stuffed a few boiled sweets in his mouth. Keeping his tongue occupied sometimes kept him quiet.

He retrieved his phone and set about editing the photos he'd taken at Pink's. He drafted a few prototype tweets and saved them. Tom didn't know much about Twitter, but he'd scheduled a trial promotion period in the New Year. Somehow, Jake had ended up in charge of it.

His phone buzzed as he was finishing. A voice mail from Cass that must have come through when the train had passed Bushey and Watford.

"Hey, Jake. Fucking crazy day, man. Got loads of prep still to do for tomorrow. I'm not gonna be home tonight. By the time I get there, it'll be time to turn my arse around and come right back. Can you call Tom for me? He must be on the underground and his voice mail's full. Gotta go. See you soon, mate."

Jake frowned. Cass had made it home every night since he'd moved in, though he sometimes didn't crawl in until the early hours and was often long gone by the time Jake woke. Something felt off. He called Tom. It took a few tries to get through, but eventually the call connected. "Cass rang. He's not coming home tonight. Said he's behind on setup for tomorrow."

Silence, then the sound of a door closing. "That's convenient."

"Um, is it? *Wankers*. Fuck." Jake glanced around, but no one was looking his way.

Tom sighed. "Never mind. We were supposed to go somewhere tonight. Guess I'll have to go alone."

"I could go with you."

"No, it's all right; this isn't a work thing. I'll see you soon, okay?"

Tom hung up without further comment. Jake put his phone away, perplexed, but there wasn't much he could do, stuck on a train by himself, and by the time Tom joined him at the house a few hours later, the frustration he'd heard in Tom's voice was gone.

"All right, mate?" Tom dropped a takeaway pizza on the kitchen table and kissed the top of Jake's head. "Did you have a good day?"

Jake nodded and turned his computer screen in Tom's direction. "Want to see?"

"Nope. Show me after Christmas. The office is officially closed. No more work."

Jake opened his mouth to protest, but Tom silenced him with a kiss, the kind of kiss that went on and on, even after Tom had pulled away. "What are we going to do instead?"

"Nothing." Tom unbuttoned his shirt. "I'm gonna put some trackies on, eat pizza, and watch Morecambe and Wise. You in?"

"Sure."

"Good." Tom held out his hand, hauled Jake to his feet, and spun them around. "Have you seen the cat? I need to feed her before she takes a crap in my shoe again."

Jake laughed. Tom seemed a little drunk. Maybe he was. "I fed her already. She's on my bed."

Tom grunted in reply. "Grab some beer, will you? Or wine. Whatever you can find."

Jake closed his laptop down properly, searched out a few bottles of beer, and found Tom in the living room, stretched out on the sofa, feet up, arms open.

"Come sit," Tom said. "Tell me about your day."

Jake settled between Tom's legs, his back to his broad chest. "Thought you didn't want to talk about work?"

Tom brushed Jake's hair back. Jake could feel his warm breath on his neck. "I don't. I want to talk about you. Tell me something you did that wasn't about work."

Jake thought on it a moment. Almost everything he did these days traced back to Tom and Urban Soul. "I met a lush Spanish guy."

"You met Nero, eh? What did you think?"

"Um." Jake shrugged, unwilling to admit just how attractive he'd found Nero, but the flush in his cheeks gave him away.

Tom laughed. "It's okay, we know he's bloody gorgeous, but he's not gay. At least, he says he's not, and I believe him. Cass isn't convinced, but I think that's wishful thinking. They're good mates, actually. Nero covers Cass at Pippa's when he takes time off."

"Once a year, then, yeah?" As far as Jake could tell, Cass rarely took more than a single day off at a time. "What happened to his hand?"

It was Tom's turn to shrug. "No idea. I've never asked."

"Why not?"

"Because it's not my business. He's worked for us for three years and never mentioned it. I reckon he would've by now if he wanted to talk about it."

Jake's phone beeped, cutting off whatever asinine question he'd been about to ask next. Another message from Cass.

Cuddle up with Tom for me. Miss you both.

That was a new one, but Jake didn't need much persuading to cuddle up to Tom. They shared a pizza and a few beers, and slobbed out in front of the TV until both of them began to doze. Tom's phone roused Jake sometime after midnight. Cass's face flashed up on the screen. Jake tried not to look at the text beneath, but his curiosity got the better of him.

Don't be alone tonight.

Jake stared between the phone and Tom's sleeping form. Four simple words, but they meant everything.

Jake rolled over, chasing the warmth that felt just out of reach. He found it, at least he thought he did, but then it was gone again. He cracked an eye open. The unfamiliar room came into focus.

Tom's room.

Cass's room.

Damn. He was in their bed.

Jake shifted onto his side. He could sense Tom beside him now, hear him breathing, slow and deep. If he closed his eyes, he could recall the dazed grin on Tom's face when he'd woken him up and told him they were going to bed . . . together. Jake wanted to reach out and mould himself to Tom's broad back, but a voice in his head stayed him.

Tom likes his space when he sleeps.

Jake closed his eyes and pushed his face into a pillow that smelled of Cass.

It was morning when he woke again. This time, he found himself wrapped around Tom like a limpet. So much for his good intentions.

He raised his head from Tom's chest and felt his nervous system come alive. His arm jerked. He whistled and buzzed. Then his whole body shuddered like a bloody car crash.

Tom, fresh faced and wide-awake, just smiled. "Morning."

Jake peeled himself off Tom and sat up. "Morning. Sorry. I didn't mean to smother you, or beat you up. Sorry."

"Stop saying sorry. You're only lying on me because I told you to."

"How do you work that out?"

Tom coaxed Jake back into his arms. "You were hanging off the other side of the bed. I was worried you were going to fall right out."

"Cass told me you like your space. I know we've slept together before, but this felt different."

Different was an understatement. Last night there had been no crazy sex, and Tom had fallen asleep first. And he'd stayed. Jake had never woken up with him before.

Tom wove his fingers into Jake's hair and rubbed the nape of his neck with his thumb. "Yeah, I'm weird. I like a cuddle when I'm conscious, but I turn into a lone ranger as soon as I fall asleep. Unless I'm drunk, then I'm all over Cass like a rash."

Jake hummed. He felt calmer now, lazy and mellow, though his tics continued. They were almost constant first thing in the morning. "Poor Cass."

"I know." Tom sounded contrite. "I think it's because I shared a room with my brother when I was little. He used to draw on my face. I didn't care for that."

Jake laughed. He could imagine it all too well. Tom liked order, both in himself and his everyday life. "How old is your brother?"

"Rich is thirty-five. You'll meet him tomorrow."

Tomorrow. *Oh yeah. It's Christmas.* Jake had forgotten he'd stupidly agreed to visit Tom's family on Boxing Day. Oh well. Maybe they could lie here forever and tomorrow would never come.

Later that day, after a long morning in bed, Jake took a shower and met Tom in the kitchen. "You cooked?"

Tom tossed a scowl over his shoulder. "No, I fried some stuff. Bacon, sausages, and eggs. Cass will feed us some real food later."

Jake's stomach growled. Certain aspects of his convoluted new life were a clusterfuck, but there was no denying the lure of Cass's cooking. The bloke was a bloody magician.

Jake sat at the table and made short work of the heaped plate of food Tom dumped in front of him. When he was done, he slouched in his chair and nursed a cup of tea. "It doesn't feel like Christmas, least not one I've ever known."

Tom pushed his plate away. "That good or bad?"

"Both." Jake remembered Christmas being the best day ever when he was little, but life had moved on since then. He'd seen the lights in the city, and the tree Tom had dug out of the loft, but it didn't resonate. It felt like there was something missing, an ingredient gone astray.

Tom said nothing. It took Jake a while to notice he was watching him, like he was weighing him up.

"What?"

Tom drummed his fingers on the table. "How pissed off would you be if we gave you a Christmas present?"

"Pissed off? I'm not that bad, am I?"

Tom's face said it all. "Cass reckons you think we're grooming you as some kind of live-in rentboy."

Jake jerked. His fork flew across the kitchen. "*Wankers*. Sorry. A rentboy? Why would I think that?"

"You don't think that?"

"No." And he didn't. "I know you're good people."

Tom grinned. "I think that's the nicest thing you've ever said to me."

"Piss off."

Tom rolled his eyes and ambled away to get what Jake assumed was his present. He returned with a wide, flat cardboard box. "I didn't wrap it."

"That's okay." Jake took the box. It felt solid, but not heavy. "Will it break if I drop it?"

"Probably." Tom seemed nervous, or as close to nervous as Jake had ever seen him. "Do you want to open it on the sofa?"

Jake pictured the box sharing the fate of his breakfast fork and the numerous mugs and cups he'd broken since he'd moved in. "Good idea."

They decamped to the living room. Jake sat cross-legged on the couch and peeled away the tape around the box. Opened his mouth. Shut it again. "You bought me a MacBook?"

"Looks like it."

"Why?"

"Because you need a computer of your own. Cass's laptop is old, and probably full of porn and pirated music."

Jake didn't know what to say. The sleek laptop was the computer of his dreams, and he *knew* how much they cost.

Perhaps reading his mind, Tom nudged him. "Before you freak out about money, you should know we get a massive discount through the business. This cost nowhere near as much as you probably think it did."

Jake shook his head. "Mate, I spent twenty-five quid on your present."

"You got me a present?" Tom's grin turned boyish.

Jake glanced up from his box of treasure. "Do you want it now?"

Tom hesitated. "What about . . ."

He let the sentence hang, but for once Jake knew the answer. "I got Cass something too. Do you want to wait until later? Open them together?"

There wasn't enough money in the world to buy the smile Tom bestowed on him then. He took the laptop and set it aside and dove on Jake, toppling him flat on his back and kissing him like he'd been waiting to kiss him his whole life.

Jake laughed and made a halfhearted attempt to fend him off. "What are you so excited about?"

Tom pulled back, his grin still rakish and bright. "I'm not sure. I just love watching you two grow. I know it's been hard . . . weird, sometimes, but I feel like us all being here, together, gets easier every day."

Jake kissed Tom, losing himself for a moment as he gathered his thoughts. "I can't imagine not having Cass in my life now."

Tom smiled. He didn't ask, *What about me?* He never did. Instead he covered Jake with his body and worshipped him with his lips until the city called them to Cass's side.

CHAPTER FOURTEEN

The dark basement club in Farringdon didn't seem like Tom's scene. At least the Tom Jake had pieced together in his mind. That Tom wore smart business clothes, drank sensibly, and conducted meetings like a fucking mafia boss. He didn't binge drink and wear Ramones T-shirts. He didn't press Cass up against walls and kiss the ever-loving shit out of him. Though Jake was willing to bet both incarnations of Tom fucked like a—

Stop it.

Jake turned his back on his two companions and ordered drinks, but it wasn't long before he found himself facing the other way again, searching out Tom and Cass. He'd left them close to the dance floor, completely wrapped up in each other, and retreated to the bar, but once he'd put some distance between them, he'd found himself transfixed. He'd seen them kiss before—a hello, a good-bye, or in passing—but he'd never seen them so . . . together. He'd questioned himself sometimes, late at night, if he'd be jealous when they finally let their guard down, let him see who they were, and what they meant to each other. Jealous of the way Tom held Cass. The way Cass leaned on him. The way they breathed each other in as though there'd never been anyone else.

But he wasn't. Beneath the haze of three-too-many drinks, he was fascinated, and he couldn't look away.

At least until the barman tapped his shoulder and held out a hand for his money. Jake paid for the three bottles of beer and zigzagged his way back to Tom and Cass. He took his time, soaking up the atmosphere. It had been a while since he'd been somewhere like this, but he'd always liked clubs, always felt safe and free in them. With the lights and the pounding music, no one noticed the twitching weirdo in the corner, or heard his muttered tics and clicks.

The fact that he was drunk as a skunk helped. After messing about on the sofa with Tom for most of the afternoon, they'd driven Cass's car into London. Tom had brought beer for Jake to drink on the way, and he'd been pretty tipsy by the time they'd reached Pippa's. Perhaps that had been Tom's intention all along, because Jake had felt no trace of nerves as he'd entered what was undeniably Cass's lair.

Christmas dinner had been a rowdy affair, shared with any Urban Soul employees who had nowhere to go. Nero had come, and a few other faces Jake recognised. No one seemed to notice Tom's arm around the back of Jake's chair, or the fact that Cass never left his side.

Cass, Cass, Cass.

Sometimes Jake studied Cass and caught that wildness Tom talked about, the barest hint of a troubled young man he'd never known. Then he'd remember the other side of Cass, the Cass who'd helped Jake pack up his few precious belongings, put an arm around him, and brought him home to share a bed with his own lover. Tonight Cass seemed to be a wonderful mix of the two, and Jake wondered who the man who was fast becoming his best friend really was. A best friend who just happened to be drop-dead gorgeous.

Drop-dead gorgeous . . .

Interesting. Jake had never completed that thought before, and he couldn't make sense of it right now. Right *now* he was battered in an underground, hipster gay club with two men he kind of idolised, and he liked it. He liked it a lot.

Jake approached Tom and Cass from behind. Tom had his arms around Cass, whispering in his ear, and it was Cass who spotted Jake first. He met Jake's gaze, held it a moment, then disentangled himself from Tom. He came to Jake and took the drinks from him. "Do you dance?"

"When I'm drunk enough."

Cass laughed. "Are you? Drunk enough? Because I am, and Tom wouldn't dance even if he was tripping on acid."

Jake eyed Tom over Cass's shoulder. He was talking to the front-of-house manager from Pippa's, but Jake knew he was watching them, and the sensation left him warm all over. Jake loved dancing, especially pissed in a club—a gay club—with his inhibitions a distant memory. Did he want to do that with Cass? Did he want to get up in Cass's personal space? Touch him? Feel him?

Jake put his hand on Cass's chest. Felt a spark jump between them which he'd never noticed before. Perhaps it was the booze, or the reckless air of the club, but yeah.

Yeah, he did.

Cass led him to the dance floor and into the throng of sweaty bodies. He put his hands on Jake's hips and drew him close. Jake sucked in a harsh breath. They moved together, and for the first time since he'd found himself under Tom's thrall, his connection to Cass, built on friendship, felt right. Real.

They danced chest to chest, cheek to cheek. Jake felt Cass's hands all over him, and his rough scruff scratch his face. It was so different from Tom's clean-shaven skin, but he loved it all the same. Felt his body respond. Heat. Blood. Sweat. In an effort to control himself, Jake pulled his body back from Cass and put his lips close to his ear. "How did you get all your staff to come and party in a gay club?"

Jake felt rather than heard Cass's laugh.

"Cheap drinks," Cass shouted. "And it's open till 4 a.m. This lot are animals when they get going."

Jake could believe that, if Tom's alcohol consumption that night was anything to go by. He said as much.

Cass laughed again. "Don't bank on seeing it often. It's a once a year kind of thing."

The music changed to something deeper. Jake let his body slow down. He felt Cass do the same and draw back, and he wondered if Cass would return to Tom.

Not for long. Cass fingered the hem of Jake's T-shirt. "Take this off?"

Jake glanced around the teeming mass of bodies. Most of the men on the dance floor had shed their shirts, and he didn't mind people seeing him. He pried his shirt from Cass and yanked it over his head. "Your turn."

Cass licked his lips, then his shirt was gone, flung over his shoulder with no care to where it landed.

Jake swallowed. Tom was a broad man, well built and strong, but Cass . . . wow. Who knew his collection of grungy hoodies and faded band T-shirts hid a body so beautiful? Covered in ink and piercings that stood out against his pale skin, Cass was stunning. Jake touched the bar in Cass's left nipple, watched it prism under the club's lights. He traced a line of ink across Cass's chest, and followed it down the light dusting of dark hair on his abdomen.

He frowned. He'd seen Cass's tattoo before on the photographs he'd tried so hard not to open on Cass's computer, though he'd managed to resist the albums that seemed to bare more skin. No. That wasn't it. Jake had seen Cass's tattoo somewhere else, but where?

An image of a simple wooden sign flashed into his mind, along with the gentle smirk behind Tom's words to him then. *"That fact that you think you have confuses the hell out of me, but I like it . . . Let me know when you see something that jogs your memory."*

"Fuck. That's the sign from the Dragonfly."

Cass caught Jake's fingers. "I thought you knew that?"

Jake shook his head, letting his fingers twine with Cass's. "I saw the sign, and I recognised it, but Tom wouldn't tell me why."

Shit. Jake realised his mistake too late. TS and a booze-loosened tongue didn't mix.

Cass stilled, then he drew Jake closer so he didn't have to shout over the music. "Why did you recognise my ink?"

"Um . . ." Jake tried not to be distracted by Cass's skin on his.

Cass began to sway with the music again, taking Jake with him in a soothing rhythm. "You can tell me, Jake. You don't have to be scared of me."

Jake snorted a soft puff of air into Cass's chest. "I'm *not* bloody scared of you."

"So tell me. It can't be that bad. Have you been spying on me in the shower?"

"What? No!" Jake shoved Cass, though not hard enough to separate them. "I . . . um . . . looked at some of the photos on your laptop."

"That all? Damn, what did you see that has you blushing like that? Was it the Thailand ones?"

Jake shook his head. "I didn't open all the albums, but I saw you on the front of some."

"Ah, bet you only opened the ones you saw Tom in, right?"

Jake didn't deny it. When Tom had first given him Cass's laptop, he'd been too lost in a haze of obsession, desperate to know more about Tom, the man who captivated him so entirely, to look for Cass. Back then, it had been easier to think of Cass as just a number on his phone, not a tangible human being. "I'm sorry."

Cass shrugged. "Don't be. Just think yourself lucky you didn't open all the holiday ones. We went through a phase of taking dirty photos a few years ago."

"You don't do that anymore?"

"Nah, not now we've got FaceTime. Means we can swap nudey pictures whenever we want."

Nudey pictures? Jake was intrigued, but Cass slowly grinding them together intrigued him more. His brain and his body often felt disconnected, but as he responded to Cass, he felt in sync for the first time in years.

Cass said something else. Jake ignored him and slid his hands over Cass's bare chest. The piercing caught his eye again, and he wondered what it would feel like between his teeth. What it would feel like for Cass if he pulled on it. Would it hurt? Or would it be the best kind of pain? The kind of pain that sent a man into that hazy place where nothing mattered but the touch of his lover.

"Jake?"

Jake jumped. Cass wrapped his arms around him and pulled him even closer. Jake hid his tics in Cass's chest for a moment, breathing him in while Cass played with his hair and hummed a tune that had nothing to do with the deep dubstep pulsing in the club.

Jake raised his head. "Why are you humming the West Ham song? Thought you were a Charlton boy?"

"My nana used to sing me that song when I had bad dreams."

Jake recalled a time West Ham had come to Leeds to play an FA Cup tie. He never went to the game, but he remembered the crowds of hard-eyed Londoners roaming the city, singing their sweet song and terrifying the locals. It hadn't seemed much of a lullaby, but the words . . .

I'm forever blowing bubbles,
Pretty bubbles in the air,
They fly so high, nearly reach the sky,
Then like my dreams they fade and die.

Yeah, he could see it, and more than that, in the dark of the club, he saw a flash of pain in Cass's brooding gaze. Jake touched Cass's face, his jaw, his cheeks, and his eyelids. There was something deep and raw in Cass he didn't understand, and he couldn't stand to see him hurting.

They stared at each other for a long time before their lips met, then Jake felt himself being sucked into a vortex he hadn't felt even with Tom. A heady black hole where there was nothing but heat . . . heat and the scent of a man he'd never believed he'd truly want.

Cass.

Jake bit down on Cass's bottom lip and shoved his hand into Cass's hair. He deepened the kiss and lost himself until Cass pulled away with a strangled groan, his eyes wide, shocked, like Jake had turned his world upside down. For a brief, heart-stopping moment, Jake caught another glimpse of the vulnerability he'd never seen in Cass before tonight. Then a hand touched him that wasn't Cass, a hand that grounded Jake. Centred him, and tied him down to the world.

Tom.

"Let's take this home."

Home for the night turned out to be the Hampstead flat. They were all too drunk to be bothered with traipsing back to the house.

The cab ride home was interesting. Tom led the way, while Cass and Jake trailed behind, holding hands, touching, and stealing kisses when no one was looking. To an outsider, Jake supposed it appeared that he and Cass were the couple, and Tom was the burly, overprotective friend, guarding them, watching over them. Standing in front of them when someone glanced their way just a beat too long.

Jake would've found the situation bizarre if he hadn't been so wrapped up in Cass. So completely and utterly under his spell. In the space of a few hours, Cass had gone from being a man Jake had grown to love as a friend, to a man he couldn't get enough of. Even with Tom right there, watching them. Seeing it all.

They stumbled out of the cab in Hampstead, Cass still shirtless. The flat was right across the road. They were inside before Jake could blink, and then Tom pulled him from Cass and pushed him against the wall.

His kiss was slow and sweet before he drew back with a soft grin. "We haven't been here for a while."

Jake swallowed. Cass was like a drug—tempting and addictive— but Tom . . . Tom was where it had all begun. Jake buzzed. "You only bring me here to fuck me."

"Not on purpose." Tom kissed Jake again. "It just worked out that way."

Jake wasn't complaining. Tom released him from his cage against the wall. He seemed calmer now than he had when he'd seized Jake from Cass, like he'd satisfied himself of a doubt he'd never voiced.

Cass. Shit. *Cass.* Jake looked for him. Found him standing a few feet away, his coat and shoes still on and his hand on the front door, like he was planning a quick getaway.

Jake's stomach turned over.

"Cass, don't go." Jake held out his hand. He didn't know what was going to go down tonight, and drunk as he was, he knew he wasn't ready to have sex with Cass, but fuck, he didn't want him to *leave*.

Cass seemed torn, and Jake felt desperate, though for what, he wasn't quite sure.

Tom stepped between them. He turned his back on Jake and gave Cass his full attention. "Don't you dare run from us now. It's Christmas Day. We're not going to bed without you."

Us. We.

Jake couldn't hear Cass's response, but he saw Cass's coat drop to the floor well enough. Heard the stuttered gasp of a crazy-hot kiss. He thought maybe *he* should leave, catch the last train to Berkhamsted, and give Tom and Cass a night alone.

Then two hands reeled him in, and he found himself sandwiched between them, Cass in front and Tom at his back. Lips on his mouth, and lips at his neck.

Jake gasped, shocked at the double-edged pleasure. Cass's kiss was electric, and combined with Tom's attention to his throat, the spark between them all went through the stratosphere. He fell slack, leaning on Tom's solid warmth. "Why is this bit so easy?"

Cass moved to claim Jake's neck as his. Tom chuckled and nipped Jake's ear. "Because articulating it is so hard."

"Hard like you?" Jake ground himself into Tom, feeling the outline of his cock, remembering the stretch and burn of Tom pushing inside him.

"Or you." Tom unbuttoned Jake's jeans and squeezed tight enough to make Jake's eyes roll. "Not sure we should do this in the hallway, though."

Something told Jake that Tom and Cass needed him to lead the way, prove to them how much he *wanted* this. He disentangled himself from Tom, pulled his shirt over his head, and walked to the bedroom, trusting that they would follow.

Cass reached him first. They kissed and fell onto the bed together. Jake strained his senses for Tom, but for a moment, there was no one else, only Cass.

Cass broke the kiss and caught Jake's chin. "You don't have to do anything you're not cool with, okay? This, between you and me, this is enough for me tonight. I want you, but I can wait. I *will* wait. With Tom . . ."

Jake licked his lips, his breath caught in his chest. This was what he'd been waiting for all along—limits, ground rules. For Cass to take some possession of his lover.

Cass touched Jake's cheek. "With Tom, you can do what you like. Don't worry about me . . . what I'm thinking, what I'm feeling. Just be you and Tom, together, like you're meant to be."

Jake wondered if Cass had planned to be so poetic, or if the booze had made him that way. Beneath it all, he felt relief that Cass didn't want to push their boundaries any further that night. Too much too soon could break them, and they both knew it.

The bed dipped. Tom lay down beside them, shirtless. Jake turned into his arms as he felt Cass slide into place behind him. He glanced over his shoulder. "You're still going to kiss me, right?"

"Try and bloody stop me."

No more words were needed. Jake kissed Cass so hard he could hardly breathe, then he turned his attention to Tom, dancing the dance they'd rehearsed before. Clothes disappeared, Tom's first, then Jake's, then they started to strip Cass.

"I just want to watch you," Cass protested.

"You can," Tom said. "Naked, right, Jake?"

Jake hummed his agreement. Cass was as beautiful bare as he had been shirtless in the dim light of a smoky nightclub. He stared at Cass's cock. He wanted to touch it, but not yet. *Not yet.*

Cass lay on his back. Jake climbed over him and kissed him. He felt Tom behind and raised his body up. Tom rubbed Jake's thighs and his back. Blew warm air over his spine until he finally—*finally*— touched Jake where he needed it most. Lubed fingers first, and then his tongue.

Oh God, his tongue.

Jake groaned into Cass's mouth, feeling him deepen their embrace, consume him with a fiery, biting kiss until Jake saw stars. He buried himself in Cass's chest, writhing. "*Tom.*"

Tom pulled back and kissed his way up Jake's spine. Jake heard him kiss Cass, then felt the latex-covered head of his cock push against him. "This what you want, Jake?"

"Fuck yeah."

He couldn't look at Cass. Wasn't sure he wanted to. All he knew was the blunt intrusion of Tom's cock was seconds away, and it was too fucking long to wait.

Cass took away his choice. Grabbed his hair and tugged until Jake found his gaze.

Fire burned between them as Tom slid into Jake, stretching him, opening him. Jake's eyes watered. Tom had never taken him from behind before and, fuck, it stung. Just for a moment, but it hurt.

Cass held him tight and rubbed his back. Their closeness meant Jake could feel Cass's cock against his. If he moved, he could rub them together, feel another kind of friction, but he couldn't move. Couldn't do anything but pant and wait for the all-consuming pressure to fade into something incredible.

Looking back, Jake would be able to pinpoint the exact moment when the disjointed desire between the three of them fell into place.

That moment when Tom began to move inside him, and Jake stared into Cass's stormy eyes, and knew he'd found his home. But *in* that moment, Jake knew nothing . . . nothing, but the wildfire brewing deep in his belly.

Time seemed to stop as Tom drew out every push and slide of his cock, but then everything got faster. The stuttered gasp of his lungs. The slap of flesh on flesh.

Jake found Cass's hands and clutched them. *Don't let go.*

Cass squeezed back. *I've got you.*

"Touch yourself," Tom said, breathless. "I want to see you come."

Jake reached for his cock, found Cass's too. He licked his hand and gripped them both. Saw Cass's eyes widen and his cheeks flush. "You too. Always you too."

His incoherent, pleasure-driven mumble made little sense, but Cass relaxed and folded his hands behind his head. Jake watched the rapid rise of his chest and knew they were all close to falling.

He moved his hand faster to goad Cass into losing his cool, and behind him, Tom groaned.

He likes this. Through the fog of feeling, Jake realised that every thrust of Tom's hips pushed his dick into his hand . . . and into Cass's dick. That Tom was in complete control of them all. What it would feel like if Jake raised Cass's legs and pushed inside him too. If Tom really was fucking them both.

Jake cried out. He spilled over his hand and onto Cass's stomach. "Oh *God.*"

So much for goading Cass.

Cass wrapped his arms around him. "I've got you. Tom's gonna come too. Can you feel him?"

Tom groaned. Inside Jake, he pulsed and swelled, then came with the whispered gasp Jake remembered from their previous encounters. Tom was a quiet fuck.

Warmth filled Jake. Though contained by the condom, it travelled through him into his blood and bones. He smiled, loopy with the beauty of it, and sank his teeth into Cass's chest until Cass squirmed and let out a moan of pleasure.

Jake lay still, boneless and dazed. The sticky mess between him and Cass was too much to be just his own, but he wasn't sure. Pride kept him from raising his head and asking.

Tom pulled out of Jake, slow and gentle, as always. Jake heard him murmur something, but felt too detached to pay much attention. The bed shifted. A cool breeze hit him as Tom got up and padded away. He shivered.

Cass pushed his sweat-dampened hair back. "Roll over, Jake. Let me clean up our mess."

Jake rolled off Cass in a heap of soft arms and legs. "I didn't know if you came."

"You're joking, right?" Cass grabbed an errant pair of boxers and wiped them both down. "I was ready to bust before you even got started."

Cass tossed the underwear away and manoeuvred himself under the covers. He held the duvet up for Jake. "Get in." Jake hesitated. Cass growled. "You leave this fucking bed, I'm coming too."

All right, then. Jake crawled into the bed and cuddled up to Cass. Tom came back in the room. Jake figured he'd get in Cass's side, but he didn't. He slipped in behind Jake and put his long arms around them both.

"Everyone okay?"

Cass and Jake hummed in unison. Tom laughed and kissed them both. "I'm so happy you've found each other."

CHAPTER FIFTEEN

Tom's family were exactly as Jake expected them to be: warm and kind, and so bloody normal, it hurt. Jake didn't know if Tom had warned them about his TS, but luckily for all of them, his blistering hangover hadn't made his tics *that* much worse than usual, like his delinquent nervous system knew his pounding head couldn't take any drama.

It didn't stop the curious stares of Tom's nephews, but Jake could live with that. After a lifetime of disastrous family gatherings, it seemed a small price to pay.

Tom and Cass stayed nearby for the first few hours, sandwiching him between them on the sofa in much the same way they'd fallen asleep the night before. Jake enjoyed their closeness—Tom's strong thigh pressed against his, Cass's palm a pulse point of warmth on his back—and he watched the rowdy Fearnes family exchange gifts through heavy eyes as he struggled to stay in the present.

Waking up at the flat had been strange . . . in a good way. Tom, as Jake half expected, had been already up, washed, and dressed by the time Jake raised his head, but Cass had still been there, fast asleep, his arm clamped around Jake's middle, and his left hand gripping Jake's as tightly as Jake was gripping him in return.

Jake had lain as still as possible and hoped his buzzing and popping wouldn't disturb Cass, until Tom had come back in the room and smiled like the early morning sun.

And Jake never did wake Cass. Apparently nothing did when he was hungover, and Jake had forgotten that Cass had worked a twelve-hour day before he'd finally sat down to eat his Christmas dinner. It was a shame they couldn't have let him sleep in. The dawn car ride home had been brutal.

Tom touched Jake's arm. Jake jumped and realised Lily Fearnes, Tom's mother, was holding out a small package with his name on. "Um . . . thanks, you didn't have to get me a present."

Lily smiled. "It's nothing much. We couldn't leave you out."

He was glad she'd waited until most of the family were distracted with their own presents, because even though the credit card–sized external hard drive for his new laptop was a simple, unobtrusive gift, the thought of Tom discussing him with his mother made Jake blush, a lot, and the gesture of including him in their family Christmas almost made him cry.

Almost. Jake thanked her and sank into the couch, hoping no one else had been so thoughtful.

Beside him, Cass sniggered. "Think yourself lucky. The first Christmas I came here, they bought me a car."

Cass had muttered the words under his breath, but Tom's father caught them and grinned. "That old Nova you drove was a death trap. I'm sure it only had three wheels."

"That's my Del boy roots. Still don't feel right driving a car without rust."

"Life moves on, son. Sometimes you have to leave your roots behind."

Jake couldn't see Cass's face, but he felt a ripple of tension run through him, felt the lazy rub on his back still and cool, like a part of Cass had clammed up and left the building. He'd noticed that before, the way Cass and Tom would both shut down when a conversation strayed too close to the missing pieces of Cass's puzzle. Jake didn't mind. Every soul was entitled to their secrets, but he didn't like the creeping feeling that Cass was upset.

Tom's father turned away, his attention diverted by one of the kids. Jake reached behind himself and found Cass's hand. Cass squeezed back, but it wasn't long before he got up and left the room.

The day wore on. Jake fought his hangover, and an uncharacteristic urge to hide behind Tom, and eventually found himself constructing a LEGO fortress on the living room floor with Tom's brother and a few of his nephews. Rich Fearnes didn't say much, but Jake felt his gaze all over him as they worked, watching his quiet tics, glancing between him and Tom . . . and Cass, taking it in. Adding the three of them together and trying to find an answer.

Jake didn't envy him there, and he was ready when Rich finally found his tongue.

"Have you been working for Tom and Cass long?"

Jake concentrated a little too hard on adding the knights to the watchtower. He had a toddler perched on his lap, a chubby, milky bundle of flesh who'd taken a shine to him. Jake had worried at first he might tic and throw the kid right off, but his fears had proved unfounded. Little Josh was pretty soothing in his own, dribble-covered way. "About three months. Tom, um, recruited me in September to help him with the Camden project."

That was one way of putting it, though it had been October by the time Jake had actually taken a job at Urban Soul. Rich said nothing for a moment, distracted by one of the gaggle of small children on the floor with them, then he fixed Jake with a shrewd look. "Tom doesn't let people help him with restaurant launches. You must have impressed him."

"Not really. Think he just needs more hours in the day."

Rich snorted. "Tom works too much; they both do. Are we building a moat?"

Jake rummaged the scattered LEGO bricks and found some blue pieces. "We can try."

"What are you going to do when the Camden project is done? Are you going to stay with the company?"

"Um, I don't know. Maybe, if they want me to." Jake tried to not to search the room for Tom. Last time he'd checked, Tom had been playing cards with his dad, both men wearing identical expressions of playful concentration.

"Mate, I think that's a given. Tom told me you designed the company a whole social media platform. I know he's been looking for someone to do that for ages."

Jake shrugged. "I'm only doing a bit of web design. Cass could do it if he could be arsed . . . sorry, I mean if he had the time."

Rich rolled his eyes. "You don't have to be diplomatic, Jake, about any of it. I don't get to see my little brother as much as I'd like, but I know him, and I know when he's happy. Cass too. No one around here is ever going to argue with that."

It was close to lunchtime when Jake realised Cass had never come back to the living room. He put off going to find him for a while, waiting for Tom to do it, but when Tom remained caught up with his siblings, Jake slipped away.

He found Cass in the kitchen, wrestling with an enormous joint of gammon.

"Thought this was your day off?"

Cass grunted and lifted the ham out of its saucepan with two carving forks. "Trust me, you'll be glad I took over the cooking when you taste Lily's trifle. She's got a heart of gold, but she's a lousy cook."

Jake ventured closer. Tom's parents had a big, country-style kitchen, with an AGA stove and an island in the middle. Jake settled on one of the stools. "Do you cook every year?"

"Yep. Learned my lesson the first time, then Rich offered to pay me to take over. I've never taken him up on the cash, but somehow, I still end up doing it."

By Cass's faint grin, Jake knew he didn't mind. "What are you making? Can I help? Unless you want to be by yourself."

It crossed Jake's mind too late that perhaps it suited Cass to be all alone in the kitchen, away from the merriment of Tom's loud, affectionate family. He could tell Cass loved them, and it was obvious they loved him, but as ever with Cass, Jake knew he was missing something.

"Nah, you're all right," Cass said. "I've got to scrape the rind off this. Want to make the glaze for me?"

"Erm, okay." Jake slid off his stool. "How do I do that?"

"Mix together all that crap on the board. There's a bowl by the sink."

All that crap turned out to be treacle, mustard, and smoked paprika. Jake stirred it up in the bowl, took it back to Cass, and watched, fascinated, as he scored a diamond pattern in the flesh of the gammon and studded it with cloves. "That looks like the ones in Morrisons."

Cass elbowed him, hard. "Bloody Morrisons? Are you taking the piss? This ain't no battery-farmed swine, you know. This is good stuff."

"Not going to lecture me on commercial farming again, are you?"

Cass rolled his eyes. "Not if you behave, and I only lectured you because you asked."

He had a point, on both counts. Tom had shown Jake how restaurants were branded and marketed to the outside world, but Cass . . . man, Cass had taken him back to the start and taught him where the food had come from in the first place, from the Kentish wild mushrooms and herbs, to the organic eggs from their neighbour in Berkhamsted. Cass had taught him a lot, in more ways than one.

"Something on your mind, mate?"

Jake blinked. Cass was staring at him, holding out his hand for the bowl of glaze. "Not really."

"Not really? Sounds like a little of something, then. Wanna share?"

"Like we did last night?"

It was Cass's turn to blink, though Jake was just as surprised. He'd had their alcohol-fuelled threesome on his mind since he'd awoken that morning, but had figured he'd find a better way to bring it up.

Cass fiddled with a pan on the hob. "Regrets?"

"What? No! I mean, no, fuck it. I *mean* no. It was great; I meant you."

Cass's lips twitched, like he was fighting a smile, but his gaze remained shrewd. "Me? In what way?"

Jake reclaimed his stool. "Have you ever watched Tom with another bloke before?"

"You want to talk about that *here*?"

Jake shrugged. He didn't *want* to talk about it at all, but he *needed* to, damn it.

Cass sighed. "I wish you wouldn't worry about shit like that. I wouldn't let it happen if I had a problem with it. I liked it, more than liked it."

"Did you feel left out?"

"No."

But did you want to fuck me too?

Jake didn't have the balls to ask it out loud, because he wasn't sure what answer he wanted to hear. He was coming to terms with his attraction to Cass, helped by the memory of their sizzling-if-drunken encounter, but did Cass feel the same?

Jake had no idea.

"And in answer to your other question, I've watched Tom with other blokes before, but never all the way. Just kissing and stuff. When we've had three-ways in the past, it's always been him watching me. He likes watching me top."

That was food for thought.

"Do you like it? Topping, I mean, because I know Tom doesn't bottom. Is that why you see other people?" Jake had asked Tom the same question once, but he figured he'd get a less polite response from Cass; the kind of response that couldn't be misinterpreted.

He wasn't disappointed.

"No," Cass said. "We fuck other people because it suits us to do it, but if you're freaking out about that, you should know neither of us has looked at another bloke since you came along. You've put a spell on Tom, and I'm not far behind."

Yep. That was Cass, all right, and his words did strange things to Jake. He'd closed his mind to the possibility of Tom hooking up with other men, couldn't see where he'd find the time, but knowing Cass hadn't either gave Jake pause. Until he'd felt Cass's lips on his in the club the night before, he hadn't known he cared.

Cass nudged him. "Don't do your nut, but I reckon you're everything me and Tom didn't know we were looking for."

Jake absorbed the compliment as Cass stepped away from him. The thought of Tom and Cass calling time on their open relationship, closing it down for him . . . around him, like a warm, safe fortress, made him feel a little light-headed. In a good way. Perhaps. Maybe. "If it was just you and me in bed, what would you do?"

"You mean, top or bottom?" Cass drained a pan of cauliflower, dumped it in a dish, and poured another pan of cheese sauce over it. "I'd do whatever you were comfortable with, but if you're asking what I'd *want* to do, then I guess I'd want to top you. Get a piece of the look you put on Tom's face last night. Pass me those bread crumbs, would you?"

Jake passed the bread crumbs. He absently watched Cass finish off the dish of cauliflower cheese, while he struggled to articulate his answer. "What about after, though. I mean, after the first time . . ."

Cass caught on without missing a beat. "Mate, I'd bottom for you in a heartbeat, if that's what you're asking, and no, before you ask, Tom wouldn't mind. He'd love it. He's totally in love with you. You know that, right?"

Jake ticked. A bowl of cherry tomatoes skidded across the counter, but he caught the bowl before it crashed to the floor. The tomatoes weren't so lucky. He got up to retrieve them. "Tom's not in love with me."

He kept his back to Cass, but he saw his knowing smirk all the same, even though it was gone by the time he made it back to the counter.

"Suit yourself," Cass said. "I reckon that photo frame you gave him will be filled with your smiley mug soon enough."

Jake covered his snort of laughter with a cough. Giving Tom and Cass their presents had turned out to be a lot of fun, though he wasn't keen on seeing his own face slapped in the picture frame.

Cass mistook his unintelligible answer for sulking and sighed. "Look, I know this is complicated, Jake, but it's here to stay, for as long as you want it, especially if you want to fuck me. Just not on these counters, yeah? Bloody granite is freezing on my arse."

The dirty joke eased some of the tension the subject had brought with it. There was a noise from the hallway, and Jake figured it was time to kill their X-rated conversation. He thought of the new hard drive burning a hole in his back pocket. "Tom's folks are really nice."

Cass turned away to open the oven. "Yeah, they're good people, and they're experts at ignoring things they don't know how to deal with. Comes in handy when you don't fit what they had in mind for their son."

"What do you mean?"

Cass came back to the counter, his gaze on the ham. "I spent some time inside before I met Tom. I know they know, but they've never mentioned it."

"Inside? Like, prison?"

"A young offenders institution, actually, but I suppose it's the same thing. I did a year in Feltham when I was seventeen."

Jake had heard of the notorious prison in West London. He'd watched a documentary once that named it the most dangerous jail in Britain. "What did you go down for?"

"Nicking cars, mostly. Selling a bit of weed. Nothing I'm particularly proud of." Cass stuck a pastry brush in the glaze Jake had made and started painting the ham with it.

"What was it like?"

"Prison? Boring, most of the time, and fucking terrifying when it wasn't. Did its job, though. It took me a while to get my head straight after, but I got there in the end. I might not have bothered if I hadn't known what it was like."

The revelation should've shocked Jake, but it didn't. He'd known from the moment he'd seen Cass's brooding eyes that he'd lived a darker life than Tom. A life Jake could only imagine. "What about your parents?"

"My what?"

Cass turned away, but even without seeing his face, Jake knew he'd made a terrible mistake.

"Um, your parents. You've never mentioned them."

"Don't have any," Cass said. "Never knew my dad and my ma's been gone a long time."

"Gone?"

"Yeah. Gone."

Cass turned back, his expression benign, but the chill in the air remained until a ripple of tics buzzed through Jake and left him half-convinced he'd imagined it.

Jake eyed the family photographs scattered around the kitchen. "Tom's the youngest, isn't he?"

"Hmm? Oh yeah. By five years. Think he was an accident, but he's definitely Lily's favourite. She's so proud of him. Arsehole can do no wrong in her eyes. Good job he's the nicest guy in the world."

Jake already knew Tom was the nicest guy in the world, and his gut told him Cass fitted that title too. He studied Cass, tried to picture him a decade younger, caged in the dark, creepy cells he'd seen on TV. "Will you tell me about it?"

"Tell you about what?"

"Prison."

Cass thought on it a moment, then shrugged. "One day."

CHAPTER SIXTEEN

A few weeks after a strangely muted New Year, Tom arrived home from the city with a boot full of sweet treats and cakes. Jake met him at the door and relieved him of some of his load. "You brought home twenty different puddings?"

"Yep." Tom traipsed through the house with Jake in his wake and spread the cartons and boxes out on the kitchen counter. "And there's more. I've got some of Cass's ice creams in the freezer. Hope you're hungry, because we're having a sugar fest for dinner."

"Um, okay." Jake hopped up on the kitchen counter, unable to hide his grin. After a crazy December, Tom had forced him to take some downtime. He'd spent his first day off alone kicking around the house by himself, completing some of the unfinished DIY, but as the day had drawn to a close, he'd begun to feel lonely, too used to spending most of his days with Tom, or at the very least, engrossed in something that involved him. "Any occasion? Or are you trying to tell me you're pregnant?"

"Very funny. If anyone's pregnant, it's you."

Jake let him have that one. Since Christmas they'd fucked a lot, sometimes with Cass present, sometimes without. Truth be told, Jake preferred it when Cass was there, kissing him and whispering dirty things in his ear, and he'd have liked it even more if Cass joined in. Not that he was going to complain about Tom fucking him every night, Cass watching or not. Hell no. Though he did wonder when Tom and Cass found the time to love on each other, because if they were doing it, they weren't doing it in front of him. "So what is all this? Ooh, are they doughnuts?"

Tom pushed a box Jake's way. "Churros. Mexican doughnuts with cinnamon chocolate sauce. We're looking at dessert options for the

Camden project. The menus need finalising, the basic blueprints, at least. Cass has done the development research, so it's down to us to pick something and roll with it."

Jake stuffed a tiny spicy doughnut in his mouth and frowned. "These are minging. I'd be right pissed off if I ate one of them after my badass burger."

"Badass? Have you been watching Sky Atlantic all day?"

"Maybe." Jake pushed the doughnuts aside and stuck his middle finger up. "But those are still disgusting."

"Okay, no churros." Tom dumped the box in the bin under the sink. "What about brownies, or here . . . try these waffles."

"Waffles? Aren't they like chips?"

Tom rolled his eyes. "Not those kind of waffles. Belgian waffles, with ice cream and chocolate sauce. Whipped cream and strawberries. Bananas and syrup. Sound good?"

Like Jake could argue with that. He sampled the waffles, all of them. "I like them."

"Yeah?" Tom wiped Jake's mouth with the pad of his thumb. "Okay, now close your eyes and imagine you just ate your badass burger and downed some bubbly. Would you want a plate of waffles next?"

Jake thought on it. "I *could* eat them, but I'd probably puke after."

Tom pushed the waffles aside, and so it went on. Brownies, cookies, and pies, washed down with some wine from the cellar. Jake was half-pissed and fit to burst by the time Cass drifted through the front door an hour later.

"Hey, you're early." Tom ditched his notebook and embraced Cass like he hadn't seen him for weeks. "Everything okay?"

Cass let Tom sweep him off his feet a moment, before he smirked and fought back, ducking Tom's shrewd stare. "Quiet night. I cleaned the canopies and caught an early train home, seeing as some fucker stole my car."

Tom's grin was infectious. Jake took his turn greeting Cass and wrapped his legs around his waist, hooking him close and holding him there. Cass felt chilled from the outside world, and Jake wanted to warm him up. Wanted to welcome him home. Recently, he'd found himself dreaming of Cass, and then jumping awake, convinced he was alone, and back in his crappy flat. Then he'd roll over and find Cass already reaching out for him in his sleep, like he sensed Jake needed him.

Jake loved him for that.

Cass kissed Jake's cheek. "Pleased to see me?"

"Always."

Tom watched the exchange with a soft smile, then he poured Cass a glass of wine and passed him a box of cheesecake. "What do you think of this? Any good?"

Cass swiped a finger through the box, then stuck it in his mouth. "I know it's good. I made the bloody thing."

"Ha-ha." Tom poked Cass, hard. "Just answer the question, will you? If I eat any more sugar my teeth are going to fall out."

"Okay, okay . . ." Cass sampled a few more boxes and considered the rest, all the while remaining in Jake's grip, but he didn't seem to have an answer more definite than what Tom and Jake had come up with. "We need something fun and cheap, but not crap. Something that proves the rest of it isn't a gimmick."

Tom nodded. "It's got to fit, and feel right. There's no point setting the tone, only to mess it up at the last hurdle."

Cass looked thoughtful. "Did you say something about giving away jelly beans on the bill trays?"

"That was Jake's idea," Tom said.

"And I was joking," he protested. "You were banging on about ice buckets and all that posh stuff I've never heard of. Figured I'd bring the conversation back to my level."

"Don't put yourself down. You sound like Cass."

Jake eyed Tom as Cass tensed in his arms. Tom smiled, but it seemed off.

"I like the idea of jelly beans, gourmet ones," Cass said at last. "We've just got to find the right platform to get us there from burgers and fizz."

He absently traced a pattern on Jake's jean-clad thigh, his sharp gaze clouded and miles away. Jake waited for Tom to comfort Cass, to put his arms around him and soothe away whatever had troubled him so suddenly, but it never happened and though the tension in Cass remained, the moment passed.

They talked in circles for next few hours. Jake mostly let Tom and Cass get on with it. Tom knew what sold, and Cass knew what the kitchen could realistically produce, and on what scale. For a while, Jake thought they were arguing, until he caught the gleam in Tom's eyes, and the smirk playing on Cass's lips. Then he realised the tension he'd seen earlier had dissipated and the banter was a weird take on flirting, that this was the part of opening the restaurants they got to do together.

It was nice to see and it distracted him, a little, from the sensation of having his legs wrapped around Cass, having his hands on his thighs, and the warmth of their hips pressed together.

At least until he'd downed his third glass of Tom's posh wine, then he could think of nothing else, and he no longer gave a shit what sweet treats the funky population of Camden Town wanted with their burgers.

He slid off the kitchen counter right into Cass's arms, and made a clumsy grab for Tom. "Ice cream. Two flavours from a choice of six. A tray of three toppings from a choice of twelve. Five quid all in. Done. Can we go to bed now?"

Jake: You left early. Something big happening 2day?
Cass: Nah. Just couldn't sleep.
Jake: Why not?
Cass: Dunno
Jake: Liar
Cass: Am I?
Jake: Dunno
Cass: Don't forget to eat lunch
Jake: I want to punch you
Cass: Do it. I like that shit

It was February when Jake took a trip to Camden Library to finalise the handover of the old fire station artefacts. As it turned out, the library had been pleased to see the back of them in return for a hefty donation, and Jake had the perfect place for the vintage fire engine in the entrance of the new restaurant. He tracked down the woman in charge of the exchange and waited in her office, trying not to call her anything rude, while she pulled the paperwork together.

He let his mind drift as she opened and shut her filing cabinets. It was Monday morning, and he'd crept out of the house in Berkhamsted while Cass was still asleep. Tom had caught him, naturally, up and at 'em early, as usual, but Jake had dodged his invitation to spend a lazy day at home. It had been a while since Tom and Cass had spent any real time together—*alone* together—and Jake wanted to give them some peace. Things were great with Tom, with both of them, but something was still off with Cass, and for once, Jake felt fairly certain the problem didn't stem from their newfound sleeping arrangements. In fact, stretched out between Tom and Jake, a hand on each of them, was the only time Cass seemed happy.

The rest of it, he seemed tired and sad, like he had the weight of the world on his shoulders, and Jake had heard him rambling in his sleep at night. He couldn't make out a word, but the hurt in his muttering broke Jake's heart. Something was tearing Cass to bits.

"Here you are, Mr. Thompson." The librarian's soft voice brought Jake back to the present. "The release papers are all there. You just have to sign here, and here."

The librarian pointed to the dotted lines, and Jake scrawled his name, all the while waiting for someone to burst through the door and remind him he had no place putting his name forward as the face of a company like Urban Soul. "Is that it?"

"For now. You'll be arranging transportation, I take it?"

"Friday," Jake confirmed. "The floors are going down in the dining area today, then the decorating starts. Did you say you had some covers for the fire engine?"

The librarian nodded. "In the storeroom. We had them made when we refurbished the children's section, to save moving everything around. I'll have them put on for the removal men at the end of the week."

Jake smiled. "Thanks. That's really helpful. We don't have anywhere safe to store it while the decorators are in, and I don't want it to get damaged."

Life would've been easier if they could've delayed the transfer of the car-sized fire engine, but with the builders' typical setbacks, they'd messed the library around enough.

"It's no problem," the librarian said. "I think I've dealt with your boss before when I worked for the mayor's office. Urban Soul sponsors the food banks in Peckham and Hackney, don't they? And I think Pippa's was the first restaurant in London to supply artisan bread to the poorest local schools.

That was news to Jake. Tom and Cass were both obsessed with ethical food production—animal welfare, biodegradable packaging, and sustainability—but neither of them had ever mentioned any charitable endeavours at street level. Bemused, Jake shook the woman's hand and left the library. As he stepped outside, he put his hat on. The new year had brought a cold snap with it, and the wind whistling through Camden was bitter.

He made his way to the unfinished restaurant. As ever on a weekday morning, the place was a hive of activity. The structural building work had finished a week ago, the open kitchen was almost complete, and the decorators were about to move into the dining area.

Jake trod carefully around the carpenters renovating the hardwood floors and slipped upstairs to what had become his office of sorts, when he didn't work at the house. A few tradesmen called hello, but most paid him no heed, used to him coming and going with no real routine. No one seemed to notice his tics anymore. The builders shot him the occasional stare, but Jake had grown up with men like that, and learned how to ignore them.

He sat down in front of the desktop computer, booted it up, and plugged his phone into the USB port. Most of his web design work was on his new laptop, but he'd stored the files for the Camden project on his phone so he could access them anywhere. He loaded up the blueprints for the completed menus—including his crackpot idea for DIY ice cream sundaes—and the table designs. Some samples of crockery and glassware had arrived at the end of the previous week, and Tom had charged Jake with going through them and making a short list.

Jake fetched the boxes and opened them up. The first sets were awful, the next lot less so, but only a few seemed like anything he could live with. He took the samples downstairs and found the funky black tables that had arrived that morning. After checking himself for incoming tics, he peeled the plastic away and set about creating a typical place setting. It didn't work, and why would it? They weren't developing a typical restaurant. The Camden project was a burger bar with ice cream and posh fizz. How the fuck did you lay a table for that? Did he even want to?

Jake had no idea, and the more options he tried out, the less inspired he became.

He bit the bullet and called Tom.

Tom answered on the first ring. "Hang on a sec."

Jake heard the sound of rustling, then a door closing.

"Sorry," Tom said. "Cass fell asleep on me."

Asleep? It was nearly lunchtime. Maybe they were . . . "Are you in bed? I can talk to you later."

"I wish. Nah, I was working in the living room. Cass is crashed out in front of *Only Fools and Horses* again."

Tom's tone was bleak. Jake waited for him to elaborate, but the silence stretched until Jake felt compelled to break it. "So . . . I looked through the tableware samples."

"And?"

I hate them all. Jake tried to measure his words. Failed. "I hate them all."

Silence, then Tom laughed. "Okay, we can work with that. What's so bad about them? Too fancy? Too basic?"

"No." Jake thought on it a moment, and let his imagination get the better of him. "Do you really want each table to look the same?"

"I hadn't thought there was an alternative. Hang on a sec." A door opened. Tom said something, but it was too muffled for Jake to hear. Then the door closed, and Tom came back on the line with a heavy sigh. "Sorry. I thought Cass was awake."

"False alarm?"

"Oh no, he was awake all right—" Another door slam cut Tom off. "And now he's gone."

"Gone?"

"Yep, with the royal hump. He gets like this when he spends all night thrashing about."

"Thrashing about?" Jake frowned. "You mean tossing and turning?"

"And the rest. I don't think he's sleeping well. He used to have . . . Fuck, never mind. It's probably me who's dreaming shit. Anyway, what do you have in mind for the tables?"

Jake blinked at the abrupt return to business. "Um, I don't know, but none of that stuff in the boxes is right. It's too, uh, clinical, I think?"

"Clinical, eh?" Tom sounded amused. "Okay, why don't you do whatever the hell you want, and I'll worry about it on opening night?"

"What?"

"You've done more on this project than I have." There was a shrug in Tom's tone. "And you've been right about everything else so far. It's your design, your vision. Do what feels right."

"What if it's crap?"

"Then we'll both be wrong, won't we?"

Bastard. But there was nothing Jake could say to dissuade Tom, and he'd spend the next few weeks putting together a plan that was either going to be brilliant, or make the Camden project look like a bloody jumble sale.

And the Camden project wasn't the only venture Jake had on his mind. The night before Pink's website relaunch—Valentine's Day—found him huddled in front of the fire at 2 a.m. with just his laptop and Souris for company. Tom had gone to bed around eleven, and even Cass had come home and gone straight upstairs while Jake toiled away in the dark. Over the past few months, he'd driven himself mad with font layouts and coding, and in a few hours, he'd see his efforts either crash and burn, or come to fruition as the biggest project he'd ever attempted. Alone in the living room, it was hard to be optimistic.

Souris batted his hand. She'd spent much of the evening draped across the back of the couch, but she'd grown agitated since Cass had come home, like she couldn't decide where she wanted to be.

Jake sympathised with her there. He felt a little torn himself, but he couldn't sleep, not yet. Not while the threat of destroying one of Tom and Cass's businesses hung over him. No. Jake was in this for the long haul tonight, and he was probably going to see dawn before he found rest.

The night crept away from him, and he felt cross-eyed by the time Souris put a stop to his frenzied triple-checking by nudging his laptop shut.

Jake took the hint and set his computer aside. It was still dark outside, but barely. Dawn was just around the corner, and he needed his—Tom and Cass's bed, and them, even if he only got to enjoy their comforting warmth for a few moments before they got up and started their respective days.

Jake fed the cat and padded upstairs. He brushed his teeth, and thought about taking a shower, but then a noise from across the landing drew him out of the bathroom and to the bedroom he'd come to share with them.

Tom held Cass like a prisoner, his arm tight around his throat, restraining—choking him. He shoved his other hand into Cass's hair and yanked his head to one side. "Say it."

Cass groaned, naked and beside himself, every muscle straining and pulsing. His answer was unintelligible, a breathless whimper that sounded like it came from someone else.

Tom tightened his grip. "Say it. Say my name."

"*Tom*. Please."

Then Cass slumped forwards, his eyes glazed and distant. Tom pushed him down face-first and drove into him, slamming him so hard the bed slid across the unvarnished floor. A flush crept over his fair skin, and a sheen of sweat glistened. With his strong body and set jaw, the dim light of the room made him look like a god. Only the tender gleam in his eyes gave him away as a man entirely human—*too* human to hurt the love of his life beneath him.

Cass let out a desperate gasp. His face was hidden, but the plaintive plea needed no explanation. He needed this, needed to feel something all consuming, but he couldn't take much more.

And Tom heard his call and pulled him up, wrapped his arms so tight around him that Cass's breath caught in his chest. "I've got you."

The words were whispered, for Cass's ears only, but from his position, frozen in the doorway, Jake felt each one like a sledgehammer.

It took him a while to realise Cass was crying.

CHAPTER SEVENTEEN

A few weeks later, Jake rolled over and his reaching hands found empty space. He let out a restless puff of air. It had been a while since he'd truly slept alone, and he didn't like it at all. Even the bed didn't feel right, though he'd spent weeks alone in it when he'd first come to Berkhamsted. With Tom and Cass stuck in London for the night, it had seemed the sensible thing to do, but he regretted it now. Their bed may have been big, cold and lonely, but at least the pillows smelled of them. Not like this bed. This bed had been neglected so long it didn't smell of anything.

A paw touched Jake's face, reminding him why he hadn't gone to the flat to be with Tom, or braved Pippa's to track down Cass. Tom thought Souris would be fine by herself, but Jake wasn't so sure. The cat was his shadow when Cass wasn't around, and he didn't want to abandon her.

Tom had found the sentiment amusing, but Cass had seemed comforted, and Jake felt like Cass needed comfort right now, though he still had no idea why. Sometimes, he could convince himself that nothing was wrong, but then he'd remember the heartbreak in Cass's face when he'd seen him with Tom, remember his tears, and he knew that Cass needed him—and Tom—more than ever.

Shame he was never home for Jake to try to take care of him. Since the night Jake had seen him crying in Tom's arms, Cass had hardly been home at all. Work, work, work. These days, it seemed that was all Cass ever did, despite his long-forgotten promise to come home every night, and Jake was astute enough to recognise when a man was hiding from the world.

He just didn't know what to do about it.

Jake fell asleep with the cat on his chest. She still seemed restless, so when he was started awake by movement in the bed some time later, he figured it was her terrorising his feet. He shifted away from the disturbance, drifting off again. A tired voice pulled him back.

"Don't make me chase you."

Jake bolted upright. Cass sat on the side of the bed. In the darkness, Jake could see he was still wearing his coat and shoes.

"Cass? Thought you were staying at Pippa's?"

"Couldn't sleep. Figured I'd come home and count sheep with the cat."

On cue, Souris padded across the bed and leaped onto Cass's shoulder, reminding Jake that she was, at heart, a one-man cat.

"What time is it?"

Cass shrugged. "Dunno. It was 1 a.m. last time I looked."

What had driven Cass to come home to him, and not take the shorter route to Tom in Hampstead? Jake rose up on his knees and put his hands on Cass, pushing his coat—and the cat—from his shoulders. "You're freezing. Did you walk home? I thought you had the car."

"Hmm? Nah, I sat on the steps and had a fag before I came in. Don't tell Tom."

Jake grinned. If Cass wanted to hide his smoking from Tom, he'd have to do it himself. He massaged Cass's tight muscles. "You should get some sleep. Wanna go to bed?"

"Kicking me out of your room?"

"No." Jake kissed Cass's cheek. "I'll come with you, if you want?"

Cass hummed and leaned against Jake. He didn't look like he wanted to move.

Jake took pity on him and unzipped the hoodie Cass was wearing under his coat. "Fuck it. Get in."

Cass didn't take much persuading. He shed his hoodie and his trainers and crawled into Jake's bed already wearing the soft tracksuit bottoms he often wore to sleep in. He looked like he'd driven home in his pyjamas, but Jake let it slide.

They lay down together, Jake on his back with Cass's head on his chest. It was an unfamiliar position, but it didn't feel strange. Cass wasn't like Tom, he didn't need to be the strong one, and how many times had Tom silently told Jake that Cass liked—needed to feel loved?

Jake wrapped his arms around Cass and kissed the top of his head. "Why couldn't you sleep. Something on your mind?"

Cass didn't respond right away, apparently distracted by Souris digging a nest behind him. Then he shrugged, like the shadows in his gaze were nothing. "Feel like I've forgotten how this week. No good at sleeping alone anymore."

"Then you should get rid of the flat and let someone else live at Pippa's. Having those places makes it too easy for you and Tom to be apart."

Cass shifted and met Jake's gaze. "It's not just Tom I miss anymore. I can't sleep without you, either."

Jake kissed Cass, one of those slow, sweet kisses he'd become addicted to, but now, without the lure of Tom to distract him, the kiss bloomed into something deeper, until Cass was on top of him, grinding them together in a rhythm that made Jake's toes curl.

Jake gasped as Cass broke the kiss and buried his face in Jake's neck. Jake moaned. *God*, he wanted Cass, wanted him so much it hurt, but despite the heat between them, Cass was clearly exhausted. When the wicked pressure of his hips faded away and his breathing slowed, Jake knew he'd fallen asleep.

Jake woke up with Cass still on top of him, and for a moment, it seemed like he hadn't been asleep at all, because Cass was kissing his neck again, and without the shadow of exhaustion hanging over them, the slow-burning fire enveloped him.

He closed his eyes and gave in to Cass's touch. For months, Cass had been careful with him, restrained, but now, floating along in that hazy place between reality and the best fucking dream ever, Jake felt his hands all over him—his throat, his chest, his belly. Sliding past his waistband and brushing the boner Jake felt like he'd had for days.

Jake arched his back as a low grumble of pleasure escaped him. Cass jumped in his arms and reared back, his eyes wide.

"Shit, sorry. Fuck." Cass reclaimed his wandering hands and rolled away. "Fuck, sorry. I was having a mega-dirty dream."

"Those are my lines." Jake chased Cass down and drew him close again. "And don't apologise. I liked it."

"Yeah?"

"Yeah." Jake swallowed Cass's response with a kiss, then put a finger over Cass's lips. "And I don't want to stop."

Cass squirmed and sucked Jake's finger into his mouth. He let it out slowly, with just a graze of his teeth. "What *do* you want?"

"You." Jake tugged on the T-shirt hiding Cass from him. "I want all of you."

Cass didn't protest as Jake stripped him of his clothes, or even when he climbed all over him, kissing, biting, and made him groan. Jake clambered out of bed and fetched condoms and lube from the other bedroom. When he got back, Cass was still sprawled out, the duvet bunched at his hips.

Jake straddled him, a condom in his hand.

Cass clutched Jake's hips. "Slow. You've got nothing to prove."

Jake didn't understand the sentiment, but it didn't matter. He was far from ever understanding Cass, or the crazy life they were forging with Tom, but he understood the deep, aching desire he felt to have Cass inside him. He caught Cass's chin in his hand. "Lie still. Raise your arms over your head."

Cass obeyed. Jake rolled a condom onto him, lubed up, then lowered himself, taking Cass in until there was nowhere left to go.

For a long moment, Jake didn't move, swept up in the dizzying pressure of Cass filling him, then he leaned down, his face so close to Cass their noses touched. "Why are you sad?"

Cass didn't blink. "I'll tell you about it one day, but not today."

"One day soon?"

"Maybe."

Jake stared at Cass and filed his words away in his ever-growing stash of Cass's promises. One day could be tomorrow, or ten years away. Why the fuck couldn't Cass just tell him now?

Frustration warred with the hornet's nest of pleasure in Jake's belly. He wanted to shake Cass until every part of him was laid bare, but the sensation of his dick buried inside him proved distracting, and the resolution of the tension that had brewed between them since Cass had caught him in Tom's bed too enticing to ignore.

Jake rolled his hips a fraction. His head fell forwards, and he moaned. "You feel so good."

"Says you." Cass panted out a stuttered breath. "Tom told me you felt amazing like this. I believe him now."

"Maybe you can show me one day."

"Yeah? Want me to ride you?" Cass's eyes fluttered closed. "I could do that. I could do anything with you."

Anything. Jake stared down at fierce, beautiful Cass at his mercy, and yeah, anything suddenly felt possible.

He rode Cass slow, like a painstaking meeting of minds. Cass felt different than Tom, smelled different, but the crazy pleasure was no less intense, Jake took his time exploring him, twisting and rolling, paying heed to what made him buck and moan. He knew from Tom that Cass was an eclectic lover—that he got off on pushing boundaries— but Jake sensed Cass didn't crave adventure from him now. Didn't want it. No. Cass wanted, *needed*, the same as him, needed to know that the spark between them was real, tangible, and that it would be there long after their blood cooled.

Jake took his control to the limit, pushing himself to the brink over and over, only to pull back at the last moment, unwilling to end this so soon. Beneath him, Cass moved in sync. His face was a study in restraint, but the sweat-sheened flush darkening his chest, and the teeth bruising his bottom lip gave him away.

Cass pulled Jake down, crushing him to his chest, and together they rolled over, moving like they'd done this every day of their lives. He pushed Jake onto his stomach and drove inside him again. Jake gasped and grabbed a pillow, burying his face even as he shoved a hand between himself and the mattress and gripped his cock. He'd pictured them like this—him facedown with Cass all around him, fucking him the way only someone who'd done it all could fuck.

Cass groaned and fell to the side, taking Jake with him. Tom was a quiet lover, but not Cass, and as the morning sun began to filter through the half-closed curtains, he growled into Jake's neck and came, the beat of his heart against Jake's back matching the pulsing warmth where their bodies were joined.

It tipped Jake over the edge. He came with a low cry and spilled into his hand.

White noise followed, and for an unmeasured moment, they lay silent and still. Jake chased his breath. He'd always known Cass would blow his mind, but this? *Damn.* He was wrecked, and wanted to do nothing but enjoy Cass's clumsy embrace and breathe.

A tic shattered the quiet. Jake jerked and threw Cass back into the pillows. He froze, horrified, but Cass's laughter reeled him in. Jake rolled over and found Cass's eyes, got lost in the depths of his dark-blue gaze. "Fly him to the moon."

Cass laughed again, and the sun shone a little brighter. "Whatever you say, Jake. You're stuck with me now."

Jake: Cass came home last night.
Tom: Good. I'll be home around six. Take care of each other.

Despite Jake's frenzy of tics, Cass drifted back to sleep, and he stayed that way for most of the morning. Jake watched him for a while, heeding Tom's advice and making the most of their quiet time together, but around nine, he got up, fed the cat, and fetched his laptop. When he got back, Cass had rolled over and his expression didn't look entirely peaceful. He muttered something and reached out. When he found nothing, he groaned and rolled again, still reaching.

Jake quickly clambered back into bed. Cass talked in his sleep most nights he came home, but this felt different, like Cass was searching for someone, anyone, to pull him back from wherever his dreams had taken him.

Cass must have sensed Jake's presence because he pressed himself tight against Jake's side. Jake hugged him with one arm, felt Cass's trembling like it was his own, and tried to channel some of Tom's warmth and strength.

A tear rolled down Cass's cheek. Jake kissed his bare shoulder. "You're not alone, Cass. I promise."

Whether Cass heard him or not, Jake didn't know, but his shaking calmed and eventually passed, and it wasn't long before he was sound asleep beside Jake once again.

Jake waited awhile to be sure, then retrieved his laptop from the bedside table and booted it up. The launch of Pink's website had been a tentative success, but he still had much to do on the Camden project and growing the social media profile for the company as a whole.

He got lost in his work. Setting up the Camden restaurant was fun, but his passion lay in coding and design, and creating new websites for each individual Urban Soul business was a task that seemed to get bigger as he worked, even with the distraction of Cass naked beside him. He'd been engrossed for a few hours when a low chuckle startled him.

"You're so cute when you concentrate."

Jake tore his gaze from the screen and scowled at Cass. "How long have you been awake?"

"Long enough to form an objective opinion." Cass shifted and stretched. "What time is it?"

"Eleven. You okay?"

Cass rubbed his eyes. "Yeah. Thanks for letting me sleep. I needed it."

"I could tell." Jake recalled Cass the night before, almost loopy with exhaustion. "Do you feel better?"

Cass shrugged. "I feel a lot of things. What about you? The fact that you're tapping away on that thing in your birthday suit seems like a good sign to me, but I've been wrong about these things before."

The uncertainty colouring Cass's features caught Jake's attention. He set his laptop aside and slid down the bed. "I don't regret anything. Do you?"

"Not at all." Cass touched Jake's cheek. "I feel like . . . I don't know, like we've resolved something we were both worried about."

Jake grinned. "Works for me, but what were you so worried about? That fucking me would be crap?"

"No." Cass cleared his throat. "I knew we'd be hot together the moment I saw you. I guess I was worried we'd wait too long, and sex would change everything between us."

"*Wankers*. Sorry. Ruin our beautiful friendship, you mean?"

Cass rolled his eyes. "Piss off. Did you talk to Tom yet?"

"Yeah, he'll be home around six. What are you doing today?"

"I might tile the bathroom, if I can be arsed, and you don't give me a better offer."

Cass coughed again. Despite his epic sleep, he sounded a little rough. Jake put his hand on his chest. Did he feel warm? Cuddled up in bed, Jake couldn't tell. "It's Monday, so you should chill out. What do you usually do with Tom?"

"I've told you before . . . walk, eat, and fuck, though I guess we started early. That was this morning, right?"

Jake smiled. "You don't remember the sun?"

"Fuck the sun, Jake. I only saw you."

It took Cass a while to get going, but after a hot shower—with company—Jake persuaded him to leave the tiling for another day and take a walk along the canal instead. On the way home, they stopped by the farm shop and picked up chicken and vegetables to continue their tradition of Cass teaching Jake how to cook Tom's favourite meals.

Jake let them into the house and took their wares through to the kitchen. Cass followed, turning the oven on as he passed, and retrieved the equipment they needed to make a roast dinner.

"Why are you and Tom so sneaky about the nice things you do for each other?" Jake asked.

"Sneaky?" Cass unwrapped the chicken and dumped it in a roasting tray. "What the fuck does that mean?"

Jake shrugged. He knew what he meant, but articulating it was difficult. "You're cooking Tom dinner under the guise of teaching me life skills. Why can't you just admit you want to make him smile?"

Cass snorted. "Trust me, mate, it'll take more than a chicken dinner to make him smile at me. I've been a twat to him all weekend. Think he's fed up with me."

"I doubt that." Jake hadn't seen Tom and Cass together, or at least, awake and together, for a few days, but he knew it would take more than a couple of grumbles to make Tom truly angry with Cass. "Tom loves you."

"I know that." Cass finished rubbing butter on the chicken and jammed a lemon inside it. "Doesn't stop me doing my best to fuck things up, though. Wouldn't blame him if he kicked me to the kerb. I've given him enough reason over the years. Here, bung some wine in this tray. I'll show you how to make gravy later."

Jake poured white wine into the bottom of the chicken tray, and for a while they fell into their by-now-familiar roles of student and teacher. Jake liked watching Cass cook, and hearing him explain the various processes, but the distraction didn't stop him pondering Cass's words. He'd never known two people to love each other as much as Tom and Cass did, and he couldn't imagine Tom *ever* turning his back on Cass. "He'd never leave you."

"Yeah, he said that once. He hasn't said it for a while, though." Cass flashed Jake a cheeky wink, but his droll grin didn't reach his eyes.

Jake swallowed the lump in his throat. "Tom told me you hate cooking at home. What's up with that?"

"Hmm?" Cass chopped a board of carrots so fast Jake almost missed it. "I don't hate cooking at home, I just break stuff. Everything's too small. I'm used to caravan-sized saucepans and nuclear gas burners. I get a bit lairy at home."

"You seem pretty Zen to me." It was true. Though talking about Tom had dampened the mood, Cass always seemed calmer when he cooked, like it took him away from the world for a while.

Cass swept the carrots into a small baking dish. "That's you, mate. You're a good influence on me. Even Tom says so."

Jake didn't know how to respond to that. Cass hadn't seemed to notice his tics all but disappeared every time they cooked together. Maybe they were good for each other. "I've done the potatoes. What's next?"

"What else did we buy?"

"Parsnips, carrots, and peas. I reckon I can manage that if you tell me what to do. Sit down. Watch someone else cook for a change."

Cass looked as though he might protest, but then he dropped into one of the kitchen stools and put his head on his arms. "You're dangerous with those puppy-dog eyes."

Jake stuck his tongue out and held up the parsnips. "Shut it. Do I need to cut these up?"

"Yeah, same as the carrots. We're going to bake them, then add some cinnamon and honey."

Jake followed Cass's instructions and prepared the rest of the vegetables. When he was done, he made Cass a cup of tea and set it in front of him. "You're a good teacher."

"Thanks," Cass said dryly. "That your idea of a chat-up line?"

"Probably. I've never chatted anyone up before." Jake brushed some hair away from Cass's eyes. It was easier to do that kind of thing with Cass than with Tom, like their shared love for him equalled them somehow.

Cass smiled. "You know, you're more like Tom than you think."

"I'm nothing like Tom." Strong, wise, and warm. Nope. That wasn't Jake.

Cass shook his head. "You don't see yourself at all, do you?"

"You're talking in riddles." Jake gave Cass a shove.

Cass sighed and slid off his stool. He looked like he wanted to say something . . . do something else, but then the phone rang, and he sloped off to answer it without another word.

After an hour, he still hadn't come back. Jake cleaned up the kitchen with his mind half on his abandoned laptop upstairs. Alongside the ongoing Camden project, Pippa's website was his next task, and he'd meant to pick Cass's brain while they'd been cooking, but being with him had proved as distracting as ever.

The oven timer went off as Jake was loading the dishwasher. He opened the oven and eyed the chicken, trying to remember what it was supposed look like when it was cooked. He took it out and set it on the side. Cass had said something about loose legs, but he may have been taking the piss.

Jake was poking at the chicken with a fork when he heard the front door open a minute later. He greeted Tom with an absent smile. "You're early."

Tom dumped his laptop bag on the table. "Didn't feel like hanging around. Something smells good. Where's Cass?"

"On the house phone."

"To who? My mum? She's the only one who ever calls that number."

"No idea," Jake said. "He's been gone awhile."

Tom's expression softened. "Fair enough. I'm going to get changed, then I'll come and give you a hand."

He disappeared. Jake called the chicken's bluff, judged it cooked, and set the potatoes on the hob to parboil. He could bodge the rest of the vegetables, but he'd have to wait for Cass for the gravy.

"You look lost."

Jake jumped and spun to face Tom. "I'm all right. Don't know what to do next though."

"Don't worry, I do. Cass has likely dozed off on the couch by the phone. My mum has that effect on the best of us, and he's probably knackered after a killer weekend. Let's finish dinner, then see if we can bully him into an early night."

"I can finish dinner." Jake considered the pans still requiring his attention.

Tom laughed. "Sounds like you want to look after him too. Is this how it's going to be now? Us fighting over who gets to love him the most?"

"How do you know I love him?"

"Because I know you've slept with him, Jake, it's written all over your face. And I know what happened to me the first time I had sex with Cass. You might not know it, but you're as in love with him as I am."

Jake scowled, though he didn't mean it at all. He'd been searching for the words to tell Tom what had transpired between him and Cass, and knowing he didn't have to was such a relief he felt like he could pass out. "He thinks *you're* in love with *me*."

Tom shrugged. "Cass is a clever bloke."

Warmth filled Jake's chest. "Guess it's all falling into place, eh?"

"I hope so." Tom stared at Jake for a long moment, like he was trying to convey something he wasn't ready to say out loud, then he broke the deadlock and peered at the dishes on the counter. "What are you making?"

"We were making roast chicken, but the gravy is a bloody mystery to me."

Tom smiled. "Well, lucky for all of us, Cass usurped my mother and taught me to cook too. Why don't we see if we can finish this off between us before he gets back?"

So that's what they did. Tom's approach to cooking was a little slapdash, but between them, they managed to cobble together a pretty good-looking dinner, and Jake felt his mood teetering around the edge of the happiest he'd been in years. He hadn't realised how worried he'd been about Tom's reaction to him and Cass fucking until Tom had come home and put his mind at ease. Which made no sense at all, because Jake had known from the start, long before he reckoned Tom knew it himself, that the three of them together was Tom's dream, a dream Jake now claimed as his own.

Tom rested his chin on Jake's shoulder. "Smells good."

Jake leaned against Tom, enjoying his comforting bulk. "Think it's up to Cass's standards?"

"Don't let his big talk fool you. Cass likes cold baked beans. He has no . . ."

Jake turned his head, searching out the source of Tom's distraction. His gaze fell on Cass, who stood in the kitchen doorway, the cordless phone clutched in his hand and his face like a ghost's. "Cass? What's the matter?"

Cass stared right through him, his eyes only for Tom. "They found my mum's body."

TOM

CHAPTER EIGHTEEN

"*They found my mum's body.*"

It took Tom ten seconds to lose Cass. Five words, and then he was gone, leaving nothing but pale skin and empty eyes.

Tom dropped the vegetable pan on the counter. He started across the kitchen, but Cass was already backing away, shrinking into himself in a way he hadn't seen in years.

"Cass—"

"Don't." Cass blocked Tom with his arm. "I need to go."

"What? Where?"

Cass didn't answer. He turned his back on Tom and moved through the unpainted hallway like a shadow. Tom caught up with him at the front door. "Where are you going?"

"Leave me alone." Cass shrugged him off and stamped into his shoes.

"No bloody chance." Tom put himself between Cass and the door. "Cass, talk to me. You can't just leave. How do you know they found a body? Did the police call you?"

"Does it matter?" Cass's voice sounded distant, like he'd already checked out. "Move."

"No."

"*Move.*"

"*No.*"

Something changed, like a haze descended over Cass and turned him inside out. He lunged at Tom and yanked him away from the door. "You can't fix this by being a bloody hero, now get out of my fucking way."

Tom stumbled. Cass was halfway to his car before he righted himself. He dashed out into the wet evening drizzle and blocked Cass's path again. "Cass, stop. For fuck's sake. Talk to me."

"Why? So you can tell me it's all in my head again? No, thanks."

Guilt burned a hole in Tom's gut. Over the years, Cass had distanced himself from his mother's absence, but in recent months he'd begun to dream about her again, thrashing around in the night, calling her name and Dolly's, like he'd lost them both just yesterday. "I didn't know. I'm sorry, okay? I didn't know."

"I need to go. I can't be here. I need to be . . ."

Cass stopped. Tom caught his arm. "Don't go. Please. Whatever's happened, we can figure it out together."

"Get the fuck off me." Cass wrenched his arm free, unlocked his car, and opened the door. "You don't get it, do you? This shit doesn't come right with a pot of Earl Grey and a fucking biscuit. Some workmen found a sack of human remains on a building site. The coppers think it's my mum. How the fuck are we going to figure that out?"

Cass slid into his car and slammed the door. He gunned the engine and drove away in a cloud of exhaust fumes before Tom could verbalise his answer.

Because we love you.

Cass's headlights disappeared into the night. Cold seeped through Tom's bare feet and into his bones. In his hand, he still clutched the carving fork from the abandoned chicken, and the other was outstretched, reaching for something that was already gone.

He turned back to the house, his mind in bits. *"They found my mum's body."* How the hell had that morphed into a sack of remains on a building site? How the hell had this happened at all? Faye Pearson's disappearance had been a cold case for more than a decade. The way Cass told it, another missing hooker had meant little to the police fourteen years ago, but then, Cass hated coppers with a venom Tom would never understand.

Tom stepped inside and shut the door. It took him a moment to notice Jake frozen in the kitchen doorway.

"What happened to Cass's mum?"

Tom wondered how much he'd heard. He picked up the phone Cass had dumped on the pile of shoes by the door and dialled 1471, but the robotic operator had nothing for him.

"Fuck's *sake*." Tom fought the urge to throw the phone at the wall. Who the hell called someone to tell them they'd found their mother's bones? Why didn't they send someone round?

He ran upstairs and shoved the loft hatch open. It had been years since he'd looked at the copies of the cold-case files documenting the disappearance of Faye Pearson, but he knew where they were. Could picture the battered cardboard box as though he'd shoved it into the attic just yesterday.

He jumped and hauled himself up through the hatch, his biceps burning. Below, he heard Jake's footsteps on the stairs, a dull thud, and a muttered curse. Jake was prone to bashing himself on the banister. His Tourette's didn't seem to like the stairs. Tom's heart ached, but Jake would be okay. Cass was the one who needed him now.

Like everyone's loft, Tom and Cass's was full of junk—books, clothes, and abandoned electrical appliances. Tom wove his way through the chaos, balancing on the wooden beams between the layers of insulation. The box he was looking for was behind the hot water tank, deliberately hidden from view. Tom retrieved it, then realised he needed Jake's help if he wanted to bring it down without dropping it out of the hatch.

"Jake?"

"I'm here."

Of course he is. Tom's heart cracked a little more. Of course he was there. Jake was everything he thought himself incapable of—strong, dependable. Tom crouched over the hatch. Jake stood below, his arms outstretched.

Tom passed down the box and lowered himself out of the loft. He took the box from Jake and carried it through to the bedroom.

Jake watched him dump the contents on the duvet and start leafing through the papers. "Tom? What's happened? Tell me? Please?"

The confusion in Jake's voice almost broke him, but it was also enough to return some perspective. He pulled out a page of the *Metro* and passed it over. "Cass's mum went missing when he was fifteen. She worked as a prostitute in Hackney. She went out one night and never came back."

"She didn't come home?"

"Wherever that was. Cass lived with his nan. Dolly raised him from a baby."

Jake said nothing for a long moment, then he pointed at a date in the article. "New Year's Eve. That's why you don't celebrate."

Tom nodded, his heart heavy. He'd seen Jake's bewilderment that night just a few months ago when Cass had stayed at work, and Tom had gone to bed at 11 p.m. like any other Tuesday night. "Unwritten rule, about the only one we ever stick to. He doesn't talk about Faye much, but New Year's Eve always finds him in the kitchen, working his arse off. Most years, he won't even look at me."

As Tom admitted it out loud, he realised for perhaps the first time how much that hurt. He'd grown used to Cass's reticence over his colourful past—drugs, crime . . . prison—but he'd never allowed himself to take stock of how painful it was when Cass shut him out of something so huge.

Jake touched his arm. "What's happened tonight? Where did Cass go?"

Cass. Fuck. Tom shook himself and rifled through the old papers until he found the contact details for the detective who'd handled the case. He pulled out his phone and tapped the number in before he gave Jake his attention. "Honestly? I have no idea. I think the police called here and told him they'd found some human remains that could be Faye. That's about all I got out of him. He was pretty upset."

Upset. The word didn't sit right. Upset, Tom could handle, but the edge in Cass tonight scared the crap out of him.

Jake moved closer to Tom and pressed himself against his side. Tom wrapped an arm around his slender shoulders and held him tight while he waited for the call to connect.

It didn't. It rang and rang until an automated voice told him the office he was calling no longer existed. Tom growled and killed the call.

I can't be here.

Tom's stomach turned over. Over the years, Cass had mostly got to grips with the real belief that he didn't deserve the life he'd worked so hard for, but Tom remembered times he'd been sucked back into the black hole he'd come from. Times when Cass couldn't hide the person he'd once been.

Tom gathered up the papers on the bed. "I need to go out."

"Where? To find Cass?"

"Yeah. He's not himself. I need to be with him."

"Okay." Jake helped Tom gather the papers. "Do you know where he's gone?"

"Nope." Tom let Jake stack the papers back in the box and opened a drawer, looking for a jumper to put on over his T-shirt. He pulled one of Cass's over his head and came through the other side to find Jake right in front of him, his phone pressed to his ear.

"He's turned his phone off. Where are you going to look for him? He could be anywhere."

Tom shook his head. He knew Cass, and there were places he went when he felt more like the troubled boy he used to be than the incredible man he'd turned out to be. "There's a few old haunts I can try . . . places he goes when he's pissed off with me. If he's not there, I'll come home again, I promise."

"I'm coming with you."

"Jake . . ." Tom stopped, and so nearly crumbled. Jake was strong and brave, but it wasn't that simple. Cass had come from a volatile place in the city, laced with crime, death, and poverty. To find him, Tom would have to search some of London's darkest places, and he couldn't take Jake with him. Whatever Cass's state of mind right now, he'd never forgive Tom for that. "No. I need to go on my own."

Jake coughed. "Fuck off, you selfish bastard."

The tic caught Tom off guard, but before he could react, Jake punched the wall. The plaster crumbled. Jake stared at the dusty crack, and then something seemed to snap in him. "*No*," he said. "You don't get to decide. You can't bring me into your life, your fucking bed, then shut me out every time shit goes down."

"I'm not sh—"

"Bollocks! You've been doing it for weeks, you both have, almost as much as you've been doing it to each other."

It was like he'd been hit in the chest. Wished he had been, because as the truth of Jake's words sank in, it would've been easier if one of his lovers had decked him. "Jake, I can't explain it all to you now, I need to go, but Cass . . . he's not himself. He wouldn't want you to see him like this."

"Why? Because I'm a stupid fucking kid? Some retarded kid you took in because he had a nice arse? Fuck you, Tom."

"Jake, please." Tom stopped. Please what? What the fuck could Jake do to fix this bloody mess? "Jake, I'm sorry, okay? I've messed up, we both have, and we were messed up long before we met you. Please, God, don't doubt anything we've ever said to you. We love you, both of us, but I need to go looking for Cass, and I need you to stay here in case he comes home. Can you do that for me? Please?"

Jake shook his head. Tom's heart sank before he realised it was a tic, and Jake was reaching for him, his shoulders slumped and his anger gone as quickly as it had appeared. Jake took Tom's face in his hands. "Do you think he'll come back?"

"I don't know, but I need you to be here. I can't bear the thought of him coming home to an empty house."

"He won't." Jake pressed their foreheads together.

Tom tried to smile, but it felt hollow. "I'm going to get the last fast train to Euston. I know a few places he might go to blow off some steam. Wait by the phone, okay? Whoever called him might call back."

"Who should I say I am if they do?"

Tom thought on it for less than a second. "Tell them you're his partner."

Tom dashed through the barriers at Euston station and jumped on the first bus he saw heading south. He'd start in Hackney, which was close to Cass's old stomping grounds and the last place Faye had been seen alive.

The journey to London's East End took twenty minutes, and as he watched the bright lights of the city trundle by at a maddeningly slow pace, Tom found himself questioning his sanity. It had been a long time since Cass had been lured back to the deprived estates he'd grown up on, and Jake was right. Driving, he could've been anywhere by now. Maybe even somewhere benign, like Pippa's, or the flat in Hampstead.

After reaching Cass's voice mail again, Tom called the flat first, knowing in his heart Cass wouldn't pick up. He never went to the flat alone unless he knew Tom was there. Tom called Pippa's with more hope, but a brief check with the manager confirmed Cass hadn't been there all day. Tom hung up and tapped his phone against his lips. His sanity might be dubious, but his gut told him he was on the right path.

The bus pulled into a stop on a street Tom vaguely recognised. He disembarked and when his feet hit the pavement, he *knew* Cass was close. Felt it in his bones. Determination surged through him. Cass's demons had been trying to pull him down for years, but now, with so much to lose, Tom would be damned if he let them.

For the next few hours, he scoured the pubs and bars of Hackney, keeping close to the path plotted out on the long-forgotten map in the box at home. Cass hadn't been through it in years, but there'd been a time, back when Tom had first met him, when he'd lost weeks to trying to retrace Faye's last movements. Cass hadn't long been out of prison and was still haunted by the isolation he'd endured, and the brutal violence he'd witnessed inside. At the time, Tom had figured looking into his mum's case gave Cass a gruesome distraction, and now he was glad of it, and glad he'd taken the time to peer over Cass's shoulder.

But he came up blank as he roamed the streets of Hackney, keeping a sharp eye out for Cass's blue Toyota. The stupidity of his search washed over him again as he approached the final pub on his mental list. The Star in Bethnal Green was a dive, but not only was it the last place Faye had been seen alive, it was also a place Cass knew well, a place where he'd come of age, drinking, fighting, and fencing stolen car parts.

Tom shuddered as he pushed the door open, forcing away visions of Cass's darkest days. He'd seen Cass unhappy, seen him struggle, but there was no doubt Cass had been on his way up by the time Tom met him. Tom could only imagine the lifetime of crime and violence that had come before.

He searched the crowded pub. A cloud of illicit cigarette smoke hit his senses. He pushed through the sea of bodies, taking care not to jostle anyone. As anxious as he was to find Cass, he also didn't want to get punched. He worked his way to the far end of the bar, searching for that mop of unruly hair he knew so well.

"Tom?"

Tom whirled around, his heart in his mouth, but instead of Cass, he found himself almost nose to nose with Nero. "What the hell are you doing here?"

Nero eyed Tom. "Might ask you the same thing. Me? I live here, mate."

He had a point. Tom had forgotten the Spanish-born chef had a flat in Bethnal Green. He hadn't seen Nero since the staff piss-up on Christmas Day. When it came to business, Nero preferred to deal with Cass, which suited Tom just fine. Nero looked exotic, but his cockney brogue was as broad as Cass's, his scowl just as deep, his temper as fierce. Tom didn't have the energy to deal with him and Cass both. "Very funny. I meant what are you doing in this shithole? Is Cass with you?"

"Cass?" Nero frowned. "Why would Cass be here?"

Tom didn't have an answer. He shook his head, for his own benefit as much as Nero's. "We might need you to cover Pippa's this week. Do you think Henrietta could handle Pink's?"

Nero scowled. "Suppose we can cobble something together. Where's Cass at? Anywhere nice?"

"What?"

"Cass. Where's he at?"

Cass, Cass, Cass, where are you? Tom glanced around the pub again. He'd walked in half-convinced he'd find Cass propping up the bar and staring down an empty glass, but Cass wasn't here, and he couldn't figure out if he was relieved or about to have the world's biggest anxiety attack.

Because if Cass wasn't here, where the hell was he?

Tom left Nero to it, unable to answer his question, and stepped out into the night. He found his phone, hit speed dial, and walked to a nearby bus stop while he waited for an answer. The call connected on the first ring. Tom sat down and closed his eyes. "Jake, I need help."

CHAPTER NINETEEN

There was a rustling on the other end of the phone. "I'm here, Tom. What do you need?"

Tom opened his mouth, shut it again. He needed . . . something, anything, to help him find Cass, but he was bang out of ideas. "I can't find him."

"Where are you?"

"Bethnal Green."

"Why? What's Bethnal Green to Cass?"

"He used to, uh, work around here, and so did his mum. I thought he might have come back here."

Jake said nothing, but Tom heard his muttered tics and his heart ached. Jake was upset, and more than that, he was alone, like Cass, and Tom had failed them both.

Then Jake made a low noise. Tom couldn't decipher it, but the sound soothed him until Jake found his words.

"I figured she'd sacked him off when he told her he was gay, or something, but . . ."

Tom waited, tapping restless fingers on his jittering leg. It sometimes took Jake a while to articulate his thoughts.

"What was the worst part of losing his mum for him?"

Tom frowned. The question was something he'd never considered before. Why would he? The whole situation was awful. No part of it was worse than any other, or was it? "Dolly," he blurted. "It killed Cass to see her so upset, even before Faye went missing."

"Nana Dolly?"

Tom nodded. "Yeah. She raised him."

Raised him, loved him, and stuck by him when the mess of his childhood and the power of outside influences inevitably sent him off the rails.

"Do you think he maybe went to see her? She's his maternal grandmother, right? Perhaps he went to tell her the news."

Tom felt suddenly stupid. All this time he'd been running around London like a twat, and the answer had been bloody obvious. "Fuck. I know where he is."

"Yeah?"

"Yeah." Tom stood and studied the bus timetable. Jake hadn't quite hit the nail on the head, but he'd done enough. Cass wouldn't have gone to the nursing home, he couldn't bear it, but he would have gone to Dolly, spiritually, at least. Tom traced the glass-covered bus routes with his fingertip until he came to Tower Hamlets. An audible click sounded in his brain, and he knew he was right.

Cass had gone home.

He pleaded with Jake to get some sleep, and hung up. Then he placed another fruitless call to Cass's voice mail, left the bus stop and crossed the road. The next bus wasn't for ten minutes, and he couldn't wait that long. Tower Hamlets was only a thirty-minute walk away, twenty if he ran.

Ran. Shit. That was a bloody joke. It had been months since Tom had last found the time to put his trainers on and pound the streets, and a ten-minute burst of speed was as much as he could manage. He jogged the rest of the way and an ominous shadow crossed his heart when he caught sight of the concrete towers Cass had once called home looming in the distance.

Tom slowed. Cass's old estate was a dangerous place, and attempting to run through it would attract attention from both the hidden eyes in every stairwell and the parked-up police on the pavements outside. He glanced between the foreboding towers. Cass hadn't let him come here much, and he could never remember which block housed Dolly's humble flat.

He took a chance on the eastern block and made his way cautiously to the entrance. He dug out his keys and found the set he'd long forgotten about. The larger key for the exterior door worked and let him inside.

Tom let the door swing shut. Cass had taught him to avoid the lifts in places like these, especially at night, but hearing echoing voices above him, he didn't much fancy the stairs.

Man up.

Tom made for the barren concrete steps. Dolly's flat was on the eighth floor, and he sensed eyes on him as he passed each landing on the way. He glanced up a few times. Regretted it. The estate had changed in recent years, but the influx of the Bangladeshi families Dolly had insisted on calling "darkies" were absent from the landings and stairwells tonight. The sullen-faced cockney boys were out in force, like time had stood still, that he was retracing his steps from the first time Cass had run out on him.

He remembered that day well. It was the first real fight he and Cass had ever had, borne of Tom pushing Cass too far, too hard, and not understanding the world Cass had come from, or the scars it had left. Cass had walked out of the converted studio flat they'd shared by the docks and come back to a place he believed was no less than he deserved. He'd stolen a car that night and driven it into a wall for shits and giggles. How he wasn't killed, or caught and thrown back in prison, Tom would never know. Perhaps he didn't *want* to know. Cass had told him years later that he'd grown addicted to the thrill and speed of racing boosted cars through the streets of London. That of everything, he'd found it the hardest habit to break.

That particular conversation, almost more than any other, had stayed with Tom ever since.

He reached the eighth floor. A small huddle of youths sat on the landing, smoking weed. Tom sidestepped them, keeping his gaze straight ahead, and made it out onto the adjunct corridor.

Tom shivered as he searched for Dolly's front door. He hated flats like these, even the refurbished ones—which this wasn't—that had been sold to the private sector. Built in the sixties during the capital's "streets in the sky" craze, they were freezing cold and ugly as sin, a thought that distracted Tom until he found himself in front of a shiny, reinforced front door that stood out in the bleak corridor.

Tom allowed himself a small smile as he remembered Cass and Dolly squabbling over the colour. Dolly had won, of course, but Cass had gladly painted the door bright red. Knowing his precious nana was safe in her home had been more than enough for him. He'd given Dolly the money to buy her flat from the council a year or so before she'd started to lose her marbles. It lay empty now, untouched since the day Tom had moved her into the nursing home on Cass's behalf.

He took a deep breath, slid the key into the lock, and nudged the door open. It took him a moment to look up, afraid of what he'd find, but at first glance he saw nothing untoward or out of place in the cold, dark flat. Nothing to make him believe Cass was or had been there.

Then his gaze fell on a crumpled cigarette packet—the brand Cass smoked when he slipped up and let his workday habit follow him out of the kitchen.

Tom's heart skipped a beat. The musty smell of Dolly's flat was testament to her forty-a-day habit, but Tom smelled fresh smoke. Someone was here.

He shut the door with a quiet *click* and poked his head into the living room. It was empty, the kitchen too. The next stop was Cass's childhood bedroom, and there Tom found him at the window, blowing smoke to the moon.

Cass let out a sigh that was barely audible. "I don't like you being in a place like this."

"So why did you come?" Tom countered. He fished his phone from his pocket and fired a text to Jake, but remained in the doorway, waiting on a sign that Cass wanted him close. "You knew I'd follow you."

"I didn't know I was coming until I got here."

Tom let that hang a moment. "Where's your car?"

"Brixton."

"Brixton? Why?"

Tom tried to keep the tension from his voice, but Cass heard it anyway, and finally turned and met Tom's gaze. "A cold-case detective asked me to meet her at Brixton cop shop. She wanted to show me some photos. I didn't feel like driving when I got out, so I left it there."

Tom took a hesitant step forwards. He wanted to go to Cass and hold him, but he knew what would happen if he did. Cass would lean on him, say he was sorry, and Tom would let it all go until the next time. And this wasn't like all the other times Cass had gone AWOL. This wasn't a fight, or the clash of their conflicting backgrounds.

Something tangible had happened, something huge, and they needed to talk about it. And, more than anything, Tom needed to know that Cass was okay. That he hadn't done something that was going to come back on all of them. "Where've you been all night?"

"I told you. Brixton."

"Brixton." Tom nodded slowly. "To the police station? You didn't go anywhere else?"

Cass stared at him before comprehension flickered over his features. He laughed, tired and bitter. "Where would I go? I don't know this place anymore. My face doesn't fit. And no, before you ask, I didn't nick any bloody cars. You're going to hold that against me forever, aren't you?"

"I've never held it against you."

"Liar."

Silence. Tom counted to ten in his head. They were getting nowhere, and all the while ignoring the elephant in the room. Perhaps Cass's intention all along. He didn't want to talk about whatever had driven him to this lifeless flat in the arsehole of London, and Tom had long ago given up trying to *make* him talk about anything.

Something on the dust sheet–covered bed caught Tom's attention. One of Dolly's picture frames. He crossed the small room with a single step and picked it up. Took in the image of Dolly and a kindly old man holding a baby Tom was pretty sure was Cass. "I've never seen this before. Is this your granddad?"

"Yeah." Cass flicked his cigarette out of the window. "He died a month later. Keeled over with the teapot still in his hand."

Tom recalled the story, but he'd never seen any photographs of old man Ken. Dolly didn't like to see photos of the dead. Said they haunted her dreams. Tom sat down. It was two o'clock in the morning, and he was flagging. "Cass, I can't do this with you again. I need you to tell me what's happened. You can't shut me out anymore. I can't bloody stand it."

His voice cracked and caught him by surprise. Perhaps it was exhaustion, but all at once he wanted to weep for Cass, for Dolly, and for Jake, home alone with just the cat to guide him through this bloody shitstorm.

Cass moved away from the window and slid down the wall to sit opposite Tom. "I *can't*. I can't talk to you about this. I look at you, and I don't want you to know shit like this happens."

"Damn it, Cass. I'm not naïve, and I'm not a child. You can't protect me from the world any more than I can you."

"I know that."

"So tell me." Tom leaned forwards. Cass was half a foot away. He stretched and touched his knee. "You don't have to do this on your own."

The silence seemed to go on forever before Cass closed his eyes and banged his head against the wall. "A detective from the cold-case squad called me this afternoon. They've been trying to reach me for a few days. Some builders unearthed the remains on a site in Lambeth. They cross-referenced it with the missing persons' database and Faye's name came up. They found some stuff with the . . . remains too. The detective wanted to show me some photos. She said it could wait until tomorrow, but . . ."

Tom felt sick. Faye had been gone for fourteen years. He could only imagine what was left of her. "What kind of photos?"

Cass opened his eyes and winced. "Not what you think. The remains were just some bones and a few teeth. They didn't make me look at those. The photos were of some items they found close to the site. Most of it was bullshit, but there was a bracelet. I stared at it for ages before I recognised it."

"Was it Faye's?"

"No." Cass got up and pried the picture frame from Tom's hands. "It was Dolly's. Look. My granddad bought it in Switzerland for her on his way home from Japan."

"When he was a POW?"

Cass nodded. Tom stared at the photo and took in the silver chain around Dolly's wrist. The piece was distinctive. "Why would Faye have it?"

"She stole it every bloody chance she got. I lost count of the number of times me and Dolly went down the pawn shop to buy it back."

"So, Faye could've sold it on to anyone, right? This, uh, body, might not be her?"

Cass shrugged. "That's what the detective said, but they'll know soon enough. They have my DNA, remember? They're going to call me in the morning."

DNA. Bloody hell. Tom remembered Cass recounting what a big deal it had been for him to hand his DNA over to the police at the tender age of sixteen. It went against everything he'd ever feared, but at the time he would've done anything to end the Dolly's pain. She'd never got over not knowing the fate of her daughter. "Where's your phone?"

"In my pocket."

"Is it on? We've been calling you all night."

"I didn't even notice." Cass pulled it out. The screen was blank. "What time is it?"

"Just after three. We should get a night bus to Hampstead and get some sleep."

Cass turned his phone on. "You go. I'm going to stay here until they call me. Doesn't feel right being anywhere else."

Tom didn't understand, but he was coming to the conclusion that he probably never would. He swiped at his stinging eyes. "I'm not leaving you, but I need to call Jake. He's worried. We both bailed on him."

Jake's name seemed to bring Cass back to life. "How much does he know?"

"Nowhere near enough. You garbled some shit at me, and ran off, then I pretty much did the same to him."

Cass swore. "I'm sorry I ran out on you. I always figured I'd be ready for that call, but maybe I didn't believe it would ever come."

"Do they, um . . ." Tom measured his words. "Whoever this, uh, person is. Do they know how they died?"

"No, but they were wrapped in an industrial-grade bin liner and stuffed in a bag, so I'm guessing it wasn't a pretty end."

Tom retrieved his own phone with shaking hands. "Don't say it like that."

"Like what?"

"Like you're a cold-hearted bastard, because I know you're not."

"Aren't I? Why are you looking at me like I killed your dog, then?"

Cass turned his attention back to the window. Tom wanted to shake him.

"Stop it," he said. "Whatever bullshit you're throwing my way to shut me down, forget it, okay? I'm not doing this with you again. It's not just about you and me anymore. What about Jake? We made him promises, and yet here we are, without him, making a fucking mess of it."

Cass made a sound. It could've been a grunt of disagreement, but Tom's phone rang in his hand before he could figure it out.

Jake.

Tom connected the call. "Why aren't you asleep?"

"Where was he?"

Tom winced; Jake sounded exhausted. "Exactly where you said he'd be."

"I didn't say he'd be anywhere. Is he okay?"

"Ask him yourself." Tom activated the speakerphone and held it out.

Cass glared, but then Jake called his name and everything changed. *Cass* changed. The hard-faced cockney boy faded away and his eyes filled with tears. "Jake?"

Jake muttered something unintelligible. "Where've you been? You drove off like a right wanker. Are you okay?"

"Yeah, I'm good. Just a rough day."

This time, there was no mistaking Jake's growl. "A rough fucking day? Jesus, Cass. Who do you think you're fooling?"

Cass took the phone from Tom's hand and turned off the speakerphone. "I'm not trying to fool anyone. There's just so much you—"

Jake snapped something. Cass smiled. "Are you doing that thing you do with your thumbs when you're really pissed off?"

Silence. Cass's faint grin evaporated. He ducked his head and brought his hand to his face. "I know, mate. I know. I will, I promise, but I've got a lot to tell you first. Make yourself comfortable."

CHAPTER TWENTY

om fell asleep listening to Cass tell Jake his life story, and he awoke slouched down on the plastic-wrapped bed with a crick in his neck. He got up, stretched, and glanced at his phone. Nine o'clock. Bloody hell. He couldn't remember the last time he'd slept that late. Perhaps going to bed at 5 a.m. was the answer.

He searched out Cass and found him sitting on the living room floor, smoking again, and flicking through some dusty photo albums. Tom paused in the doorway. He was two years older than Cass, but he'd had a good life, a safe life. He'd only seen the dark parts of the world through Cass's eyes. And at twenty-eight, Cass had seen *far* too much, so why did he look so young right now?

Cass stubbed out his cigarette. He stood, and for a moment, they stared at each other, then Tom crossed the room and folded Cass into his arms. He buried his face in Cass's hair. "I'm so sorry. I should've done this last night."

"Don't be sorry, Tom." Cass trembled. Tom hugged him tighter until Cass pulled away. "It's not like I haven't fucked you over before."

Tom shook his head and kept Cass close. "This isn't your fault, Cass. None of it is, and I'm sorry I got angry, okay? I was worried and—"

"Scared?" Cass let Tom draw him to the couch and sit them both down. "I was scared too. I didn't want . . . I've *never* wanted this anywhere near you, but Jake . . ." Cass blew out a breath. "I didn't want him to see this either, but I talked to him for a long time while you were asleep, and he chewed my fucking ear off. And yeah, maybe it wasn't my decision to make. I get that now . . . maybe. Thanks to Jake."

Tom smiled a little, though it didn't feel quite right in their bleak surroundings. "He's like that. I worried for ages that he let this . . . thing develop between us because he had nothing else, but I see the way he looks at you now, and I know he loves you."

Cass snorted. "And there's never been any doubt he loves *you*. Poor kid was head over heels from day one."

Tom let his smile widen, then he sobered. "Was he okay? He doesn't do so well when he's tired."

"He didn't sound great, but I got him to promise he'd sleep all day until we came home. Figured that was the best I could do."

"Have *you* slept?"

Cass shook his head and glanced at his phone lying dormant on the coffee table. "I will, but I need to know first. I feel like I'm in some weird vortex."

Tom let him have that, and got up to find something to drink. He washed out two dusty glasses and filled them with water. Cass had his nose in another photo album when he came back. Tom gave him some space, but eventually the silence began to grate, and he felt the need to break it, fill it, anything to stop it choking him. "I'm trying to picture you going willingly to a police station. I can't do it."

Cass kept his gaze on the album. "It wasn't easy. I've been dragged into Brixton before, kicking and screaming, but they've done it up. Hardly recognised the place."

"That's good, right? Maybe you've moved on."

Cass chuckled, though it held little humour. "I still hate cop shops, Tom. I threw up as soon as I got out. Felt like I'd escaped a bloody apocalypse."

A cacophony of images flickered through Tom's mind, none of them pleasant, of Cass so distressed and alone he'd made himself sick. Perhaps silence was better after all.

Tom reclaimed his space on the couch. He put his arm around Cass and peered over his shoulder for a while, but when he saw Cass begin to lose his battle with fatigue, he gently took the album away and persuaded Cass to lean on him. He held him for a long time, and Cass grew so quiet and still he was almost convinced he'd dozed off.

Then Cass's phone rang, and they both jumped out of their skins.

Cass lunged for the phone. Tom caught him before he fell off the couch and kept him upright as he connected the call.

Cass listened. His face became a study in impassivity, and Tom strained to hear both sides of the conversation, anything to clue him in to what would come next. For endless minutes, his world narrowed to the frustrating mix of Cass's one-word answers and inscrutable frown.

Then Cass hung up. He set his phone on the arm of the couch with undue care. "It's her."

Nausea burned in Tom's stomach. He thought of his own mother, like he had so many times before, and tried to imagine she'd been left to rot in a bin liner for fourteen years. His stomach turned over again. He made a clumsy grab for Cass's hand. "Shit."

Cass nodded. He looked as stunned as Tom felt, but his reaction seemed muted, like he'd exhausted himself worrying and the end result was an anticlimax.

Tom didn't know what to say. Cass got up and walked to the window. He stared out over one of London's most deprived boroughs and shook his head. "The detective said they've got a few vague leads for how she died, but I feel like it doesn't matter, like I don't really care, even if we never find out. That's weird, right?"

"I don't know." And, really, who did? There was nothing normal about the situation they'd found themselves in. "Are you . . . Do you need anything?"

Cass shook his head again and reached for the pack of cigarettes he'd stuffed in his pocket. Tom waited for him to shake one out and light it, but he didn't. He dumped them on the windowsill and turned his back on them. "Can we go to Clapham? I need to see Dolly."

They went to Brixton first and retrieved Cass's car. Dolly's nursing home wasn't far away, but despite his eerie composure, Cass wasn't happy leaving his car in the car park of a police station.

Tom drove them back to the East End. Cass said little for much of the journey, and the silence got under Tom's skin again. The round-trip, though short in distance, took an hour in the city traffic, and he felt ready to combust by the time they reached the nursing home.

Cass got out of the car and glanced around. He'd only visited Dolly here once, a long time ago, and the converted factory had changed a lot since then. A recent refurbishment had transformed the exterior of the home, and perhaps Cass was looking at the landscaped car park and swish revolving doors and thinking they'd come to the wrong place.

Tom took his arm. "Come on."

He led the way into the spotless reception area. The woman behind the desk smiled, handed him the visitor's book and cast a curious gaze over Cass. Tom filled out the visitor form and took his sticker from the receptionist. Cass did the same, but seemed lost.

Tom squeezed his hand. "Her room's this way. She used to have pottery in the mornings, but she likes to take a nap now."

That was putting it kindly. Dolly hadn't taken to any of the therapeutic treatments the home offered as part of its dementia care package. Music, art, and exercise: she'd shunned them all, preferring to scream rude things at her fellow patients and throw her belongings at the staff. It wasn't an uncommon reaction, according to the nice nurse who'd once mistaken Tom for Cass, but it meant Dolly spent much of her time alone in her room, a far cry from her days as a trader on the rowdy East End markets.

Dolly's room was on the first floor. They found the door open. Tom half expected Cass to freeze up in the corridor, but he didn't, and if he was shocked by the wizened creature dozing in the rocking chair, Tom couldn't tell. Cass walked into the room like he'd done it a hundred times.

Cass drew a chair up close to Dolly. He stroked her white hair away from her face and took her hand. "Nana?"

Tom's heart broke. Cass had never called Dolly "Nana" in front of him before, at least not when he'd been aware of his presence. The term of endearment had been one he saved for her, and only her.

And Dolly heard him now. She stirred and opened the dark-blue eyes that held so much of Cass. She didn't speak, but for a moment, Tom saw recognition flicker in her cloudy gaze, a gaze that had once been sharp enough to make grown men shake.

The spark faded even as Tom convinced himself it was real, but Cass didn't seem to notice. He squeezed Dolly's hand. "I'm sorry I haven't been by in a while, but I've got something to tell you. They found Faye. The police. They found her body. She died, Nana. She died a long time ago, like we always thought."

Dolly's eyes watered, though that wasn't unusual. Cass pulled a tissue from a nearby box and wiped her tears away. "They found her in Lambeth. Remember you used to say you could feel her close by? Turns out you were right. The police think she could've OD'd in a squat somewhere, and someone hid her body to stop the police raiding their stash. Or . . ." Cass paused, like he was steeling himself, though he was surely past the worst. "She could've been killed . . . murdered, by a john, or someone else. They reckon they'll let me know if they find anything, but I'm not sure I want them to. You always said it didn't matter . . . that you just wanted to know one way or the other. I didn't get it at the time, but I think I do now."

Cass stopped for breath. Dolly stared at him, and something seemed to pass between them that made Cass smile. "There's something else I need to tell you," he said. "Me and Tom, we've met someone else. He lives with us now, and he reminds me of you sometimes. He's clever and kind, and he has this honest grin that lights up the world."

Dolly smiled at that, a loopy half smile that said though Cass's words meant little to her anymore, she'd understood the sentiment.

"He says weird things too," Cass went on. "Stuff that sounds like a riddle, until I realise it makes perfect sense. You'd love him, Nana. We do."

Tom had heard enough then. He slipped unnoticed out of the room and left Cass to it. The nursing home had a pretty garden, part of the reason he'd chosen it for Dolly, to give her something she'd never had, and he drifted along until he found a bench by a patch of lavender. He closed his eyes for a while and breathed it in. He wasn't much for sleeping, but the snatched few hours bent in half on Cass's childhood bed hadn't been nearly enough. He felt shattered, wrecked, and more than anything, he wanted to wrap Cass in his arms and take him home. Home to Jake.

Jake. Tom opened his eyes. He wanted to call him, but knowing he'd been on the phone with Cass until sunrise, he let him be. Exhausted, he stared up at the sky and considered calling his own mother, but he didn't know what he'd say to her. His parents had welcomed Cass—and Jake—with open arms, but they'd never understood the fire that burned for Cass deep in Tom's belly. Never understood how a broken East End car thief had stolen his heart so entirely.

But stolen his heart he had, and Tom felt the world shift when warm hands touched his shoulders from behind. He turned and smiled up at Cass, squinting in the sunlight. "All right?"

Cass stooped a little so Tom could see his face. He looked drawn and tired, but there was a peace in his gaze Tom hadn't expected. "I'm so fucked. Can we go home?"

"Of course." Tom stood and stretched. He felt a hundred years old. "How did it go with Dolly?"

Cass shrugged. "I promised her I'd get the bracelet for her. I hope the police let me have it in time. I think she's going to die soon."

Tom couldn't argue with that. "Are you going to come back, then?"

"Yeah. Tomorrow. Do you think Nero would cover Pippa's?"

Tom cupped Cass's face and traced the shadows under his eyes with his thumbs. "I sent him over last night, and he's there for the rest of the week. Take as much time as you need. We'll figure it out."

Cass closed his eyes. "You always know what to do."

If only. "Can I ask you something?"

"Anything."

Tom pressed his cheek against Cass's and searched for the words to voice what had been on his mind since that fateful phone call the night before. *Shit. Was that only yesterday?* "Do you feel different now that you know?"

"That Faye's dead?"

"Yeah."

Cass thought on it a moment, then lifted his shoulders in a listless shrug. "Maybe. I feel . . . I dunno, lighter, I s'pose, like I can get on with my life. It never felt right before, knowing she was out there somewhere while you made me so fucking happy."

Tom pulled back and tilted Cass's face until he found his gaze. "*That's* why you've pushed me away all these years? Because you didn't think you deserved a life while Faye was missing? Fucking hell, Cass.

You're not her. You never have been. You had the same shitty start in life and look at what—look at who you are. You deserve everything."

Cass shook his head. "No, I don't, or at least, I didn't. Maybe now, shit. I don't know. I don't know anything except I love the bones off you and I need to see Jake before I bloody combust."

Tom held Cass firm for a long moment and felt the weight hanging over them break its bonds and float away. "You can't hide from me anymore. I can't bloody stand it, Cass. I need you and Jake as much—more than you think you need me."

Cass opened his mouth, but Tom silenced him with a kiss.

"I don't need your promises. I just need you to do it." Tom released Cass and nodded towards the car park. "Let's go home. I need our bed, and so do you."

Tom drove them home. He expected to find Jake passed out on the couch, or even in bed, but the front door opened before he'd killed the engine.

Jake met them on the path, barefoot and dressed in a pair of Cass's tracksuit bottoms and one of Tom's sweatshirts, hair sticking up in every direction. The jumper was huge and made him feel even lighter as Tom lifted him off the ground.

Jake hugged him tight, then squirmed and reached for Cass. He embraced him so hard Tom was sure Cass could barely breathe. "I'm so sorry you had to do this. I love you. Shit. *Wankers*. I do. I love you."

Tom would never know if Jake meant to articulate himself so beautifully, and hearing Cass return the sentiment was better than bloody Shakespeare. He took them both by the arm and steered them towards the open front door. "I love you both, but I'll love you even more if you take this indoors. It's bloody freezing out here."

He guided them inside and dispatched Cass to find some comfortable clothes while he built a fire. They regrouped in the living room and set up camp on the couch with a bottle of wine and a bowl each of Cass's secret stash of Angel Delight.

"We need a bigger sofa," Cass said later from his position squished between Tom and Jake. The wine had gone straight to his head, and despite the horrendous twenty-four hours he'd just lived through, he seemed content.

Tom rolled his eyes. "It's a corner couch. How much bigger can you get?"

"There's no room for the cat." Cass put his bowl on the floor and dumped his feet in Tom's lap. He was already using Jake as a pillow. "And she hates this couch."

Jake laughed. "How can you tell?"

"Because . . ." Cass broke off to yawn. "She always dumps dead mice down the back of it in the summer."

"They're not always dead," Tom said dryly. "Remember the live one she dropped in the CD rack?"

"No." Cass seemed bemused. "I think you made that up."

"Whatever." Tom retrieved his bowl from the arm of the couch, scraped the last of his Angel Delight onto his spoon, and held it up to Cass's mouth. "Perhaps you weren't here. You know how she likes to torment me."

Cass licked Tom's spoon, then his face fell serious. "I want to do something about that, about me, and you, not being around enough." He glanced at Jake. "I'm going to offer Nero the rooms over Pippa's, maybe get him out of Pink's a bit more, and I think we should ditch the flat. Buy it and rent it out, or just sack it off completely. I want to come home every night . . . come here. I don't want work to get in the way anymore."

Jake said nothing, but the gleam in his eyes told Tom this was something he and Cass had cooked up between them.

Tom rubbed Cass's feet and wished he could reach Jake without bending them all in half. "I want what you want, but I don't want you knackering yourself. Driving in and out of the city every day is brutal."

Cass opened his mouth, and Tom knew he was gearing up to say he didn't care, but Jake cut him off.

"Wouldn't matter if you worked less. I think you should take Friday nights and Sundays off, both of you. Cass, Gloria told me you have a second chef bloke who can handle Sundays, and Tom, *you* told me you only work Sundays because Cass does."

Jake rounded off his lecture with a flurry of tics. Cass passed him the wine and rubbed his chest. No one spoke for a while, but Tom could see the storm raging behind Cass's tired eyes. Pippa's had been his baby from the moment they'd drafted the business plan and taken it, cap in hand, to the bank. It was the first time they'd combined their skills and passions and created something together, and leaving the Sunday service to someone else would be a huge deal for him.

So Tom expected Cass to shrug it off, to deflect it as a pipe dream to come back to another day. He nearly fell off the sofa when Cass answered at last.

"My second at Pippa's is a banging chef, and he's better with the team than I am. I'm going to train him up to take over from me. After that, who knows? Maybe I'll get that dog Tom won't let me have."

Warmth crept through Tom's chest and into his veins. Cass could have a whole pack of bloody dogs if it meant he was home to take care of them. He met Jake's bright grin, absorbed his muttered tic about flying to the moon, and felt like his heart would combust.

Cass put his half-empty wineglass down and snuggled into Jake. He was knackered, and Tom knew he'd be fast asleep the next time he turned their way. Jake slouched down too, resting his cheek on Cass's head. Tom wanted to carry them both to bed, but failing that, he got up to search out some blankets. They were sound asleep when he got back. He knelt on the hardwood floor, a hand on each of them, and in awe of the men who made his life complete. Cass was the love of his life, and Jake . . . Jake had taught them to love each other better.

Jake had taught them to live.

CASS

EPILOGUE

Cass Pearson dusted off his nana's headstone. It had only been up a few weeks, but it was already losing the glittery sheen it had come with. He traced the engraving with his fingertip. His granddad had been in this grave for twenty-nine years, but Cass had ditched his old headstone and ordered a new one for them both. Dolly had loved shiny new things.

He sat back on his heels and inspected his handiwork. Daisies, lavender, and thyme. In the spring he'd plant daffodils. A stray dandelion caught his eye. He left it there. Dolly had a thing for dandelions. Said they were wild and free, like the birds.

Cass closed his eyes. In the sky above, he could hear the starlings calling each other, and the distant hum of the traffic. A sense of calm washed over him, the kind of peace he only ever felt when he was visiting the dead. Graveyards were tranquil places, even in the hustle and bustle of east London, and he sat, content, until a stirring in his heart told him it was time to go.

He stood and brushed the dirt from his knees. In the distance, he saw Jake loitering by the cemetery gate, smoking, and clearly doing his best to be quiet. Cass smiled. Jake always made him feel better. Dolly had died ten days after Cass told her Faye was dead. He'd been by her side, his fingers hooked in the bracelet on her wrist, and afterwards, he'd driven to Bites and found Jake making banana cake with Ethel. That day, despite his grief, all had seemed strangely right with the world. Like a chapter of his past had come to an end, but his future remained entwined with everything he had left.

Cass reached Jake and pinched the last of his smoke. Jake scowled, but punctuated it with a gentle kiss that smelled of smoke and Jake. A kiss that smelled perfect. They'd promised Tom they'd quit the fags, but sometimes, these stolen moments felt too good to give up.

Jake snuggled closer and put his hands in Cass's back pockets. "Are you ready to go?"

Cass cast a final glance behind him and nodded. "Damn straight."

They caught the underground to Camden Town. On the crowded train, Jake stood behind Cass and buzzed away to himself while Cass stared at the empty black windows. At home when the TS took over, Jake would curl into Cass and hide his face while Cass rubbed his back. Often the tics would subside, but on the Tube two blokes embracing attracted as many stares as the ticking, so Cass let him be. Instead, his mind drifted. It had been six months since Faye's remains had been found in Brixton, and the police had yet to release them to Cass. Not that he knew what he'd do with them. Bury them? Burn them? Put them in the ground with Dolly?

No fucking way. Cass shuddered. He wasn't much for religion and faith in an afterlife, but he believed Dolly was at peace now. He couldn't bear the thought of Faye tormenting her beyond the grave.

Jake nudged him. Cass looked away from the window, unsure if Jake needed him or had hit him by accident.

"Shh. *There's rats in here.*"

An accident, then, but Cass gave Jake his full attention. The rats tic often meant he was nervous, and Cass was pretty sure he knew why.

"Chill your beans, mate. He's going to love it."

Jake rolled his eyes. "How do you do that?"

"What?"

"Read my mind."

"I don't read anything. I listen."

"Eh?" Jake's puzzled frown made him seem far younger than his twenty-five years.

Cass held up his hand and counted off his fingers. "Flying to the moon makes you happy. Wankers annoy you. Rats make you nervous. And the only thing I can think that's making you nervous right now is showing Tom the restaurant tonight."

Jake growled. A nearby man stared, but Cass stared right back until he dropped his gaze. Jake trod on his foot. "Stop it."

"What?"

"Being aggressive. You promised Tom you wouldn't hit anyone for a whole year."

Jake had him there. The three of them had sat up many nights over the past six months and hashed out what they all needed to make their unconventional relationship work, but it turned out each of them wanted very little in return for their love and trust. Tom wanted Jake to believe in himself, and Cass to think before he lost his rag and punched people. Think before he flipped his shit and ran off into the night.

"Don't run from me anymore," he'd said.

Cass couldn't argue with that, and he could argue even less with Jake's desire for them all to just *be*.

The trained grumbled into Camden. They jostled their way off and made the short walk to the restaurant site. The old fire station was beautiful, as always, but something caught Cass's eye.

"Wow. They fitted the sign."

Jake bounced on the balls of his feet. "There's rats in there. Do you like it?"

Cass took in the simple, clean branding. Took in the name that had come to Jake and Cass late one night while Tom slept between them. *Misfits.* It was perfect. "I love it, and Tom will too, so stop jigging about and let me inside to see what else you've been doing."

Jake pushed open the restaurant door. Cass had spent the past few weeks training the Misfits team at Pippa's, but though he'd seen the prep areas of the new restaurant and developed the open-plan kitchen himself, he'd yet to see the dining areas set up for service, and Tom hadn't either. The Camden project had changed their lives in more ways than one, and Misfits had become entirely Jake's vision. Tom had given him a budget and taken a big fat step back, and it had turned out to be the most canny business decision he'd ever made.

Not that he knew it yet, and Cass couldn't wait to see his face when he did. The funky, hipster burger bar was everything Tom had dreamed of when he'd founded Urban Soul all those years ago. Unique, eclectic, and cool, it was Jake all over, but it fit their core values and ethos like a glove. Style with a conscience.

Hell yeah.

Cass gazed around the dining area. Most of the tables were still bare, but Jake had laid out the one closest to the vintage fire engine the night before. He moved past Cass and turned on the low-hanging lights. The restaurant caught the best of the sun during the day, but in the evenings it was going to look epic.

It's all going to be epic.

Cass stared at the table. It looked awesome, but it took him a minute to figure out the punch line. "Bloody hell. Nothing's the same."

Jake snorted. "Took you long enough to notice."

"Shut up." Cass bent over the table and stared, but sure enough, no glass, plate, or piece of cutlery was the same. Nothing matched, nothing at all.

Misfits. Fuck. Cass burst out laughing. "Fuck me. When you named this place, I thought you were talking about us. You could've told me you meant the plates, mate."

Jake stepped into Cass's personal space. "I was—I am talking about us. The plates are a coincidence, and I'm thinking a pretty dodgy one now. Tom's going to go ape, isn't he?"

"You're taking the piss, right?" Cass held a smoked-glass champagne flute up to the light. It reminded him of a bowl Dolly had kept behind the cheese grater for the sole purpose of mixing egg mayonnaise for picnic sandwiches. To use it for anything else had been considered sacrilege. "You spent less than half the money he gave you and the place looks—"

"Fucking incredible."

Cass and Jake jumped in unison. Cass spun around and found Tom behind them, his smile a mile wide. "Hey! You're not supposed to be here until tonight."

Tom shrugged, unrepentant. "So call me an impatient twat. I don't care. I'm done waiting. I want to see it all."

Later that day found Cass in a place where, professionally at least, he felt most at ease. Misfits's kitchen was exposed, and the pressure of supervising a fledgling team on an opening night was always brutal, but tonight, the kitchen was flying. Opening nights were usually Tom's thing, but it felt different this time, and with the buzz of the kicking restaurant and Nero along for the ride, Cass was on cloud nine.

He checked his whites for obvious grease stains, then left the grill in Nero's capable hands and searched out his partners in crime.

Tom was easy to spot. He'd cut his teeth in the restaurant business as a student waiting tables in a busy London gastropub, and the opening night of any restaurant found him bussing tables and scraping plates with the troops. Cass caught his eye and grinned. Tom returned the smile and inclined his head to the old fire station's open staircase. Cass followed his gaze. Jake stood on the second floor of the restaurant, leaning on the railing, watching, taking in the result of a year of hard work. His hard work.

Cass headed over and climbed the stairs. Jake saw him coming and raised his hand in an absent wave. Cass took his place beside him and looked out over the restaurant. "You done good, mate."

Jake shrugged. "You and Tom are good teachers, and I had a lot of time to get it right."

He wasn't wrong there. The Camden project—Misfits—had fallen way behind schedule when Tom and Jake had taken a few weeks out to support Cass through Dolly's last days. The whole company had felt their absence. As if Cass had ever needed reminding how hard Tom and Jake worked. How hard they *all* worked, and how much that needed to change.

Jake touched his arm. "It feels weird seeing it in motion. It's been on my computer screen for so long."

"Think you've got the bug?"

"Um . . ." Jake thought on that a moment, then shook his head. "I started this because I needed a job, then I carried on because I fancied Tom. I finished it because he convinced me I'd be proud of it, and I am, but I wouldn't want to do it again."

Cass chuckled. Jake looked worried, like he thought Cass would be disappointed, but he wasn't, far from it. They all knew Jake's passion lay in web design and managing the company's growing social media presence, and that he was far happier working from home with the cat for company than negotiating planning permissions and sourcing crockery. "Then don't do it again. You can do whatever you like."

"I liked watching you cook tonight."

"Yeah? Why's that?" Cass glanced at the kitchen, but Nero appeared to have everything under control. "You've seen me cook a hundred times before."

"Not like this. You're different at home. Here . . ." Jake popped and shook his head. "You look like someone else."

Cass rolled his eyes. "And you like it? Cheers, mate."

"I didn't mean it like that, I just meant it was hot, and I know Tom thinks so. He can't take his eyes off you."

Cass felt the part of his heart reserved for Tom light up. He knew Tom was proud of him, of them all, and knowing Jake knew it too made him feel more sentimental than he cared to admit in the middle of a crowded restaurant. "Did you call your mum?"

Jake shrugged. "Last night while you were out getting dinner. She invited me to my stepdad's birthday party."

"That's good, isn't it?"

Jake clicked. "I don't know. I think she'd had a few vinos. She might change her mind."

Cass didn't know what to say to that. He found Jake's hand and squeezed. "Well, if she doesn't change her mind, you should take Tom with you. Everyone loves Tom."

"Would you come?"

"Me?" Cass hadn't considered that. Tom's family had accepted their three-way relationship with little comment, but Cass wasn't naïve enough to believe they'd be so lucky with the rest of the world. If Jake wanted him there, though, he'd be there. He'd always be there. "Sure. Just let me know the date. I'll get Pippa's covered."

"Not if it's a Thursday."

Jake shot Cass a sideways grin, and Cass grinned right back. In the last six months, he'd cut his hours at Pippa's in half and every Thursday he got Jake all to himself, since Tom made a point of being elsewhere, much like Jake did on Mondays. With Saturday's being Jake and Tom's day, and Sundays the sacred day they all spent off together, life was good. Better than good. Life was awesome.

Cass took Jake's arm and tugged him towards the bar. "Come on. Let's kidnap Tom and go get drunk. We've earned it."

Jake pushed Cass down on the bed. Clothes had disappeared long ago, littering the stairs and the landing, and now it was just them, bare, and wanting.

And, fuck, Cass was wanting. He wanted it all.

He kissed Jake hard, reaching for Tom. His hands found the warm flesh of his chest—fine hair, muscle, and bone. He grasped at it with clumsy hands until Tom's lips replaced Jake's.

Tom's kiss was rough and bruising, the way Cass liked it. They wrestled for dominance until Cass fell slack, content to let Tom own him.

Let them both own him.

Cass shared another biting, bruising kiss with Tom as Jake climbed over him. "I want you to fuck me, and I want Tom to fuck you. That okay?"

Jake bit down on Cass's pierced nipple. Cass gasped and arched his back, wondering how this was going to play out. Jake had fucked him a few times, but never in front of Tom, and he'd never been the one in the middle. Being the most versatile, Cass usually got that privilege, but he didn't want that tonight. Tonight was about Jake, in every way.

Tom moved behind Jake and rubbed his back. "I'd like to see that," he whispered. "I've never seen Cass get fucked before. Never could, but I'd like to see you do it."

Jake groaned. "I want to do it, but I don't know if I can handle you both."

Cass understood his desperation. The first time he'd found himself in a Tom-Jake sandwich, he'd shot his load in ten seconds flat.

He tugged Jake down for a kiss. "We'll look after you. Just enjoy it."

It was persuasion enough for Jake. He took Cass into his mouth and worked his fingers inside him until Cass writhed and begged for more. His legs shook and his back arched. He needed Jake.

But he had to wait. Tom had a big cock, and Jake needed to be readied too.

Jake rose up on all fours while Tom prepared him. Cass gripped Jake's dick, found the rhythm of Tom's tongue behind and matched it.

"*Fuck.*" Jake hung his head. His arms trembled. "I can't . . . God, you're going to make me come."

Tom eased off and kissed his way up Jake's spine. "Yeah? You ready?"

Jake nodded, breathless. "Cass first."

Cass lay still; it was best for everyone if he let Jake take charge. Sex between them all was sometimes too hot to handle. Often, Cass got rowdy and people fell over. Then Tom got cross and Jake laughed, and no one got to come. A bloody shambles, that's what it was unless Jake called the shots.

And it wasn't about who put what where. It never had been. It was about holding Tom and Jake in his arms and loving them for everything they'd done for him.

Jake rolled a condom on and climbed over Cass again. He was still a nervous top, but they'd practiced this when Tom wasn't home and they had it down. Cass widened his legs and raised his hips, met Jake in the middle, and took him deep inside his body.

His breath caught in his chest. Jake wasn't as big as Tom, but there was an edge to the push and slide of his cock that made Cass's eyes water.

Jake gentled his movements to a barely there rhythm. He stared at Cass, and in the dim light of the room, his dark gaze seemed to gleam. "Okay?"

Cass nodded. He was more than okay. "I'm good."

Jake rolled his hips. The motion was nothing like the slamming thrusts Cass often craved from Tom, but he felt it in every part of his body. He let out a long breath and gripped the hand Tom offered him. "Yeah, do it like that."

"Like this?" Jake teased.

Cass groaned and screwed his eyes shut. "Just *do* it."

Jake laughed and fucked Cass for a while, slow and deep, a way he never knew could feel so good until the first time Jake had eased inside him. Cass shook and whimpered, and it was only Tom's grounding hands that kept him from screaming and blowing his load.

Then it all stopped. Tom kissed Cass's fingertips, one by one, then moved behind Jake and pushed him down, chest first, onto Cass.

Cass gasped. Jake was still buried inside him, and everything was about to get a million times hotter. He held Jake tight, soothing him as Tom breached him. He'd watched Tom and Jake fuck more times than he could count, but it never got old. From the very first time, it had blown his mind.

Jake panted out a curse, cheeks flushed, eyes wide, and from that point on, Tom had them both, owned them both, and they were powerless beneath him, enthralled by him, as they always had been.

Tom took his time, holding Jake in place in a gentle grip with one hand, and soothing Cass with the other, constantly mindful of the care and balance it took to keep them all joined together, in every way possible. Cass watched Jake's heated blood bloom beneath his pale skin, and the vein throb in Tom's temple. Felt them sweat and shake until his own climax crept up on him.

Cass grabbed the headboard and gritted his teeth, trying to delay the inevitable, but it was no good. It was Jake's cock inside him, but, fuck, he felt Tom too, felt them both, everywhere, and it was too much. He came with a guttural shout; Jake wasn't far behind, and they clung to each other, trembling.

Afterwards, Jake lay prone, exhausted. Tom withdrew from him and disposed of the condom. Cass put an arm around Jake and beckoned Tom closer. Tapped his lips. "Come in my mouth."

Tom slid his cock past Cass's lips. He was rock hard, legs shaking, and it wasn't long before he tensed and groaned. The gravelly moan rumbled through Cass who opened his throat and grazed Tom's cock with his teeth.

"*Cass*." Tom jerked. Release ripped through him, and Cass felt every shudder and jolt like it was his own. "Fuck, Cass . . . Jesus Christ."

Panting, Tom pulled his dick slowly from Cass's mouth, kissed him, murmured his love, then turned his attention to Jake, who was already half-asleep. "Jake, wake up a sec."

Cass chuckled as Jake moaned. Sex always knocked him out, but Tom manoeuvred him enough to retrieve the condom and wipe the sticky mess of Cass's release from between them. He left the bed to get rid of the detritus. While he was gone, Jake rolled over, taking Cass with him, and curled into his chest.

Cass wrapped his arms around him. His heart ached for Tom, but he was back before Cass could really miss him. Tom pulled the covers up the bed and tucked them tight around Jake, then he lay down behind Cass and kissed his cheek. "Hold him, and I'll hold you. All night, I promise."

Cass woke up wrapped entangled in Jake, with Tom's warmth at his back. Jake was fast asleep, sprawled out on his stomach, but Cass knew before he even opened his eyes that Tom was wide-awake. Of course he was. A lot had changed in the past year, but never that.

Tom rubbed Cass's arm. "You with me yet?"

Cass smiled and stretched, and then, because it felt wrong to turn away from Jake, he climbed over him and held Tom's hand over Jake's back. "My head hurts."

Tom rolled his eyes. "Not surprised. Anything else sore?"

"Very funny." Cass quite liked it when he woke up aching from his encounters with Tom, but he didn't miss it this morning. Getting topped by Jake, even with Tom calling the shots from behind, had been a whole new world. Jake's loving was a beautiful contradiction of fierce and gentle, and even with a brewing hangover, Cass felt amazing.

A flash of colour caught his eye. "Did you put flowers in here?"

"Yep." Tom glanced behind him at the vase of pink dahlias on the bedside table. "They're from the bush my mum planted when we first moved in. I caught Souris gearing up to piss on them, so I thought I'd bring them indoors. They've been in here two days."

Cass hadn't noticed, but the thought of Tom picking flowers in the garden made him smile, especially with the added image of Souris stalking his every move. "You're so gay."

Tom raised his middle finger. "Lucky for you, eh?"

Cass squeezed Tom's other hand. "Lucky for all of us."

Tom smiled, but Cass could tell his thoughts were elsewhere.

"Something on your mind?"

"Hmm?" Tom brushed his thumb along the bumps in Jake's spine. "Oh, not really. At least, nothing bad."

Cass yawned. "Spill. It's too early for introspection."

"It's not that early," Tom countered. "But if you really want to know, perhaps you can tell me something."

"That doesn't make any sense."

Tom rolled his eyes, but then his gaze fell on Jake, still sleeping peacefully, and his expression softened. "How did you really feel when you first found him in our bed at the flat?"

That woke Cass up. "You're asking me *now*?"

"I asked you at the time, but you never gave me an answer."

Cass took over tracing patterns on Jake's beautiful bare skin and thought back to another morning he'd found Jake in bed, fast asleep. "I didn't feel anything to start with. Messing around with other blokes had always felt right until that point."

"What changed?"

Cass considered the question, and found his answer was more convoluted than he'd ever realised. Jake and Tom were two of a kind, both one of those rare beings that set the world alight with just a gentle smile. Cass had felt no jealousy when he'd discovered Jake in their bed, the sheets rumpled with sex and sleep. No, he'd only felt hope . . . hope that Tom would finally get the life he deserved, a life where his lover didn't beat him back and shut him out. A life that made his smile reach his eyes every bloody time.

But it was more than that. Deeper. Cass kissed Jake's shoulder. Breathed him in. "He didn't hear me come in that morning. I'd watched him for ages before he woke up and punched himself, really hard, you know? Like he hated himself, then he looked at me, and I just wanted to rub his chest better. I never really got over that."

"Know the feeling." Tom sounded wistful. "When I figured out you felt the same way about him as I did, I thought I was the luckiest bloke in the world."

"And now?"

"I still feel like that, but it's changed over the past few months. I feel like it's . . . I don't know, solidified? Like it's permanent. I don't feel like we're searching for something anymore, that make sense?"

It did. The bond between the three of them felt perfect. Tom and Cass had their past, and Jake was their future: the link they'd never known was missing. Cass had always believed Tom to be his one great love, but he loved Jake too, just as much, and somehow it all seemed to work.

"It makes sense," Cass said. "I was lucky before, but now, I can hardly remember what it was like without him."

Tom smiled, and he didn't need to say he felt the same. Tom had never hidden his heart from Cass. It was in every touch, every kiss. It was in the gentle fingertip he traced over Cass's lips. He loved Cass, lived for him, and that would never change.

Jake stirred. His hand twitched and he muttered something into the pillow. Tom and Cass leaned away in unison. Jake's tics were often explosive when he first woke up, and he got upset if he hit one of them.

But that didn't happen this morning. Jake buzzed a few times, then opened his eyes and stretched like a cat. He stared, sphinxlike at Cass for a moment before his gaze flickered to Tom.

"Why are you both looking at me like that?"

"Because we love you." Tom kissed Jake's cheek. "Cass was just telling me how smitten he is."

Jake scowled. Cass took pity on him and ruffled his hair, but with Jake awake, he was reminded of something important he'd forgotten to do the day before. Something really bloody important.

Damn threesomes are too distracting.

Cass slid out of bed and felt Jake's curious eyes on him. Unless he was working, Cass never got out of bed first.

"Don't worry," Tom said. "He'll be back in a minute."

Cass padded downstairs to the kitchen where Tom had dumped his bag the night before. He flipped through the papers in the laptop case until he came across a nondescript folder and took it back upstairs with more trepidation than he cared to admit. The folder contained something that would either make Jake's day, or *really* piss him off.

Jake jerked upright, like he knew Cass was handling an unexploded bomb. "What's that?"

Cass stalled. He wanted to pass it off to Tom, so he got the blame if it all went wrong, but he couldn't do it. Tom had given Cass everything—love, security, a home, but more than that, he'd given him a life, a life with promise, prospects, and a future.

It was time to pay it forward.

Cass pushed the folder into Jake's hands. "It's for you."

"For me?" Jake opened the file. "What is it? Something for the new project?"

"Not quite." Cass waited, tense. He and Jake had recently started work on setting up a new food bank in Stratford, supplied with surplus goods from local restaurants, but the folder contained something else, something that linked back to where they'd all started in Camden.

Jake pulled out the headed paper from the law firm Urban Soul used to handle their legal business. Stared at it. "I don't understand."

Tom nudged him. "Yes, you do. Read it again."

Silence. Cass could almost hear the cogs turning in Jake's brain. "You're giving me Misfits?"

"Kind of," Tom said. "Technically, it'll still belong to the company, but it's in your name. If anything happened, or you left the company for whatever reason, the restaurant, and the brand, belong to you."

Jake seemed too stunned to be angry . . . yet. "What? Why?"

Tom shrugged and looked at Cass. "Care to explain?"

Cass crawled back under the covers and pointed at the documents Jake clutched in his hands. "Tom gave me Pippa's a week after we launched it. Said I deserved it, but I think it was his way of telling me I didn't need him to be safe . . . secure, you know? That I didn't have to stay with him to have a good life. I thought he was bloody mad, but I get it now."

Jake reached out for Tom, like he so often did, for reassurance.

Tom took his hand and gestured between them all. "Jake, we want you to have options. We don't ever want you to feel you'd lose everything if you decided that this wasn't what you wanted."

Jake said nothing for a long moment, and Cass felt each second tick by. It had been his idea to sign Misfits over to Jake, but now he wasn't so sure. Jake's pride made him stubborn, and Cass remembered his own reaction to Tom's staggering gift—swearing, stamping, slamming doors. It had taken him days to get his head around it.

But Jake did none of that. He released Tom's hand, eased the papers back into the folder, and set it aside. "I don't have to go to those boring meetings, do I?"

Tom opened his mouth, but Cass cut him off. "Hell no. It's just a bit of paper that gives you some choices. Don't worry about the corporate bullshit."

Tom sighed. "Yeah, just leave the corporate *bullshit* to me, right, Cass?"

"Right. You can do that while me and Jake go to Battersea and get that pup you promised us."

Tom rolled his eyes. "Give up the fags and you can fill the house with bloody dalmatians for all I care."

"Careful what you wish for, mate." Cass flopped onto his back. He felt lighter somehow, like they'd cleared another hurdle and there wasn't much left in their way.

Jake got up and went to the bathroom. Tom stole his warm spot and pulled Cass close.

"That was easier than I expected. Maybe he's not as pigheaded as you after all."

"Shut up." Cass moulded himself to Tom's side and put his head on his chest. Heard his heart as steady and strong as it had ever been. "I feel good. Don't spoil it."

"I'm so bloody proud of you."

"Shut *up*."

Tom chuckled, but said no more. He didn't need to. They were on the same page at last. Misfits gave Jake a safety net, whether he knew he needed it or not, and Cass would sleep easier now, knowing he was taken care of.

Jake came back to bed, and hovered a moment, as he sometimes did, still unsure of his place, but Cass wasn't having that. Not today.

Cass held out his hand, pulled Jake close, and tucked him into the warmth of Tom's chest, the chest that was made for both of them. They were at the beginning of an uncertain journey, but right here, right now, he had everything he'd ever wanted.

AUTHOR'S NOTE

It will never be possible for me to know all there is to know about Tourette's syndrome; and when I sat down to write this book, I didn't want to write a character based on a cursory Google search.

Enter Rico, a wonderful young man I met on my quest for knowledge. Rico opened his life for me, guided me, and taught me. He made me laugh and cry, and above all, taught me that though TS is a condition a man can't hide from, with the right support and a whole lot of love, life can become something wonderful.

The terminology I've used in this book may not be textbook correct. Rico told me that he defines each tic by sensation. Buzzing. Popping. Rippling. He has some ruder terms too, but I'm taking those to the grave.

Jake's interpretation of TS may not be yours, or even mine, but know that I put everything I had into bringing Rico's experience of this condition to life. Rico, I thank you from the bottom of my heart for your generosity and patience, and for the company. You are an epic human being.

Dear Reader,

Thank you for reading Garrett Leigh's *Misfits*!

We know your time is precious and you have many, many entertainment options, so it means a lot that you've chosen to spend your time reading. We really hope you enjoyed it.

We'd be honored if you'd consider posting a review—good or bad—on sites like **Amazon, Barnes & Noble, Kobo, Goodreads, Twitter, Facebook, Tumblr,** and your blog or website. We'd also be honored if you told your friends and family about this book. Word of mouth is a book's lifeblood!

For more information on upcoming releases, author interviews, blog tours, contests, giveaways, and more, please sign up for our weekly, spam-free newsletter and visit us around the web:

Newsletter: tinyurl.com/RiptideSignup
Twitter: twitter.com/RiptideBooks
Facebook: facebook.com/RiptidePublishing
Goodreads: tinyurl.com/RiptideOnGoodreads
Tumblr: riptidepublishing.tumblr.com

Thank you so much for Reading the Rainbow!

RiptidePublishing.com

ALSO BY
GARRETT LEIGH

Roads series
Slide
Rare

Only Love
Heart
More than Life

Blue Boy series
Bullet
Bones
Bold

ABOUT THE AUTHOR

Garrett Leigh is a British writer and book designer, currently working for Dreamspinner Press, Loose Id, Riptide Publishing, and Black Jazz Press.

When not writing, Garrett can generally be found procrastinating on Twitter, cooking up a storm, or sitting on her behind doing as little as possible.

As an artist, Garrett works freelance for various publishing houses and independent authors under the pseudonym G.D. Leigh. For cover art and author branding info, please visit blackjazzpress.com

Social Media:

Website: garrettleigh.com

Twitter: twitter.com/Garrett_Leigh

Facebook: facebook.com/garrettleighbooks

Cover art enquiries: blackjazzdesign@gmail.com

Enjoy this book?
Find more UK contemporary
romance at RiptidePublishing.com!

Country Mouse:
The Complete Collection
ISBN: 978-1-62649-044-4

Trowchester Blues
ISBN: 978-1-62649-199-1

Earn Bonus Bucks!

Earn 1 Bonus Buck for each dollar you spend. Find out how at
RiptidePublishing.com/news/bonus-bucks.

Win Free Ebooks for a Year!

Pre-order coming soon titles directly through our site and you'll
receive one entry into a drawing to win free books for a year! Get
the details at RiptidePublishing.com/contests.

9615

Made in the USA
Lexington, KY
20 April 2017